CARRION SCOURGE
PLAGUE OF MONSTERS

JONAH BUCK

SEVERED PRESS
HOBART TASMANIA

CARRION SCOURGE
PLAGUE OF MONSTERS

WWW.SEVEREDPRESS.COM

ISBN: 978-1-925711-72-1

For Frank, Don, Phoebe, and Billie

It was a miracle of rare device,
A sunny pleasure-dome with caves of ice!
A damsel with a dulcimer
In a vision once I saw:
It was an Abyssinian maid
And on her dulcimer she played,
Singing of Mount Abora.
Could I revive within me
Her symphony and song,
To such a deep delight 'twould win me,
That with music loud and long,
I would build that dome in air,
That sunny dome! those caves of ice!
And all who heard should see them there,
And all should cry, Beware! Beware!
His flashing eyes, his floating hair!
Weave a circle round him thrice,
And close your eyes with holy dread
For he on honey-dew hath fed,
And drunk the milk of Paradise.

-Samuel Taylor Coleridge, *Kubla Khan*

ONE
BUTTS MCGEE & THE SQUIRES

September 2, 1926

A large crate of animal heads sat in the corner of the office. "Make an offer. Buy two, get one free," read a sign taped to the rim of the crate. The heads were all mounted and stuffed, ready to be placed on someone's wall. There were a couple of antelopes, a wildebeest, a medium-sized Nile crocodile, and a lion with a chipped fang. A layer of dust had settled on the animals' glass eyes.

They were some of the remnants of Denise's old business, a big game hunting and safari expedition office that she used to run with her father. The times had changed, though. Her father had disappeared on a trip through the Namib Desert a few years ago, and Denise didn't offer sport hunting expeditions anymore. The preserved trophy heads, which had once decorated the walls of the office as a sign of her experience and skill in the field, were now relegated to the crate in the corner.

Even if she didn't hire out for safaris anymore, that didn't mean Denise wasn't still involved in the hunting business, though. A life of thrills. Excitement. Danger around every corner.

Or something.

"Go fish," Cornelia van Rensburg said.

"Crap," Denise said, drawing a card from the pile on her desk. It was a three. She didn't need any threes.

Cornelia had her prosthetic leg propped up on the desk. The artificial leg was the same kind that a lot of former soldiers had, people who had been blasted out of a trench by a mortar shell or had their legs cut out from under them by machine gun fire in a dash across no man's land. The leg attached just above where Cornelia's knee would have been. She walked with a bit of a hitch, but she managed to get around pretty well.

"Got any threes?" Cornelia asked.

"Crap," Denise said again. She tossed her newly acquired card across the desk, and Cornelia added it to her hand.

"That's right. Come to Mama."

Denise DeMarco was one half of DeMarco & van Rensburg Specialty Hunting Services. Cornelia was the other.

Denise grew up at her father's side, hunting the veldt and living in tents under the baking African sun. She knew how to track creatures through almost any kind of terrain, and she was a damn good shot. The animals with their heads in the crate could attest to that. She spoke English and Afrikaans, and her Zulu and Xhosa skills were passable enough that she could communicate with just about anyone she met in the bush.

Denise surveyed the creased cards in front of her. "Got any...eights?"

"Nope. Go fish."

She sighed and drew another card. This was the third round of cards they'd played today. Cornelia had already won the first two.

Just another day in the life of a professional monster hunter.

DeMarco & van Rensburg Specialty Hunting Services sounded a lot less crazy than "monster hunters for hire." When Denise had come up with the name, she'd hoped that the slightly obfuscated name would help keep cranks out of her office. Mostly, no one at all came into their office.

They'd been open for less than a year, and they'd only been hired twice. Both cases were for big cats that had discovered a taste for human flesh and become man-eaters. Neither instance was quite what Denise had in mind when she opened her new business.

When she'd been a normal big game hunter, she'd heard plenty of rumors. Creatures that swept down on isolated farms under the cover of darkness. Things living among ancient ruins that were best left undisturbed. Isolated valleys and caves where evolution had gone awry. She never put much stock in those stories. That was up until a couple of particularly unpleasant incidents, though. Now, she knew there really were a few dark and unexplored corners of the earth, and sometimes that darkness tried to crawl out to the rest of the map.

Denise's eyes drifted over to the half-finished library book on the edge of her desk. It was full of stately manor houses, handsome suitors, crass interlopers, and heaving alabaster bosoms. It was absolute dreck, but it was starting to sound pretty good compared to somehow getting card-sharked in a game of go fish yet again.

Her gaze drifted from the book up to the opposite wall. A large picture hung across from her desk. Unlike the mounted animal heads in the crate, it was one of the few decorations she'd decided to keep when she got out of the big game hunting business. The blown-up black and white photo showed Theodore Roosevelt, the former American president, with a big grin on his face and a rifle in his hands as he stood in front of a downed rhino. Another man with a matching grin stood next to the ex-president. That was Cedric DeMarco, Denise's father.

Denise was in the picture, too. She was a gawky teenage girl in pigtails holding an elephant gun almost as long as she was tall. She was grinning too as she stood next to the slain animal.

"Got any aces?" Cornelia asked.

Denise had two aces, and she was about to tell Cornelia exactly where she could stick them when there was a knock on the door. Denise put her cards down and looked up. Cornelia pulled her leg off the table and let it rest on the ground.

The door opened, and two people stepped inside. The man wore a suit that looked like something a particularly stern London financier might enjoy, and his spectacles glinted in the sunlight. The second person was a black woman with her hair tied back.

The man glanced around the office for a second before his eyes settled on Denise and Cornelia. "Would I be correct in assuming that you two are Ms. DeMarco and Ms. van Rensburg?"

South Africa had a lot of different accents floating around, but the man in their doorway spoke with an English accent. That meant he might be here on a vacation or a business trip. Somewhat less likely was the possibility that he had recently moved down from the foggy, smoky heart of the empire to sunnier and warmer climes. He didn't really look like one of the colonial administrators London sometimes dispatched.

"That's us," Denise said. That accent made her immediately suspicious about what their visitor wanted. Sometimes, she still got potential clients who wanted to be taken out on sporting expeditions. A lot of them were visiting Europeans or Americans. Most of the locals had written her off as an occasionally useful nut some time ago. She wasn't interested in being hired out on some new big game expedition, though. Those days were over.

"Good. I have a job you might be interested in," the man said, not bothering with any sort of opening pleasantries.

Denise looked the man over again. He stood very straight, and his hair had been combed in such a way that it looked like he was trying to punish it for something. There was a decent chance that he was ex-military.

First thing was first. "What sort of job?"

"It should be a relatively simple matter. It's something I understand the two of you are qualified for. We'd like someone to evaluate a situation for us."

Well, the man in the suit had passed the first test. He hadn't said he wanted to hire them to go traipsing across the landscape and take potshots at some of the local wildlife. That meant she wouldn't have to turn him right back out the door. She also noticed that his answer was spectacularly vague.

"Perhaps some introductions are in order," Denise said.

"Not required. I've read reports on both of you. I'm familiar with your work."

Denise made a face that could castrate a bull from twenty paces. She didn't like being jerked around.

"Allow me to rephrase that. We like to know who we're working with. Tell us who you are, or get out of our office." She pulled a pen and notepad out of her desk to take down and cross check any information he gave her.

"I see. We're with the St. George's Squires."

"Never heard of them," Cornelia said as Denise scribbled *St. George's Squires* down in her notebook.

"You some sort of charity group or something?" Denise asked.

"No, not precisely. Our interests are aligned with the public good, though. I trust you're both familiar with the story of St. George?"

"Patron saint of England. Killed a dragon. Yeah. That guy."

"Yes. The classic version of the story says that a dragon terrorized a small kingdom, and it could only be appeased if the people offered up a regular sacrifice to the beast. They chose young women by lots, and one day the king's own daughter was selected to be staked out for the dragon. Saint George happened upon the woman while she was tied up and awaiting her fate. The princess tried to warm him away, but he refused. When the dragon appeared, he successfully killed the creature and returned the princess to the city."

"Ducky for her. I'm guessing you're not St. George, though. And neither is she." Denise gestured toward the black woman, who hadn't said a word yet. "I'd still like to know who you are before we conduct any business. We like to check records."

"You won't find any records about me," the man said.

"I'm just going to write down 'Butts McGee' as a placeholder, then." Denise's pen scratched across her notepad.

The man's jaw tightened almost imperceptibly. He pulled an envelope out of his suit jacket and peeled it open. Denise had been hoping that needling him a bit would give her more information, but her visitor was made of sterner stuff.

"Let me lay down the parameters of what you'd be doing. If you don't like the sound of the job, we will leave and find someone else. This need not be a difficult process."

"The floor is yours, Butts."

4

"There are essentially only two things you must agree to." Butts McGee brushed past the placeholder name Denise had given him. He was either unflappable, or he really wanted something. Both could be trouble.

"The first condition is simple but non-negotiable. You'll have to take Metrodora with you on your expedition." Butts gestured to the woman standing next to him.

"We don't really need any additional porters," Denise said.

"She's not a porter. She's an expert on regional mythology and biological abnormalities. We've been cultivating her for years. She'll be the eyes and ears of our organization on the expedition."

"I, uh, sorry," Denise said to the woman, suddenly feeling like a gigantic ass. "It's just with the way things are…I assumed…you know."

South African society was heavily segregated. Much of the urban black population lived in shanty towns around the edges of the cities and needed special permits or work orders to enter the white sections. The state had set aside a number of black "homelands" on small, mostly worthless lands to shunt the rest of the black population out of more economically valuable areas. Because the homelands were nominally nations, they also stripped the black population of full South African citizenship.

Denise thought it was an ugly system. But she was so used to it that it was easy to make assumptions. There weren't a lot of non-whites involved in anything but subsistence farming and menial labor. For the first time in the conversation, she was on the back foot, and she felt like a git.

"It's alright," Metrodora said, speaking for the first time since she'd walked into the office. She didn't show any more emotion than her colleague.

Cornelia looked at Denise. She obviously found the pair a little puzzling as well. Despite their weirdness, they didn't strike Denise as cranks. They weren't like the folks who sometimes walked into here and tried to convince her that their neighbor was Dracula. They seemed deadly serious about all this.

"So, what's this second condition you were talking about?" Denise asked, eager to shuffle right to the next topic.

"The British Empire is a very large place. The sun never sets on it, as they say. We have some need for new affiliates in some of the more far-flung corners."

"Is the 'we' in this case St. George's Squires? Not the government itself?"

"That is correct."

"Maybe you better spell out exactly what your organization does."

"We aren't so different from you. We're a collection of experts interested in tracking, studying, and sometimes eliminating biological anomalies. St. George's Squires was founded by people very much like yourselves. The main difference is, with a certain amount of government patronage, we've grown into a fairly significant operation, with branches in every section of the Empire."

"So, you're saying that you're basically monster hunters, too?" Cornelia asked.

"Neither of us are personally, no," Metrodora said. "I'm working on a research project."

"And I'm merely a facilitator," Butts said. "We require people such as yourselves for some of the more, shall we say, direct involvement. If you accept the offer we're about to make you, we'd like to make you affiliates of the organization."

"You won't even give us your name. That doesn't exactly inspire the trust it would take for us to want to join your organization."

"You wouldn't be joining. You would be independent contractors. It would mean you'd periodically have the opportunity take work offers from us. It is my understanding that your establishment here could do with more such offers."

"Our establishment is doing just fine, thank you very much."

"You've taken two jobs, both involving lions that started preying on people. One of the jobs was on behalf of a black village in the north. Due to a lack of capital, they mostly paid you in crops. Corn, I believe."

That wasn't readily available information. Evidently, St George's Squires had access to her DeMarco & van Rensburg Specialty Hunting Services' tax data. Their visitor had simultaneously called her bluff and intentionally tipped his hand a bit. He told them enough to let them know he had some pull in the government and also tell them that he knew they could use the work. It was a subtle way of pointing out that he was someone powerful, someone who was best not trifled with.

But if Denise was really good at anything, it was trifling.

"Alright, Butts. We're not committing to anything yet. We don't necessarily know if you're somebody we'd be interested in selling gum to, let alone working as some sort of affiliate with your organization. Tell us what you want done, though."

"I'm curious, too," Cornelia said. "As far as I knew, we were the only game in town when it came to the monster business. Now you're telling us that you've got a whole organization set up. What's this all about?"

The man pulled a couple of photographs out. He laid them down on the desk in front of Denise and Cornelia.

The black and white photos were a lot more black than white. One of them was almost completely black, with only a couple of little pinpricks to break the darkness up.

Denise squinted at the first picture and realized that there was actually a little more going on in it. In the center, she could see a sort of blot. There was a darker shape amid the main blackness, but she couldn't really define its contours very well. The picture simply wasn't detailed enough to give much of an indication what she was looking at or why she was looking at it.

The second picture wasn't a whole lot better. She couldn't see the larger black blob anymore. Instead, it had been replaced with a narrow white streak that she initially assumed was a scratch in the film or some other photographic flaw.

Then she realized what the white streak was. It was a falling star, a meteor burning up as it fell through the atmosphere. The scattered white specks making up the rest of the picture were stars. Both photographs were pictures of the night sky.

But if that white streak was a comet, what in the hell was that black blob in the night sky? Denise laid a finger on the first picture and tapped the weird black shape.

"What is that?"

"We don't know."

"You're not saying you want us to go after...whatever that is?" Cornelia said. "You'd be better off calling the army and asking them to send their planes up after it. We're not pilots. I can't even tell how high up that thing is from the pictures. A plane might not even be able to fly up that high."

"We're not asking you to go after that. These photographs were taken from an observatory in Australia. We think it might be an asteroid that flew past our atmosphere, but we honestly don't know. The main mass continued on its way without any further incident, as far as we can tell. We're more interested in the portion that seems to have broken off. We were able to track it, and we're fairly certain that it landed in some territory administered by France." Butts pointed toward the little white streak in the second photograph.

Denise stared at the photos for a couple more seconds. "Okay, you've officially lost me. So this thing landed in France. I'm not seeing the issue."

"French-administered territory."

Denise decided he must mean one of the French territories in Africa, like Algeria. The French didn't have much territory that was close to Cape Town, though. France controlled a lot of northern and western Africa, a historical remnant of the mad scramble for colonies over the last couple of generations.

Denise looked over at Cornelia. Cornelia looked back over at Denise. Cornelia had a lot of talents. During the Great War, she'd worked as a military nurse and she had a knack for medicine. She'd studied geology at one point, but she wasn't any sort of expert or learned scholar on asteroid debris, though she knew a bit about lunar meteorites. Neither of them knew how to study a meteor impact site, though.

"Right. So, this thing landed somewhere in French-administered territory. I'm not sure what that has to do with us, though. I can track an animal down a game trail. It's not like this thing left a bunch of tracks and spoor. You'd be a lot better off hiring an astronomer or a geologist or basically anyone else, if you're trying to find the impact crater."

"Oh, no. We know more or less where the impact crater is. Our problem is that we know very little about anything else going on in the area. It landed in a very isolated region, and the French have been very resistant to any attempts to muscle in on their studies. What we want is to send someone unaffiliated with the government out to examine the situation."

"You want us to…spy for you?"

"It is substantially less involved than that."

"It sure as hell better be. I have no intention of being carted off to some French prison or lined up against a wall for espionage."

"All we need to know is whether we have any cause to be alarmed or not. The area where we believe the meteorite fell is also under some British territorial claims. A day of looking around the countryside should be plenty to tell you whether or not there is anything unusual happening."

Cornelia spoke up. "So, I still don't see why you need us, specifically. If you just want somebody to wander over and look around for an hour, why not ask some expert on asteroids? Or just have someone ask the locals if they've seen anything out of place?"

"We're asking you because of who the French have asked to investigate the situation. They initially sent a small team of geologists. After that, they called in a large number of biologists. Dozens and dozens of scientists and aides. There's been an unprecedented flurry of construction in the area, and we believe it's connected."

"Are you saying they found something alive? Something from space?"

"We have no idea what they found, which is precisely the problem. We don't need you to steal research papers or decipher every aspect of what they may or may not have discovered around the site where that meteorite landed. We just need some experienced eyes on the situation. If things are under control down there, then it will be a matter for British diplomacy and intelligence services to pry any worthwhile secrets out of the French and their researchers. If things are going badly down there, we calculate that your experiences and skills mean you are moderately more likely to survive any catastrophe than most other people we could send."

"How flattering," Denise said.

"And the French will just accept us there at their secret project site?" Cornelia said.

"We've made arrangements with the French government to allow a couple of adventurers into their territory. They've accepted, given certain conditions. Initial access should not be a problem. Again, this is not some infiltration commando raid. We only need observations and impressions so we can evaluate whether or not further action is required. Then the real professionals can step in."

Denise was pretty sure that line about the real professionals was meant to bait her. Well, if Butts McGee wanted to pretend he was Mr. Slick Knickers about everything, she could play that game, too. She gave him a smile that was all teeth.

"So let me see if I have things straight here," Cornelia said, shifting forward in her seat. The joint in her artificial leg made a little squeaking noise as she moved. "You mentioned biological aberrations a couple of times."

"As I said before, the British Empire is a very large place, and it has some very dark corners. My organization has several centuries of experience in flushing light into those places and studying what we find among the shadows."

"I know. A group that hunts and studies monsters. Sounds crazy, doesn't it?" Metrodora said, her tone completely deadpan.

"If your organization is so widespread, why are you bothering to recruit us at all? Don't the Squires already have somebody else in the region?" Denise asked.

"We used to. They died."

"Ah. Doing anything related to this job?"

"No."

"So what about supplies? Equipment? Logistics?" Denise asked. "What will we need for this?"

9

"Well," Butts McGee said, "we will provide you with some specialty gear. Clothes, mostly. We don't think you'll need much in the way of equipment, but we hired a pilot to help you navigate when you reach the site. Naturally, we will be paying for all your expenses in this matter, including transport and lodgings on site. You'll also receive a small premium."

"We'd like the premium up front. As a sign that you're really on the up and up. I've never heard of your organization before, and I don't trust you any further than I can spit right now."

Denise leaned back in her chair and eyed her two visitors. On the one hand, she didn't like the way St. George's Squires seemed to operate. This cloak and dagger business wasn't how she liked to do things, and it certainly wasn't something she liked in her clients.

Bringing this Metrodora woman along would be a mixed bag. On the one hand, Denise didn't like the idea of anybody looking over her shoulder or jogging her elbow while she was trying to work.

On the other hand, if St. George's Squires were willing to loan out one of their people, it presumably meant that they were serious about ensuring there weren't any shenanigans happening behind the scene. If something went wrong, they couldn't just cut and run, leaving Denise and Cornelia stranded in the middle of nowhere.

Plus, the Squires weren't necessarily offering a bad deal. This was, in fact, a lot more pleasant and cordial than meeting with some other prospective clients, not that a veneer of manners necessarily guaranteed that things would work out in the end. Still, there seemed to be some indication that these people were serious about seeing that things went off with a bare minimum of fuss and the maximum chance of success.

Paying some money up front was a good sign. Some preparation work regarding logistics was a good sign. Some modest and articulable goals about what they wanted her to do were a good sign. Hell, just the fact that they weren't obviously hucksters was a good sign.

Denise glanced over at Cornelia. Cornelia gave Denise a quick nod.

"Alright, I think we can work something out. We'll check this place out for you and report back if anything is terrorizing the countryside. Where exactly do you need us to go?"

"Antarctica."

TWO
THE SHRIEKING SIXTIES

The icebreaker moved across the waves with all the grace of a hog stuck between some fence posts. The deck of the *HMS Sulaco* rolled under Denise's feet whenever she tried to walk anywhere. There were handrails everywhere to try to counteract some of the problem. In their cabins. Along the edge of the deck. In the biffy. Despite the handrails, Denise had still been tossed around a couple of times as the ship chugged through the waves.

They were deep in the southerly latitudes, where the wind could swirl around the entire southern ocean without any landmasses to break the momentum. Denise had learned from the crew that passing forty degrees south latitude had brought them into the Roaring Forties, where things started to get rough. Further south took them into the Furious Fifties, which combined everything unpleasant about the Forties and dipped it in hot sauce. Denise had a strong stomach, but being rolled violently up and down for hours on end had turned her guts into a mass of lukewarm jelly.

Denise had expected the final stretch of the journey, the Shrieking Sixties, to swirl them around like a dead goldfish being flushed toward the pearly gates, but the weather had temporarily broken. The seas themselves were relatively calm, which came as a blessed relief.

The Shrieking Sixties had brought something new to torment them, though. Great chunks of ice floated in the water. The *Sulaco*'s captain steered around anything too large. Denise was grateful that he hadn't sunk them yet. However, the captain simply smashed through anything small enough, and that was slowly driving her insane.

Denise grabbed onto the railing as the reinforced hull bashed its way through another tiny white island. The entire ship shuddered and gave a lurch. There was a tremendous cracking noise as the ice split apart, and then there was a sound as if demons were pounding on the hull with hammers as the disparate pieces of ice scraped and crunched against the entire length of the ship.

Denise gritted her teeth against that noise. It was all too easy to imagine some oversized hunk of ice lurking just beneath the surface of the choppy water, like a crocodile watching the shore with just its snout and eyes poking from the muck. Every single time the icebreaker smashed through some new obstacle, Denise's heart gave a little leap. The angry clatter of ice against the hull always sounded like it was doing some catastrophic damage that would surely send them down to the cold, cold silt thousands of feet below.

Below them, the churning sea was only a few degrees above freezing, and no one would last long in that choppy mess. Hypothermia would claim anyone unlucky enough to fall in the water. At best, a person who fell overboard might last an hour. Most likely, the frigid sea would take them faster than that, though. She tried to focus on something else and avoid thinking about buckling metal.

Metrodora continued to sketch in a notebook she'd brought along. She'd barely said anything since she came aboard the *Sulaco* with Denise and Cornelia, and most of Denise's attempts to strike up any sort of conversation had puttered out in short order.

Denise turned her attention from the window and craned her neck over to see what Metrodora was working on. The sketch was pretty good, all things considered. It was a pen and ink drawing depicting something whose head looked like a sphincter with teeth and a single large horn. Several parts were carefully labeled in neat handwriting, and there were spaces in the corners of the paper that were apparently reserved for more detailed drawings of particular pieces of the creature. Denise had never seen an animal quite like the thing Metrodora was drawing, and she hoped she never did.

Metrodora noticed Denise staring. She carefully tucked her pen behind her ear and closed her notebook, blocking Denise's view.

"What is that?" Denise asked, pointing toward the notebook.

"It is an *emela-ntouka*," Metrodora said, without bothering to open the notebook back up.

"Huh." Denise tried to think of something else to say. "Have you and the Squires dealt with them much?"

"We have a breeding pair at our main facility. I don't deal with them directly myself. Dr. Smithback is in charge of their upkeep." Metrodora spoke in precise, clean language that still had a trace of accent from some native language.

"I see." Denise did not actually see. "Are they big?"

She was relentlessly probing into the unknown with these scintillating questions today. The field of aberrant zoology would never be the same after she was done with it. Are they big? Inquiring minds needed to know.

"Very," Metrodora said before shifting around a little to face more toward the window and block off Denise from seeing what she was drawing.

Denise got the feeling that Metrodora thought she'd been stranded with the loser kids at the playground. Maybe she was still sore about being mistaken for a porter. Or maybe she just preferred not to talk to them for the same reason veterans didn't bother socializing with the new recruits. Maybe they would be worth talking to if they survived long enough. Perhaps she just preferred to keep to herself.

Denise turned back and glanced at their equipment. Most of their gear consisted of protective clothing like parkas and jackets. Technically, the temperature was a couple of degrees above freezing, but it sure didn't feel like it. The constant, sheering wind cut through even thick clothing. Whenever she took her gloves off, it felt like someone was peeling the skin off her hands with tongs. The environment out there was unlike anywhere Denise had been before, and it made her feel unprepared for what she was about to do.

St. George's Squires had come to her because she and Cornelia were the closest vaguely qualified people for the job. It seemed strange that they were the nearest, but it was true. Antarctica didn't have any sort of permanent population, so the mere fact that her office was on a relatively nearby continent was enough to make them the most convenient people to send.

She still wasn't sure exactly why *anybody* needed to be sent, though. The fact that the French had shipped a bunch of biologists down here didn't prove anything. That they'd sent them down after the meteorite impact was interesting, but hardly definitive. Granted, it did make her wonder what they were up to down here, though.

The only people who could answer that question were the French researchers they'd be staying with. One of the more exciting possibilities was that maybe there had been some sort of life amid the meteor debris. That would indeed be cause for a stir. Denise wasn't sure how likely that was, though.

The meteor had apparently detached from a larger asteroid. To the best of her knowledge, the typical comet and asteroid was just a big hunk of rock floating through space. No atmosphere. No water. Nothing that could sustain any sort of organism.

On the off chance that anyone really had discovered genuine life amid the debris, Denise figured it would probably turn out to be some Earth-borne microbe that had contaminated the site. Maybe a fungus or something.

Even if the lifeform were from the depths of space, it would have to be a microbe or a single-celled blob of some sort. Not that something like that wouldn't be incredibly interesting and a huge development in the study of life. It just wouldn't be Denise's job to deal with it.

She, Cornelia, and Metrodora were basically down here to check under the earth's bed for monsters. Even if there was some great and amazing discovery to be made down here, the odds that she would need to concern herself with it were basically zilch.

That was assuming that Metrodora, St. George's Squires, and Butts McGee were straight shooters, though. Everything she'd been told indicated that she and Cornelia were just down here as a prophylactic measure. They were the B-team, sent here to soothe some nerves amongst the people who liked to study biology's weirder corners.

But Denise had learned a long time ago to prepare for the worst. That's why she and Cornelia had brought some of their special tools along with them. There were a couple of .577 Nitro Express elephant guns locked away in their baggage along with five hundred rounds of ammunition. About half the rounds had a silver coating. Denise had seen enough to know that it was better to have and not need than to need and not have.

She'd seen too much for her tastes a couple of times, in fact. There had been incidents when all hell broke loose. In her experience, it paid to bring enough supplies to stuff every last devil back through hell's gates and then lock the doors behind them.

Denise cringed a little as the *Sulaco* crunched its way through another stretch of sea ice and jolted her forward. The captain sounded the horn in belated warning as they bashed into another clump of ice.

Fletch Adams walked through the doorway, using the handrails to expertly guide himself along even as the ship shuddered with each hit from the ice. The American pilot was the only one among them who had experience in the Antarctic, serving as a supply runner on a couple of prior expeditions.

"We're almost there, ladies," he said. "If you want, you can come to the front of the ship and see the shore through the binoculars. You can just barely make out Delambre Station. It's a lot bigger than I was expecting."

"Compared to the expeditions you've been on, just how much bigger?" Cornelia asked, looking up from her inventory of equipment.

"The last expedition I was on had a research station. It was exactly one shed. About ten feet by twelve feet. There weren't any other buildings. Everything else was either a tent or some half-assed igloos that a couple of guys tried to make. When you hired me to guide you around down here, I thought you might be a little soft in the head. Pardon my saying so. But no one would want to go to Antarctica just as an adventure vacation. Not the version of Antarctica I remember, anyway. You got lucky, though. Our French friends have built the Ritz Carlton compared to what I was expecting."

Technically, it was St. George's Squires who had hired Fletch. He just didn't know that. As far as both he and the researchers at Delambre Station were concerned, she and Cornelia were just a couple of diehard explorers who wanted to be the first women to step foot on this particular stretch of Antarctica. Harmless thrill chasers. Denise was pretty sure that was the only reason the French had agreed to host them for a few days. That, and a generous research grant that had also been plucked out of the Squires' coffers and filtered through her account.

"So what can we expect?"

"It's a whole compound. Looks like permanent structures. Concrete walls. The whole shebang. I'd never even heard of this place until a few weeks ago, but they invested in a major building effort down here."

"Can you tell what any of the buildings are for from here?" Denise asked.

"One of them's pretty big. I would assume that's some sort of crew area. Bunks and a common room. Maybe a mess hall. That sort of thing. I guess we'll know within the hour. Best get your things ready to unload."

Bernard Poole, the *Sulaco*'s first mate, appeared in the hallway behind Fletch. He touched the pilot on the shoulder as the ship rocked again under another icy impact.

"Afternoon." Poole nodded at Denise and the others before turning his attention fully to Fletch. "Hey, the captain asked me to find you. We've been in contact with a whaling ship in the area. They're going to be in this stretch of ocean for the next week. You're in luck. If we have to leave in a hurry for some reason, you won't be stranded."

"A whaling ship? Huh. Okay. Thanks. Good to know."

Poole nodded and retreated up the hallway back toward the bridge.

"That sounds like it's a good thing," Denise said.

"Yeah, I suppose it is," Fletch said. "It's just changed a lot down here over the last few years. Even five years ago, anyone who came down here for a scientific expedition was on their own. There was no help coming. It was just you and whatever supplies you could carry with you." A wistful note had entered Fletch's tone.

"You almost sound like you miss it that way."

"Oh, don't get me wrong. If we get to sleep behind some solid walls on full-sized cots and eat warm food from an honest-to-God kitchen, I won't miss it a bit. I'm just dating myself here. People only discovered Antarctica in the 1820s. It took most of a century for anyone to actually trek all the way to the South Pole. But things are changing. Better generators and radio equipment mean that we can apparently set up some pretty extensive bases down here and wave to industrial whaling boats as they sail past. It used to be just you against the elements. Next thing you know, the place will be a tourist trap. No offense meant, of course," Fletch said, looking back and forth between the women in front of him.

"None taken," Denise said.

She knew something of the same feeling. When she was a young girl, the big game on the veldt used to be a lot more plentiful. Those numbers had dwindled with the influx of poachers looking for ivory and new settlements that paved over grasslands and forests. The savanna was a very different place from the one she grew up with. Areas that used to be almost uninhabited were populated by small towns and farms, now. Seeing that same process play out on the ice would be even stranger, though.

"There was something that would have sent the great Romance-era poets panting about the place ten years ago. To be here, just to survive for any length of time, was an accomplishment. A feat among the tumult of nature. The journey of hungry, cold men through the windswept crags as they raced to make discoveries before the environment could suck the life out of them. It was the stuff of heroic legend. Antarctica was the last place on earth mankind ever set foot on, and it was a personal test just to survive."

"I think I'm glad we're here when it's a bit less likely we'll freeze to death if we miscalculate the weather," Cornelia said.

"Fair enough. By itself, progress certainly isn't bad. I talk about it now like we spent the old expeditions performing the twelve labors of Hercules and feats of manliness and then boasting about it all night over a fountain of mead. Not that I didn't personally perform many feats of courageous manliness myself. Obviously, my companions were in constant awe of me." Fletch mimed flexing in his baggy jacket and flashed a smile.

"But most of the time, we were just hungry and cold and miserable. Nobody was too interested in doing anything other than accomplishing their individual goal and getting back to civilization before the weather turned and killed us all. I just worry that things are going to have a different timbre now that groups seem intent on setting up semi-permanent bases down here. Before, you didn't much care whose claimed territory you were in. It wouldn't matter much if you froze to death in the French section or the British section or the little rump that Norway wants to muscle into. It was all the same, no matter which government had to go dispatch a team to collect your iced-over corpse the next summer.

"It was about endurance. Now, with people creeping in and setting up places like this, I'm worried it'll start to be more about conquering the landscape. If people can actually survive down here long enough to enforce the claims they've made, it's only a matter of time before some damn fool manages to spark a diplomatic fight about whose borders end where or who can or can't build a research station on some particular outcropping of rock. Eventually, you might have military bases out here on the ice and warships patrolling the ice flows. I think I like it better when it was something you could only step foot on for so long before you had to flee the elements. Nobody could really own it then. If somebody thinks they can own this place, then the whole area is just like any other spot on earth except cold as a well digger's tit."

A person could die of acute nostalgia poisoning thinking about such things for too long. Denise tried to steer the conversation toward something more practical. She'd be better off gathering a little more information beforehand.

"What sort of animals can we expect to see around here?"

"Well, I would imagine we'll see the occasional seal out on the shore. Mostly, you're going to see penguins, though. Lots and lots of penguins."

"So the French have all these people here just to study penguins, you think?" Denise knew perfectly well that the French government wouldn't want to build an entire research station down in one of the most ungodly environments on earth just to poke and prod at some sea chickens. She knew more about the current situation than Fletch did because she was aware of the meteorite landing. That didn't mean it wouldn't be useful to hear from someone who had some experience with this territory. Usually, the stupidest thing anyone could do on a big game hunt was to assume they knew everything they needed to know about an area, its inhabitants, or the creatures that lived there.

"Nah, they won't all be here for the penguins. Not a facility like this. Maybe a couple of people will be here for the penguins. Or the krill in the ocean. Or the lichen under some rock. A lot of the people here will be geologists or meteorologists, though."

Denise knew that the French government had specifically sent biologists down here, not geologists or meteorologists, but she nodded anyway. She'd already learned a little something by comparing her own notes with Fletch's first impressions, even if she wasn't sharing any of that information with him.

The mere fact that the French had undertaken a major construction project down here was telling. It would be difficult and expensive to build anything here. Delambre Station was apparently unlike anything their experienced guide had ever seen before, so it was obvious that somebody was serious about whatever was going on down here.

That all but satisfied the first part of Denise's little inquest down. Was there anything important happening down here at the ass end of the world? Apparently so.

The second question was more important, and it would take a little snooping to answer. Whatever was happening down here, was it both alive and dangerous?

"C'mon, let's gather your stuff and head for the skiff. We're going to make landfall soon," Fletch said. The ship hit another chunk of ice, and his voice was nearly drowned out by a sound like frozen thunder.

THREE
WHATEVER YOU DO, DON'T TRY TO HELP THEM

Denise felt like a cat that someone had sprayed with a hose. Sour. Cold. Wet. The little boat bobbed up and down in the choppy water. Sometimes a little mist of salty spray would splash into the skiff as it moved toward the shore, and she would shy away from it.

It hurt just to be alive in this weather. Every single inch of exposed skin on her body tingled like as if she'd just been slapped with a slab of frozen beef. The wind cut right through her parka and the other layers she was wearing, and it never seemed to let up. She'd given up on trying to talk to anyone else in the skiff over the noise of the wind whipping past their heads and the whine of the boat's engine.

Even though they weren't moving particularly fast, Denise felt like she was sitting on top of a car as it sped down the road. She wore a set of tinted goggles against the glare of the ice all around them, but the wind still managed to dry her eyeballs out. If she didn't keep her eyelids squinted down to little slits, it felt like her eyes were in danger of withering to the consistency of dried apricots. It felt like the air itself was trying to push her back from the rocky shore ahead of them.

Despite the weather, Denise actually felt a small thrill of excitement inside her, buried far beneath her layers and layers of clothing. Until a couple of months ago, when the French set out to investigate the meteor strike in their southernmost territory, very few people had ever set foot on this stretch of land. As far as she knew, none of them had been women. She, Cornelia, and Metrodora would be the first to visit the French territory.

Now that she was almost here, she could better understand some of the things Fletch had said earlier. There was an undeniable allure in getting to explore the world's only continent that lacked a permanent human population. If she wandered over the horizon in the right direction, she might see something that no other human being had ever seen before, even if it was just another hillock of rock and ice. Of course, if she wandered off in the wrong direction, it might take them months to find her body, stiff as a board and attached to the ice by a thin layer of frost.

That second option was none too appealing. Denise didn't think she'd need to do much wandering, though. Mostly just a little snooping.

She'd poke around outside a little with Fletch and some of the researchers, if they'd allow her along. She figured she'd have a better chance of finding out the general nature of the research station form the inside, though. Plus, whenever she was all suited up for wandering outside, it would take her half an hour to remove everything if she needed to pee. No, hopefully, she could get most of what she needed while remaining inside the research station.

They were moving closer to Delambre Station itself now, skirting around bits of ice as they moved. Fletch was right. The place was huge. Denise wasn't sure exactly what she had been expecting to see when she reached the French outpost. In her head, she'd sort of pictured wooden cabins and sheds, maybe frosted with snow like some sort kids' camp in the winter.

Instead, Delambre Station looked like an industrial outpost that had been built out in the middle of nowhere by mistake. The largest building, which she figured was probably the main crew quarters, was a big concrete rectangle squatting in the center of the facility like a mother hen guarding her chicks. There were a number of smaller buildings spread across about an acre of ice and rock. Seeing this kind of construction effort amid such a barren landscape was almost surreal. It was like visiting the surface of the moon and finding a department store.

She could see a small contingent of men in brightly colored parkas waiting for them at the docks. The *Sulaco* was too large to fit at the concrete docks, but Denise could see that a much larger docking facility was under construction nearby, something big enough for a couple of supply ships to sidle up to at once. Without the benefit of the larger facilities though, the *Sulaco* would simply remain anchored just off the coast for the few days Denise and company were scheduled to be here. It would only leave if the ice started to close in around their little harbor and risked stranding them all here.

The sun hung low in the horizon, giving a false impression that it was about to dip below the horizon. It kept the sky cast in a sort of orange and yellow glory, but it never actually slipped all the way down into the embrace of dusk. At this time of year, there would be sunlight for twenty-four hours a day down here. The famous midnight sun would give them light to work by no matter the hour. Denise was at least thankful that they hadn't been sent down here during the winter, when there would be weeks or months of darkness at a time. The false sunset painted some of the ice sheets in brilliant shades of red and orange, almost like a lake of shimmering, frozen fire. She had to squint even further against the dazzling sight.

Poole, the *Sulaco*'s first mate, piloted the little skiff toward the shore. Within a few minutes, they'd navigated the minefield of floating ice and arrived at the docks.

One of the French researchers stepped forward and offered his hand to help Denise out of the boat. She hopped out on her own and then took the proffered glove in a handshake instead.

"Welcome to *Terre Adélie*. I'm Dr. Jacques Benoit. A pleasure to meet you. Let me be the first to congratulate you on a successful journey to our little corner of paradise." He shook her hand with the energy of a terrier trying to kill a rat.

"Denise DeMarco. Excited to be here." Her teeth chattered a little as she spoke.

Terre Adélie, or Adélie Land, as the English-speaking world called it, was the French sector of Antarctica. She'd read up on the legal situation a little bit before travelling down here. The question of who actually owned Antarctica was a matter of some dispute.

The British claimed the whole of the continent for themselves. Every last square meter was part of the British Empire, to be administered by the governments of Australia and New Zealand. That was only according to the British, though. Lots of other governments claimed individual chunks, although no one else had the diplomatic chutzpa to try to claim the whole pie for themselves.

Chile and Argentina had claims on a couple of areas based on treaties involving Spanish conquistadors and the Catholic Church from the fifteenth century. They said that the old claims of the Spanish Empire to anything south of the Straits of Magellan gave them a right to their corner of the frozen continent. Meanwhile, Norway was trying to force its presence into some of the same areas.

Adélie Land encompassed a stretch of about three hundred and fifty kilometers of coastline and theoretically extended all the way down to the South Pole. Nominally, it was a narrow triangle of French territory penetrating deep into the continent's ice-choked heart. The basis for the French claim came from when the explorer Jules Dumont d'Urville discovered the area and named it after his wife.

The various sectors didn't line up all that well. Even ignoring the fact that Britain had claimed the whole thing for themselves, the miscellaneous boundaries overlapped with each other in places. If the continent was actually inhabited, it would have been a source of constant diplomatic tension trying to sort out just which territory belonged to each nation. The fact that there were no permanent residents made the point moot, but Fletch was right. If countries like France started building up their territories down here with permanent installations like Delambre

21

Station, somebody was going to have to sort all those claims out at the League of Nations or through some complex series of treaties that would no doubt leave some country or another pissed that it had lost its stretch of icy wasteland. Wars had been fought over less.

"Thanks for hosting us, Dr. Benoit." Denise smiled and reached down to haul her baggage up out of the boat as Cornelia and Metrodora clambered up onto the docks. If Dr. Benoit thought it was odd to be standing out here like a tour guide, he didn't give any indication of that fact. Either the research grant the Squires had funneled down here or the sheer excitement of seeing new faces in this isolated little community was enough to drag him out here in the cold.

"It's Jacques, please. My research students are the only people who call me Dr. Benoit. Come, I'll take you all to your quarters. I'd imagine you would like to get out of this weather. I have the best English of anyone stationed down here, so you can think of me as your minder while you're visiting us."

She glanced out over the landscape again. The shore leading up to the compound was mostly a jumble of rocks with the occasional glint of frozen sea ice hanging off in little icicles like frozen boogers. The first ten feet of the continent didn't exactly inspire the sort of awe that might be expected when stepping foot on a barely explored land.

The horizon was considerably more interesting, though. The ice on the ground rose up away from the shore to create a relatively flat plane of glistening white. In a few places, the underlying rock managed to poke a finger of stone up through the ice and create a jagged little break in the landscape, like skeletal fingers clawing their way up through the hard-packed dirt of an old grave.

Further off in the distance, Denise could see mountains erupting up out of the ice. The compacted flatness of the ice made it difficult to determine distances. There were almost no reference points to draw on, just a low, flat featureless plain that seemed to stretch on forever in haunted loneliness.

High above them, there were a couple of stretched, anemic-looking clouds. There was no moisture in the air. Even the clouds looked like they'd been drained dry by some sort of atmospheric vampires.

"What do you think? Everything you expected?" Dr. Benoit asked.

"I was expecting more snow," Denise said lamely. It was true, though. In her mind, there had been great snowbanks drifting across the land like sand dunes, the wind occasional whipping the stuff into playful flurries. There wasn't so much as a single flake of snow on the ground though, despite how cold it was.

"A lot of people ask about the snow, actually. The truth is, there's basically none, though. Antarctica's climate is technically a desert. The world's largest desert, as a matter of fact. There's almost no precipitation on any given year. However, the ice on the ground is actually the result of what little snow we do receive here. It hits the ground, freezes in a thin layer, and then another layer paves over it the next year. All the ice you see here is actually made of layers and layers of compacted snow, built up over tens or hundreds of thousands of years. It's kilometers thick in places."

Dr. Benoit continued to expound on the natural marvels of the continent as they walked toward the facilities. One of the other scientists had grabbed onto the opposite end of her baggage and was helping her carry it. She didn't really need the help, but she appreciated anything that would speed her way toward the relative warmth of Delambre Station. She nodded a thanks to the man, who wasn't much more than a vague shape under his layers of clothing. He didn't bother to respond. Maybe he didn't speak English.

Then Denise noticed something she hadn't seen before. The man's clothing had shifted because of the way he was holding onto her baggage. The butt of a revolver poked out of his jacket pocket. When the man was at rest, it would slide back down into the depths of his parka, but the stooped, awkward way he was forced to walk pressed the gun upward until it was peeking out at her.

Denise filed that image away in her mind. Why would they need guns here? It certainly wasn't because of the wildlife. This was the Antarctic, not the North Pole. There wouldn't be any polar bears around here. They lived on the opposite side of the planet. The South Pole didn't really have an equivalent to the polar bear. She couldn't think of a good reason why someone would need to traipse around with a weapon down here, not unless they were worried about something.

She took a moment to glance at the other French scientists who had come out to greet them. None of them spoke except for Dr. Benoit. She couldn't tell if any of the rest of them had weapons ferreted away in their jackets. All of them were moving quickly, as if they were anxious to get back inside, but that didn't necessarily prove anything. Any sane person would be eager to get out of this. Even with all their layers, the wind could cause frostbite and hypothermia.

They passed the research station's first building, a little concrete blockhouse. A small fleet of motor sledges was parked next to it under a small overhang. The unfastened end of a tarp flapped wildly in the wind as they trudged past.

Dr. Benoit was still talking, evidently enjoying his role as the group's unofficial tour guide. "And just over that ridge there is the penguin rookery. We'll make sure to get you over there at some point when the weather calms down a bit. It would be a bad idea to try to trek out there right away, though."

"Of course. Of course. We'll be here a few days. Plenty of time," Denise said, just responding without thinking too much. She was more interested in taking in as much of the facility as she could right now. That's what she was here for. The Squires wanted her opinion as a monster hunter as to whether or not there was anything to be worried about down here. The fact that one of the researchers had come out to greet them with a gun in his pocket was a bit odd, but it wasn't as if Delambre Station was on fire and full of bug-eyed aliens when she arrived. So far, there wasn't any serious sign that anything the Squires would be interested in was going on.

They passed another building on the edge of the compound, and Denise realized it was a hangar. There were a couple of small biplanes parked inside along with a large tank of fuel. Maybe she could talk Benoit into allowing Fletch to take her up in a plane to reconnoiter the area a bit better. All she could see from ground level was ice, rock, and more ice.

"Oh, good. Airplanes. If it's alright with you, we'll want Mr. Adams here to take us on a little air tour eventually."

"That can probably be arranged. Under the right conditions of course. You'll have to stay away from some areas, though. There's unstable ice. And poor weather. I'll give you a map when we get inside so you can avoid certain areas. Mostly, you should stay near the coast. The interior is...not a pleasant place to find yourself. Yes, quite dangerous. You should stay away."

Behind her, Cornelia and Metrodora were trudging along with their own luggage. If they were here strictly on as a pleasure trip, they wouldn't need entire trunks just to carry their cold weather gear. A .577 Nitro Express was a large weapon though, and it had to be buried under a lot of jackets and parkas to completely hide it. The same went for the ammunition, which had to be packed in tight to prevent it from rattling and making too much noise. Denise would be perfectly happy if she only had to break out the clothing items and not the weapons.

A couple of paces behind Cornelia and Metrodora, Fletch had noticed the planes parked in the hangar. He looked out at the ice in front of the building, the station's makeshift runway, and then he glanced back at the planes. Denise couldn't tell if he was hoping to try one out later or if he was exasperated that this place was even more developed than he initially thought.

After what seemed like an interminable amount of time, Benoit led them to the door of the largest building. Denise looked back, her legs aching and her face stinging, to look back at the shoreline. It was less than a quarter of a mile away.

Denise was in good shape. She'd spent years traipsing across the grasslands and forests of southern Africa, carrying supplies on her back and a rifle in her hands the whole time. She hadn't let herself slip since retiring from the big game hunting business.

Even so, just trying to move in this environment was exhausting. Shuffling around in multiple layers of thick, padded clothing slowed her down and threw off her stride. Trying to keep her balance on the ice, which bulged or sank ever so slightly based on the contours of the landscape beneath, was also surprisingly draining. Plus, she was used to travelling in the heat, not this biting, infernal cold.

Looking back at the shore, so surprisingly close, she realized that if she was going to do any exploring or surveying, she would need to do most of it with the aid of one of the motor sledges or the station's airplanes. Trying to get anywhere on foot would be a quick way to end up exhausted out in the blinding white yonder, and that was a good way to end up stone cold dead.

Dr. Benoit pushed the door open, and the wind nearly sent it crashing inward. He managed to get a grip on the handle before the door crashed all the way open, though. "Now, allow me to show you to your quarters. This is the main living area and research center for the entire base. Most of the other outbuildings you've seen house supplies or other necessities. This is where all the real activity is, though."

Denise stomped her feet on the ground, partly in a vain attempt to warm up a little and partly to scrape some of the ice off her feet. She stepped inside and blinked against the glow of the fluorescent lights, so different from the glare of sunlight against ice.

The first thing she noticed was the surprising amount of medical equipment. Off to the left, she spotted several gurneys lined up against the wall. Each gurney had thick leather straps attached to it. Denise looked at the restraints for a moment.

The gurneys were both empty. There was also a folded-up wheelchair, also with restraints. They were all lined up near a door labeled *radiographie*.

Denise didn't speak French. She had no idea what *radiographie* meant. Probably the radio room. The medical equipment was odd, though. A research station of this size no doubt had an infirmary, but she didn't see any indication that there was one hidden away in this hallway.

Benoit noticed her gaze. "The science quarters are that way. It takes up most of the building, actually. You will have to excuse our mess. We are always swapping out equipment and haggling over space for some new device or another. It is nothing personal, but we will have to ask you to stay out of that end of the building. We have some very sensitive and delicate instruments through there, and it would cost us weeks of data if they were disturbed in the slightest. You understand, I'm sure."

"Oh, yes. Of course," Denise said. She understood, alright. Now she knew she needed to find some way to stick her nose in there, if only for a moment.

Now that she'd had a couple of seconds to look around, she couldn't help but notice just how new everything looked. There wasn't any wear or tear on anything she could see. She looked up and noticed a set of metal pipes running the length of the ceiling. The metal shone like it had just come off the factory floor. There wasn't a spot of corrosion or any chips around the casing. It didn't even look like there was much dust up there.

"Follow me," Benoit said, leading Denise and her companions in the opposite direction of the *radiographie* room.

"I must admit that I'd never heard of Delambre Station until quite recently. Only once I started looking for a way to visit Antarctica a couple of weeks ago, as a matter of fact. When was this place built?"

"It's quite new," Benoit said, not really answering the question. "Do you like it? They spared no expense."

"Yes, it seems very nice," Denise said.

"You flatter us."

Denise probably was flattering the place. It was an extremely utilitarian space. The walls were poured concrete, lacking decoration. The doors were all made of heavy duty metal, again always spotless. The floor was just concrete too, but it had some sort of rubberized matting over it so people with ice stuck on their boots were less likely to either trip or track slush everywhere. It reminded her more of a prison than anything else, but it was still impressive that the French had built it at all.

They turned down a corridor and went through the mess hall. It was a large, brightly lit room with tables enough for maybe fifty people. There was one somber-looking man with a beard sitting at a table, reading a book and trying to spoon some sort of gruel into his mouth without losing too much of it in his unruly facial hair. He glanced up as the little parade meandered past him, then he went back to his book.

"We'll have proper introductions once you're all stowed away, but that's Dr. Louvain. Brilliant surgeon, but he doesn't speak much English. You probably won't have much to do with each other."

The fact that the bearded man was a surgeon reminded Denise of the medical gear she'd seen near the science wing of the building. Then she realized that she hadn't seen anyone else here except for Dr. Louvain and the party that had come to the docks to greet her. That was only seven people in total, but there was enough space here for many more people than that.

"How many people work here at Delambre Station?"

"Does it seem a little empty to you? It probably does. When it was being built, the construction teams also lived onsite. We're just the first group of researchers to use the facility. The population will expand a bit once summer rolls around and conditions become a bit more hospitable. Plus, we hope to eventually have more stations deeper into the interior of Antarctica itself. In a couple of years, this place may be more of a waystation for people travelling further inland. We built it with some extra space with that in mind. It may seem a bit lonely now, but maybe even we will host more tourists such as yourself in the future."

They entered another hallway and stopped in front of a doorway. Benoit pushed the thick, metal door open and revealed a space not much larger than a prison cell. There was a cot and a cheap dresser, neither of which looked like they'd ever been used before.

"You'll be staying here," Benoit said. "It may not look like much, but it's a lot nicer than sleeping in a tent outside. Just having an indoors to come in to is quite a step for Antarctic exploration."

"This will do nicely. *Merci*," Denise said, busting out one of the few French words she actually knew. Best to stay on Benoit's good side if she really wanted to know more about what was going on here.

"But of course. Glad to be of assistance." Dr. Benoit started to turn around to talk to one of the other scientists before something occurred to him. "I suppose I should make you aware of one last thing. It will be better to get it out of the way now."

"Oh?"

"Yes. You will have free access to the crew area here on the station. Your room here. The mess hall. You can even visit the small library we keep, if you wish. All the books are in French, though. However, as I said before, you must not, under any circumstances, enter the science facility. Our equipment is exceptionally sensitive. We cannot have any accidental influence in the data."

"Of course." Denise would try to worm her way into seeing what was inside there later, but it was better to seem agreeable first.

27

Benoit glanced at some of the other French researchers gathered in the hallway before he said anything else. He licked his cracked lips. "There is something else, though. I realize you will want to explore a bit outside, especially if we get a break in this wind."

"Absolutely," Denise half-lied. Being one of the first women to ever walk around on the southern-most land in the world was fun on an intellectual level. Feeling the cold slap her in the face like a drunk husband took the charm off real quick, though.

"We have a few teams out in the field. This is very important. If you encounter any of our people out there on the ice, don't approach them. Come back here and tell us where you saw them, if it looks like they might be in trouble. Whatever you do, don't try to help them. We have the proper equipment here at the station to deal with any problems. Do you understand me? Don't try to help them."

Denise nodded. The truth was, she didn't understand at all.

FOUR
WHEN HELL FREEZES OVER

Denise sat in the mess hall, spooning her meal around. Cornelia and Metrodora sat on either side of her. Technically, it was late in the evening, and they were having dinner. With the perpetual sunlight outside and the buzzing overhead lights inside, it didn't really matter, though. Denise could see how that could quickly grow disorienting. If someone's sleep schedule were thrown off, it would be hard to distinguish three o'clock in the morning from three o'clock in the afternoon. It all looked the same.

One of the French researchers was also in the mess hall, sipping from a bowl of steaming soup. Benoit had given them the man's name in a whirlwind of introductions earlier, but Denise had already forgotten it amid the rapid-fire list of new names and faces. She had no idea if the man spoke any English.

"We'll wait until he leaves," Denise said in Afrikaans, nodding in the man's direction. She would have carried out the whole conversation in that language; she was fairly confident that none of the scientists here spoke the tongue. However, Metrodora could understand a lot of Afrikaans, but it was harder for her to speak it. They were going to have to use English for any conversations that involved all three of them. Plus, Denise was worried that the gears of suspicion would start turning in Benoit's head if he walked in and heard them talking in a language no one else on the station could understand.

She and Cornelia started a half-hearted conversation about the weather while the Frenchman finished his meal. He didn't seem to be paying any attention to them, but Denise wanted to discuss some sensitive matters, and their rooms were too cramped to host three people very easily. Metrodora scratched out notes in her journal while Denise and Cornelia chatted.

Finally, the researcher picked up his bowl and retreated out of the mess hall, meandering off in the direction of the laboratories in the science wing of the facility. Denise waited until she'd heard the man's footsteps recede down the hallway before she got down to brass tacks.

"Alright, let's pool our impressions here. We've all had a little time to wander around the facility and gather our thoughts. Metrodora, you're the one who probably has the best idea of what the Squires are looking for. Have you spotted any smoking guns yet?"

Metrodora closed her notebook and put her pen away. "There is some unusual activity here."

"Want to unpack that for us a little?"

"Fine. This facility is extremely new. Just constructed."

"I noticed that, too."

"Everything I've seen points to this place being thrown up quite quickly. Within the last few months or so, probably. They aren't even completely done building their main docks, yet. They would have started construction during the last few months of winter. Normally, there would be no reason to be so eager to start building at that time. It would be cheaper and safer to wait until the warmest months to undertake such a project. That timeline seems to match up with roughly when the meteorite fell to earth here. Give or take the couple of weeks it probably took to find the impact site, of course."

"Can I ask you something?" Cornelia asked, craning around to look at Metrodora.

"I reserve the right not to answer."

"Alright, fair enough. How'd you get involved with St. George's Squires?"

"They found me as a child wandering near the edge of a containment area, a region they'd fenced off due to the dangerous or unusual fauna there. There was a breach, and one of the specimens escaped. I don't remember any of it very well, but the farm I grew up on was destroyed when the creatures escaped. It was apparently a matter of luck that I survived. Someone thought I showed promise, so they kept me around instead of giving me to an orphanage."

"How many of these containment areas you mentioned are there?"

"In Africa or the world as a whole?"

"Let's stick with Africa."

"Several dozen, spread out in remote locations. There's considerably more elsewhere, though. India and Australia are particularly rich in unusual biological specimens."

"And what exactly counts as an unusual biological specimen as far as St. George's Squires are concerned?"

"It's a multi-prong test. Something can fail part of the test but still catch our interest because it satisfies the other elements. First, we ask if the specimen in question is biologically divergent from its closest living relatives. What are its closest living relatives, and just how different is it from them? Then, we look at the creature's natural range of habitat. How widespread is it, and how many specimens are likely to exist in the wild?

Finally, and this is perhaps the most important question, just how dangerous is it?"

"So what exactly does your organization do when it finds a new monster?"

"Monster is considered a plebeian term among the Squires."

Denise was rapidly coming to the conclusion that Metrodora was kind of a snot. "Yeah. I know you're here to play nanny to us on this job because your boss is interested in whatever's down here, but Cornelia and I are monster hunters. If it's eating people, folks can hire us to deal with it. We've seen some things. You don't have to talk to us like we're children."

Metrodora scoffed. "Please, you're not monster hunters. That would imply you're professionals. You're just a couple of regular hunters who have been lucky enough to survive some unpleasant incidents and think you know everything now. You don't have protocols. You don't have facilities. You're a couple of ad-hoc cowboys who have caught our attention. If you impress us here, we might give you some real training and access to our archives so you actually know what you're talking about in the future."

"First of all, I've had more time out in the field than you ever will. I know what I'm doing. Second of all, you can eat a burlap sack full of dongs."

"You'll be thankful to work with us someday. Assuming you don't go out of business or get yourself killed in some spectacularly stupid fashion, first."

"We'll work for you when hell freezes over."

"Well, I'm stuck here with you, and I don't know if you've looked outside recently…"

Denise was about to say something snide when she heard footsteps approaching from the hallway. She closed her mouth, and her teeth clicked together. An uncomfortable quiet fell over the group.

Who the hell did Metrodora think she was? She only knew two members of St. George's Squires, Metrodora and Butts McGee, and they were both unpleasant. Assuming what she'd gathered about the organization as a whole was accurate, they had a lot of resources and experience at their disposal. She might lack the resources, but that didn't mean she was some sort of naïf about surviving dangerous situations and creatures, though. Nor did it mean she was ready to jump at the chance to join their organization. Better funding would be nice, but it wasn't worth it if everyone she had to deal with was a bastard and a half.

She'd quit sport hunting because she couldn't take it anymore. She'd grown up with her father on the plains and grasslands, learning everything there was to know about the great animals of the savanna. She knew how to track elephants and lions, and she knew how to follow the great, wandering herds of grazing animals that moved across the lands. She knew where their vital organs were and what bait to use to lure predators into a kill zone and which watering holes were the best to lurk near.

She'd learned all that, but the things she hadn't really understood were what caused her to give the life up. It had taken a tour group of Belgian dentists out for a hunt to show her that. They'd been tracking a group of elephants for days, and Denise had picked out a particular older female from the herd that would be a good target.

Her tour group had different ideas, though. Sometime when she wasn't paying attention, they'd decided that they all wanted an elephant. When she gave the signal, the bellow of gunfire nearly knocked her over. Half the elephant herd went down in the span of a couple of seconds. The earth shook as their huge bodies collapsed under their own weight, and they smashed into the dust.

The image that always stuck with her, the one that gave her the cold sweats when she tried to go hunting after that, was the baby elephant she saw trying to stir its mother with its trunk. That baby elephant had already had one of its ears blown off by a stray round, but it was desperately attempting to rouse the great bulk of its mother as it stood on the suddenly red soil.

When the hunters started reloading, Denise had yelled at them to stop. They didn't stop. They raised their guns and started firing again at the fleeing elephants, issuing a second ragged volley. She punched one of them out, knocked a tooth out in fact. It hadn't done any good, though. They'd wiped out nearly the entire herd, including the baby elephant standing next to its downed mother.

That was the thing she couldn't stand anymore. That moment of relative stillness before the second round of gunfire, the moment she saw that young elephant, had taught her something she hadn't learned on the trail before. The animals she was hunting weren't so very different from her in some ways. Maybe they didn't have clearly articulated thoughts, but they knew distress and pain and fear. Before it had all been a game, the thrill and the triumph of the hunt, of besting a wily opponent with skill and finesse. But the sudden realization that she was inflicting pain for sport, removing something living from the world for no better reason than idle amusement, that realization had hit her like a burst of thunder. Predators maimed and killed because they needed to in order to eat. She'd been doing it in order to decorate her office.

She'd already rearranged her life once because she didn't want to deal with the responsibility of making the world a worse place. Telling Metrodora and the Squires to shove it where the sun didn't shine wasn't such a big matter compared to that.

She liked her new gig a lot better. It managed to utilize some of the skills she'd developed, and she got to make a positive impact on the world. Even though her business was geared toward monsters...or aberrant zoological specimens or whatever Metrodora called them, most of her work so far had been a little more down to earth.

A few hundred people every year were eaten by lions or crocodiles. Man-eaters were a genuine problem in some parts of South Africa, especially once the creatures fully developed a taste for human flesh. She didn't mind hunting creatures like that because they were a menace to society. Getting rid of them actually did people some good.

There were creatures more dangerous than lions and crocodiles out there, though. She'd only found herself on her current career path after some unpleasant circumstances forced her to reacquaint herself with the art of survival. Sometimes she still had bad dreams about those times. Flashing teeth. Crashing through the jungle. The sound of leathery wings flapping across the night sky. The veldt burning as dark, seething figures shambled forward. Cornelia's missing leg.

It was all a kaleidoscope of blood and screams. She'd learned something valuable from those times, though. Her skills could be used for something good. She could help people who needed aid against the creatures of the night. That didn't mean she needed to use those skills helping a bunch of jerkoffs, though.

Denise would do this for St. George's Squires this time because she'd already agreed to do so. Curiosity and excitement and the promise of a nice payment had temporarily eclipsed her better judgement. But once she was back in Cape Town, that was the end of it. She'd do the bare minimum to establish if something dangerous had come from that meteorite or not, and then she wouldn't raise another finger for them.

Well, maybe one finger in particular.

She did her best to wipe the sour expression off her face as the sound of footsteps in the hallway grew louder. Turning around, she glanced out at the entrance to the mess hall to see who was coming.

Dr. Benoit walked past. When he noticed the three of them, he stopped. "Is everything alright?"

"We're fine. Just eating some dinner before getting some sleep. We want to be well-rested for some exploring tomorrow," Cornelia called. Hopefully, the mention that they were going to bed soon would help shoo Benoit off.

33

It didn't. "Ah, that is good thinking. You have had a long journey down here. I would imagine that must be tiring. Mr. Adams is coming back from the *Sulaco* with some of the crew. They have promised to start a poker tournament with us at some point. We could use some fresh excitement around here."

"Sounds fun. We'll turn in soon, though," Denise said. She turned back around to face away from Benoit, hoping he'd get the message and leave them be. Part of her wanted to finish her verbal scrap with Metrodora and the rest of her just wanted to get back to business as quickly as possible so she could get away. Both parts made her want to snap at Benoit.

"But of course. Say, what do you think of our marvelous cuisine?" Benoit seemed determined to hover around for another few minutes.

"It's, uh, pretty good," Denise said, stirring her food around a bit more.

"Thanks for trying to shield my feelings, but believe me, I know it's awful. Nothing is fresh down here. It all has to be packaged thousands of miles away. Dreadful," Benoit tsked. He glanced back and forth between the three of them. "Very well. I'll bid you good evening in case I do not see you again before you turn in."

"Good night, Doctor," Denise said as Benoit sauntered off in the direction of the research center.

Denise turned her attention back to the matter at hand. She glanced at Metrodora but decided not to say anything else. They'd end up stabbing each other with forks if they got into it again, and she didn't want to try explaining that to the station's physician.

"Alright, we know Delambre Station is very new. Unusually new, even," she said when the sound of Benoit's footsteps faded away. "Does that give us anything concrete, though? It seems a bit odd that they'd rush to build a station just to study a meteorite, but that's not really proof that there's something nefarious out on the ice. What else have we got?"

"Did you notice they have a gun locker near the entrance to their science quarters?" Cornelia asked.

"No," Denise said.

"It's built into the wall. It's a bit hard to see because it's partly blocked by a gurney at the moment. I never saw it open, so I don't know what's actually inside. Maybe they repurposed it to hold something else. Could be sensitive equipment. Could be guns. No idea."

"Alright, that's something. Maybe," Denise said.

"And the men here," Metrodora said. "They're all relatively young. Military age. You would expect at least a few older, esteemed professor-types around at a brand-new facility like this. These are all relatively young men, though."

"Meaning?" Denise had noticed too, but she didn't want to let Metrodora off the hook so easily. She was going to have to show her work.

"It's impossible to draw any conclusions from that, but it does strike me as unusual. Uniformity is suspicious. It implies there's some criteria beyond simply academic skill."

"Might just be the environment. They didn't want to post anyone down here that might be too feeble if there was a problem." Denise was still feeling petty and probably would have tried to refute it if Metrodora had said it was a little chilly outside.

"And have you noticed how several of them seem to lurk behind our shoulders from time to time. Like Benoit just now," Metrodora continued. "They seem interested in keeping an eye on us."

"I'm not sure how unusual that is," Cornelia said. "They haven't seen any new faces in quite a while. Let alone women. I'm surprised we don't have half of them hanging off us like leeches right now."

"But what I find unusual about that is—"

Denise cut Metrodora off. "The thing that I find the most peculiar was the warning that we should stay away from anyone we run into outside. Even if conditions are bad, hell, especially if conditions are bad, I don't know why we would come all the way back here in case someone needed help."

"Crevasses? Unstable ice?" Cornelia volunteered.

"Maybe. Still, it's odd. I'm not sure it gets us anywhere, though. We've got a number of odd little elements that don't seem to go together." She thought again of the gurneys and their restraints parked outside the main entrance to the research wing to the building. "But we don't have anything that points in any particular direction."

"I think it's all probably pretty innocuous," Cornelia said. "At least as far as our concerns go. The French government dispatched people here as part of some political gambit with research benefits attached. They get a permanent foothold in the area, and a better claim on the continent. The scientists here are eager to spend some time around new faces, but they're supposed to be secretive about their research, so we get a bunch of things half-explained to us, and we're turning it into something more suspicious than it is. It could all be *realpolitik*, with the meteorite as a convenient catalyst for a power move."

That sounded fairly reasonable to Denise. Maybe it didn't explain absolutely everything about what it was going on here, but she was only supposed to look out for a fairly specific set of problems. So long as there weren't any little green men with bug eyes wandering around the place and attacking people, it didn't matter much to her one way or the other what the French were up to down here. It would pique her curiosity, and there was nothing so fun as rampant speculation, but it wasn't really her problem. They were probably studying that meteorite and half a dozen other projects out in the research wing.

"There's still something I don't like," Metrodora said.

"What's that?"

"About the men stationed here. How many of them have you seen? I count about ten in total."

"Yeah, that's about what I've seen. Somewhere in that ballpark."

"That's what's been bothering me. And the ages again. According to the records we acquired, the French government dispatched a large number of biologists down here. Close to sixty. Enough to leave this mess hall crowded. And those were just the ones we know of. There could have been more. The oldest one we know of was seventy-two years old. Have you seen any of those people here?" Metrodora asked.

Denise realized this was the point she'd cut Metrodora off from making a minute ago. "Sixty scientists?"

"At least. Those are just the records we had passed to us. Could be more. Probably more, with support staff to consider."

Denise was pretty damn sure there weren't sixty people at this station. Even if the majority of them were devoted to their work, they would have to come out of the research wing to eat sometime. Plus, Benoit hadn't said anything about there being more people here. The way he'd run off introductions had implied that she'd met most everyone except for a couple of people in the lab. That was maybe twelve people total. *Maybe* twelve. Only about twenty percent of the total number of people Metrodora was saying should have been here.

"Alright. Quick tally of early conclusions."

"Some things don't add up," Metrodora said. "I don't like what I've seen so far."

Denise nodded. "Cornelia, you seem less convinced."

"When I was taking my nursing classes, there was a saying the instructors liked. If you hear hoof beats, think horses, not zebras. When they said it, they meant when we saw symptoms consistent with both a bout of flu and some ultra-exotic death plague, we should start out assuming it was the flu. I'll grant you, this whole situation has some fishiness to it, but it's not really inconsistent with the French trying to flex some diplomatic muscle, either." She looked at Denise. "You want to grace with your opinion, glorious leader?"

"I'm still kind of agnostic about my conclusions so far," Denise said.

"Boo. Cop out," Cornelia stage shouted.

Denise continued. "There's something weird going on here, but I don't think we have any real proof about what it might be. We certainly don't have anything to connect it to that meteorite we're here about. If the Squires are worried some sort of creature got loose down here, I'm not sure there's anything to worry about. The researchers seem to have control of the station."

Denise shushed her last words down to a whisper as she heard more footsteps out in the hallway. She twisted around to see who was coming again. There were two sets of footsteps this time.

A second later, Fletch and Poole appeared in the doorway. Fletch glanced in and noticed the three of them. "Hey, I asked if we had permission to borrow a plane tomorrow, and Dr. Benoit gave the okay. We'll have ourselves an air tour once the wind abates a bit."

"That's great. Thanks. I appreciate it."

"By the way, we're going to set up a poker tourney in here pretty soon. You three want in?"

"We're good. Thanks. How are things on the ship?"

"Doesn't look like we're going to get blocked in by ice. At least not tonight, anyway," Poole said. "That whaling ship is still somewhere nearby, too. They're keeping their distance, but they're sticking to this general area. Other than that, not much going on out there."

"Alright, good luck with your cards, then. We'll see you in the morning." Denise did her best to shuttle them off before turning back to Denise and Metrodora. "Right. It sounds like we don't have a lot more time before this place starts filling up. Cornelia, any last thoughts?"

"I'll play the devil's advocate here. Yeah, there's some stuff that doesn't seem quite normal, but that doesn't mean that anything's actually wrong. Those biologists could have been shipped down here for a very short period of time, maybe for a specific whale migration event or something. If they aren't here now, it might just mean they're already on their way back to Europe or something. Benoit and his team might just be the skeleton crew. I don't think we can jump to any conclusions here yet."

"Fair enough about jumping to conclusions. We don't have a lot to go on right now. Metrodora?"

"We need to break into the research wing of the building."

"Wait. Hold on. What?"

"It's important that we start eliminating some possibilities. We're not going to do that just sitting around in our rooms and this mess hall.

We can't rule out much of anything right now. Maybe this expedition is a big waste of everyone's resources. Maybe it's not. I intend to find out one way or another. That seems like the most direct route."

"Slow your butt down for a minute. We haven't exhausted all our options yet. Not by a long shot. We're going to have more chances to investigate outside tomorrow. Fletch just said he can show us around from one of the planes. That could tell us something."

"Getting into the laboratories could tell us something right now."

"No. We'll only do that as a last resort, something for in case we're really stuck for answers. If we get caught doing that, it'll be hard to squirm out of it. If the French are really serious about this place, they won't take too kindly to having us wandering around in there. Maybe Cornelia is right and this place is supposed to be a stepping stone for the French military. For all we know, they're developing weapons in there. If we get in there and find something like that, they're going to think we're spies. We play this smart."

No sooner had Denise finished her little spiel than an alarm sounded over their heads. The sudden wail of the klaxon nearly blew her off her seat. She jumped up, her hand pawing at her hip where she was so used to the weight of a revolver. There was nothing there, though. Her weapons were still buried in her luggage, hidden under clothing and the trunk's false bottom. She half-expected French commandos to sweep into the room and throw handcuffs on all three of them for plotting against the state's interests.

There was a gunshot from deeper inside the facility, from the direction of the research ward. Denise's head whipped around at the sound. In the hallway, two researchers pounded down the corridor in the direction of the science center. A second later, there were another couple of gunshots, and then the alarm shut off. It had only been on for perhaps fifteen seconds, but the silence in its wake suddenly seemed to fill the world.

Dr. Benoit came down the corridor at a rapid clip. He stopped in the mess hall's doorway when he spotted them. He had a scratch under his right eye that wasn't very deep but was still bleeding quite a lot.

"There's been a technical malfunction. It's been taken care of, but you three should retire to your quarters now."

Cornelia took a step closer. "I was a nurse during the war. Let me see your eye. I can bandage that up for you."

"No." Benoit threw a glance over his shoulder at something Denise couldn't see. "You should go. Right now. Everything is under control, but we need to do some maintenance immediately."

Denise stood up and edged a little closer to the door. She caught a brief glimpse of the two scientists she'd seen running down the hallway before. Now one of them was wheeling a gurney toward the research wing of the building, and the other had a jerry can of gasoline in his hands.

Then Benoit moved to the side and blocked her view. Denise had already seen enough to reevaluate Cornelia's idea that maybe everything was fine here, though. They were going to have to find some conclusions at this station, and Denise wasn't sure she was going to like them.

FIVE
THE BIG WHITE EMPTY

The little biplane bucked in the air again as another gust hit it. Denise grabbed onto the side of her seat as the plane tilted for a brief but unpleasant second, threatening to roll onto its side like it was performing some kind of barnstorming stunt.

She hadn't particularly enjoyed the ride on the *Sulaco* through tumultuous seas and churning waves. This was worse. This was a thousand times worse. Denise held onto the seat harder as the plane shuddered before flipping back onto its proper axis.

Even though she was strapped in, it was all too easy to picture the small plane hitting a particularly rough patch of turbulence and launching her right out of the open-air passenger seat. And it was equally easy to imagine one of the wings simply shearing off and sending them on a spiral toward the packed ice below, almost as hard as cement.

"Sorry about that," Fletch yelled from the forward seat. The wind tried to whip his words away, but Denise managed to hear. Even so, conversation was nearly impossible, even if she felt much like talking. That didn't stop Fletch, though.

"So like I was saying, they taught me to fly planes during the war. I flew a reconnaissance plane, the ones that fly over the enemy trenches and bunkers and snap pictures for the generals to look at. The fighter pilots like to hog all the fame, but they get to fight back. We had to fly steady while the Germans were firing at us from the ground or sending their own fighters in. Most of the other guys in my unit, Littlejohn, Pennington, O'Malley, pretty much everybody mustered out and went back to civilian life after the war ended. I stayed in, and they asked me to start doing supply runs for some of the Antarctic expeditions down here. The next thing you know, everybody wants to hire me out because there's not many people with the experience to do that. Of course, the planes today are a lot better built than they were ten years ago, so that helps." Fletch kept talking, and Denise listened with half an ear to the parts she could understand over the wind.

They were buzzing around a few hundred feet in the air, sweeping back and forth into the interior. They were moving generally toward the mountains Denise had seen off in the distance yesterday when they landed at the docks.

The winds today were less intense than yesterday. Before they took off, Fletch had explained that the pervasive gusts were something called katabatic winds. It was a strange phenomenon driven by geography rather than any particular weather system. Because the ice sheets around Antarctica rose to levels far above sea level, the entire continent was basically one gigantic plateau. Due to the extremely cold temperatures, it created a sheet of unusually dense air high up on the continent's shelf. That air then tried to disperse off the Antarctic plateau. Because the air was extra thick, it was almost like rolling a bowling ball down a hill. The winds were actually driven mostly by gravity.

Just because the wind was less intense today didn't mean it was gentle, though. Denise felt the plane shift under her again and she grimaced under her ski mask. Or she tried to anyway. Her face had gone mostly numb but for an unpleasant tingle. The wind itself was already deathly cold. Combined with the air rushing past the open plane seats, it was like getting into a slap fight with Father Winter. She would have rubbed at her face to try to press some feeling back into it, but that would require her to release her white-knuckled death grip on the sides of the plane's seat.

They always said not to look down when heights were involved, but that was exactly what she needed to do. She was out here to see if there was anything unusual down there on the ice. Some things would be a lot more obvious from the air than they would be from the ground. Bits of scuffed ice where many feet or vehicles had traveled would be hard to spot just hiking around. So would any individual creatures or people, who wouldn't be much more than specks on a glittering horizon from the ground. Up here, they would stand out like individual dots of paint on an otherwise blank canvas.

The problem was just that the canvas was very, very large. That, and the risk that they might fall out of the sky fast enough to leave a big smear of red paint. Denise scanned the horizon from behind her tinted goggles, squinting against the ice's bright reflections.

After last night, she knew there was something happening down here at the bottom of the earth. Benoit and his men had shuffled her, Cornelia, and Metrodora off to their rooms as almost as soon as the echoes of gunfire had faded completely. The poker tournament had been cancelled, too. Benoit told them this morning that they'd overloaded a piece of equipment in the science ward, and it had exploded. He said that a little piece of shrapnel had grazed him, and that was why he had the cut under his eye.

Maybe taken on its own, that story was believable. Denise knew the sound of gunfire pretty well, but the pops she'd heard had been pretty muffled by the concrete walls all around them. A generator backfiring or a piece of mechanical equipment suffering a catastrophic engineering failure might very well be able to be mistaken for gunfire.

But there were too many other niggling little doubts for Denise to believe that story right now. A lot of little things seemed to point to the idea that there was *something* bad happening here. She just didn't have an inkling what it was.

Metrodora was right about one thing. Breaking into the science labs would give them the quickest answers. Metrodora wasn't in charge of this little venture, though. She was just a chaperone for the Squires. Denise still wanted to take a more circumspect approach with her snooping before she tried anything rash. Now wasn't the time for rashness.

Especially if the French team was quick with their guns. Despite Benoit's story, Denise was inclined to trust her first instinct and assume that she had in fact heard gunfire last night. Naturally, that raised the question about what they had been shooting at.

Maybe she could gather some clues out here. Or at least some ideas that would point her in the direction of some clues. She really didn't want to try breaking into the research wing until they'd run out of other options. She didn't know what those guns might have been pointed at last night, but she intended to avoid any sort of situation where they might end up pointed at her.

So far, she couldn't tell if her strategy of playing things smart was actually panning out. She didn't actually feel that smart riding around in the little biplane as it farted across the sky and rattled like a toy every time the wind kicked back up. Climbing into this death trap actually seemed real dumb, now that she was up here.

But there was still the possibility that she was onto something. From up here, she could see where motor sledges or other vehicles had chewed their way across the ice. They left marks on the surface as well as the occasional oil stain. The paths and tracks carved the ice up a little, like a crack in a mirror.

There were lots of the little trails in the region right around Delambre Station. They led from the docks up to the buildings, and then there were smaller paths leading between all the outbuildings where the scientists had trudged across the ice enough times. There were also a few trails that led away from the station to various points of interest nearby.

She'd told Fletch to circle around to some of the trails. She hadn't bothered to tell him that she wanted to know what the researchers were up to down here. In fact, she hadn't told Fletch much of anything. She'd generally avoided talking to him or the crew of the *Sulaco*. As far as any of them knew, she was just some modestly wealthy kook on the vacation of a lifetime with a couple of friends. The fewer people who knew she had been sent here by a shadowy group she only barely trusted in order to investigate whether anything dangerous had crawled out of a meteorite, the better. Not that anyone would believe her if she told them the truth.

Fletch had buzzed around the various trails, just as she'd requested. One of them led over a ridge toward what appeared to be the penguin rookery Benoit had mentioned the other day. Another extended onto a stretch of sea ice where the researchers had drilled some holes and seemed to have some instruments dipped down into the water below. Neither of those paths held Denise's interest for long. They looked like more or less what she expected a normal, ordinary science team would be doing down here.

There was another path that extended away from the station, though. There were deep tracks in the ice, as if the trail was well-travelled. They extended away from the coast and deeper into the big, white empty.

Sometimes the ground below dipped in little valleys or crevices. Other times, spires of rock poked out through the ice. The earth beneath must have been fairly rugged terrain. Further out, closer to the center of Antarctica, the ice would be so thick that there wouldn't be any indication about what the land was like below. If the ice sheet was massive enough, it had probably flattened everything beneath it, actually.

Closer to the shore though, the tracks she was following had to weave around occasional outcroppings or short dips. They were already a few miles out from Delambre Station. Even so, she still couldn't see what the tracks were actually supposed to be leading to. They simply continued on toward the horizon as if they were marching toward the South Pole. For all she knew, maybe they were. If she ordered Fletch to book it, they could cover a lot of ground fast in this little plane. As it was, she was having him sweep back and forth, covering as much ground as possible and giving her a chance to scout the trail out more.

Denise squinted down at the ground, trying to see if she could tell what had actually beaten the trail through the ice. She assumed that a collection of motor sledges probably made the trail over many trips. It could have been dog sled teams. Delambre Station had a small collection of sled dogs, but they were mainly used for short distance trips. She couldn't imagine that the trail had been made by people on foot. That would take dozens, maybe even hundreds, of trips to wear the ice down like that. Motor sledges were heavier and a lot more convenient. They'd wear a rut in the ice a whole lot faster.

Another gust of wind blasted them, and the plane shook like a wet dog. Denise stopped focusing on the ground below and went back to focusing on keeping her butt glued to the seat. Due to the creeping numbness in her hands, she could only feel her grip on the plane as a sort of vague pressure. She wished her hands were warmer so she could be sure she had a tighter grasp. She wished everything was warmer.

Finally, the wind finished toying with them, and the plane settled into a more stable flight again. That's when she saw it.

"There's something on the ice down there," she shouted, touching Fletch's shoulder to make sure he could hear her. "Take us over it. I want to see what that is."

Fletch nodded and banked the plane a few degrees to the right. The wind buffeted them again, and Denise did her best to calm the little edge of fear that tried to whisk her thoughts apart.

Down below, the trail passed beneath a sheer outcropping of rock. There was something just off to the side of the path, resting in the shadow of the outcropping. From here, it didn't look like much more than a little black dot. However, that was more than Denise had seen in the entire rest of the time they'd been out here.

As they drew nearer, the dot resolved itself into a more defined shape. It was a motor sledge. The vehicle was tipped over on its side, and Denise could see a tumble of supplies around it like a splash of arterial spray. Oil and gasoline had leaked out of it and formed dark puddles on the ice nearby.

The motor sledge didn't keep Denise's attention for long, though. She spotted a flash of color in the shadows under the outcropping. She looked around, trying to get a fix on what she'd just seen. Then she saw the flash of yellow again. It was a man in a brightly colored jacket moving among the rocks. He stumbled and lurched as the plane banked around for a second pass.

"There's somebody down there," Denise shouted above the wind.

"I see him. They look like they're in trouble. Did Dr. Benoit tell you not to try to help anyone we found out here?"

"Yeah."

"Screw 'im." Fletch worked the stick, and the place circled away from the outcropping toward a flat surface, losing altitude as it went. He was going to land.

SIX
FROSTBITE

Denise looked at Fletch. She couldn't see him except for the back of his head and his shoulders, and both of those were wrapped up in cold weather gear. She felt a swell of respect for him. And with that came a dip of guilt for dragging him into the middle of this. He had no idea that St. George's Squires suspected there might be something seriously wrong down here. She was using him as a sort of patsy.

There wasn't time to delve too far into her own feelings, though. The plane touched down on the ice with a jolt, bounced, and then came down for good. Fletch worked the engine, throttling the propeller down and slowing the plane as it slid across the ice. They skidded and slipped for the length of a football field before the tiny plane finally lurched to a stop on the ice.

Denise hopped over the side and stumbled a little. She felt a little funny after being jostled through the air for so long. It was disorienting to be standing where the ground wasn't heaving and bucking each time the wind kicked up now. She shook her limbs out for a second, trying to throw off some of the numbness that had settled over her skin.

Then she started walking toward the outcropping of rock. She'd lost track of the man with the yellow parka again. He must have been behind one of the boulders that had crumbled off the side of the outcropping. The tall ledge had a number of small hollows and crevices. One of them appeared to be the entrance to a cave.

Marching across the ice, she kept an eye on her surroundings. She didn't know why there was a man stranded out here, his transport tipped over; she just knew that something wasn't right. There weren't any obvious signs of bug-eyed monsters from outer space, but Denise knew better than to let her guard down.

After last night's incidents in the lab, she wasn't completely unprepared. She had a heavy revolver tucked into the pocket of her outermost jacket. The weapon was the same kind game preserve rangers kept on them when they were wandering a park. If something jumped out of the grass right in front of them, the idea was that a point-blank shot to the face would take down anything short of a rhino.

Right now though, Denise wished she'd brought her Nitro Express elephant gun. There was no way to hide it on the plane, and it would have been awkward trying to explain its presence to Fletch. She continued forward with her hands in her pockets, both to keep them warm and to keep one wrapped around the grip of the revolver.

Denise approached the outcropping slowly, moving as deliberately as if she was walking through the African tall grass. She had better visibility out here than she would out on the savanna, but she was on less familiar territory. The sudden blasts of freezing wind and the white expanse extending out toward the horizon were both disorienting. The wind threatened to smear ice chips across her goggles. The white field in front of her made it hard to gauge distance.

She still didn't see the man in the yellow jacket as she drew nearer to the overturned motor sledge. She'd reached the outer ring of the debris field around the vehicle. There were cans of food, several of them bent and burst open. They'd sprayed their contents across the ice like exploded bug guts on a giant windshield. Other cans were intact and unopened.

Denise spotted a tent peg but no tent. The wind might very well have blown it away right after the accident, sending it over the horizon like an autumn leaf plucked from a tree and hurled into the October sky. There were other miscellaneous items. She nudged a shredded rucksack with the toe of her boot. A single brass bullet casing lay nearby, but there was no sign of a gun. The debris was spread out in all directions around the overturned sledge like little planetoids orbiting a dying sun.

Looking around, Denise had a bad feeling about what she was seeing. The scene looked like an accident of some sort. She tried to picture that flash of yellow she'd seen from the air. Was she sure the little speck of color was moving? Could the man be laid out dead behind those rocks?

Something stuck out of the torn backpack near her feet. It was a laminated sheet of paper. She bent down and picked it up. It was a map of the coast and part of the Antarctic interior. Delambre Station was clearly marked on the map right next to the coast.

However, there was something else marked down deeper inland. Denise checked the scale and realized that whatever else was located there was almost thirty miles away from the edge of the sea. It was a roughly straight shot south from Delambre Station.

The map simply marked Delambre Station as a dot with the word *Delambre* hovering above it. There was a second dot labeled *Merovée*, though. The map didn't give any indication what Merovée actually was. Some of the more prominent natural formations nearby were drawn in and labeled, too.

Whatever Merovée was, it was located on the far side of the mountains, just through a narrow pass. As far as Denise could tell, the trail she and Fletch had been following before they stopped here was the path to this Merovée. She wanted to know more about it, whatever it was.

The base of the outcropping ahead was littered with fallen boulders and stones. As Denise looked up, a couple of small rocks shifted and fell down the small slope to the very base of the outcropping. They'd come from behind one of the larger boulders about halfway of the slope.

Denise stuffed the map in a pocket and took another couple steps closer. She waited a moment, but no one appeared. "Hello?" There was no guarantee that anyone could hear her with the wind whistling across the ice.

They drew closer, and the man in the yellow jacket reappeared. His hood was drawn tight around his face, and Denise couldn't make out his expression. He could be either very happy or very annoyed to see them, but until he stepped out into the light, Denise wouldn't be able to see anything other than a dark shadow under that hood.

"Are you alright? Do you need any help?" Fletch called. The wind tore the words from his mouth and scattered them before they could get halfway to the overturned motor sledge. Denise could barely hear him, and she was standing ten feet away.

The wind plucked at the man's yellow hood as he started picking his way over the rocks toward them. Denise and Fletch moved closer, hoping that the outcropping would offer some kind of windbreak and a chance to speak to the man.

"*Parlez-vous anglais?*" Fletch shouted, trying again. He turned to Denise and shrugged. "That's about as far as my *français* stretches. Other than that, I can ask him where the bathrooms are or to bring us more wine. I learned a couple of essential phrases during the war, and that's about it."

Denise nodded. She was busy watching the man approach them. He was either so numb he was having trouble walking or he was injured. Maybe frostbite. His movements were jerky and uncoordinated. It was like watching a drunk who was receiving electrical shocks every few seconds.

The man passed the overturned motor sledge, stepping on a satchel bag with a crunch. It sounded like there was something breakable in there. He lurched forward into the sunlight, and Denise got her first good look at her face.

That's when she realized she'd been able to see his face the whole time. There was nothing wrong with the light. She just hadn't realized what she was looking at.

The man's face was black with frostbite. The skin and tissues on his face had swollen and disfigured themselves under Antarctica's intense cold. In places, the skin was dry and flaking off in shreds of great black dandruff. Other sections of his face seemed to have ripped off entirely. Denise noticed the man didn't have lips anymore. There were just ragged ridges of flesh surrounding his teeth. His nose was a cavernous ruin, and his eyes looked like green grapes that had started to rot on the vine.

Denise knew a little medicine. Not nearly as much as Cornelia with her nursing experience, but she could set a broken finger or tie a tourniquet in a pinch. This was far beyond anything she knew how to deal with, though. Frostbite wasn't really a going concern on the veldt.

The man's mouth opened into a gaping pit. His gums were swollen like balloons filled unto bursting with gelatin. A number of his teeth had fallen out, and his tongue looked like a big, boiled slug. The cold must have completely destroyed his outer layers of skin and chewed its way down to the nerves.

Another gust of wind blew the man's hood back away from his face more. His scalp was peeling away from the top of his skull. Hair clung to his head like patches of bracken and gorse where his scalp hadn't cracked and split. The man's ears were little more than black crusts, like something scraped off the bottom of a baker's oven at the end of the day.

Denise had no idea how the man was alive, let alone moving about. He must have been caught out here for days or even weeks. Everything from muscles to tendons must be partially mummified.

And they were supposed to leave this man out here even longer to go get Benoit and his team before dealing with this? No.

"Fletch, help me guide him over to the plane. We need to load him into the passenger seat and get him back to Delambre Station."

"We'd have to leave you behind."

"It's the fastest way. Besides, you can drop him off and get back here in less than an hour. It's ten minutes out, if you press it. You know how to find this place again. Just follow the trail leading out here. I'll make it for that long. I can take shelter in one of those crevices. I think I see a cave, too. That's probably how this guy survived as long as he did out here. Now, come on. Help me get him in the plane."

Denise stepped forward with Fletch next to her. The man was still creaking toward them. She didn't know if the man could really see them, given the state of his eyes. Maybe he was just following where he'd heard the plane touch down. Then again, she wasn't sure if he could hear anything at all either given what had happened to his ears.

Even if they got him back to the station right now, Denise wasn't sure the man would survive very long. They'd have to amputate the most damaged tissue so it didn't become necrotic and gangrenous. That wouldn't leave the man with much flesh left to spare. And Denise had read somewhere that warming a person up after they contracted frostbite would damage the salvageable tissue even more. It was like dipping bread in water, freezing it, and then letting it thaw out. The result wasn't so much reconstituted bread as it was something resembling oatmeal.

She gestured with her hands in the direction of the plane. "It's going to be okay," she lied. She spoke loudly, hoping to guide the man to the sound of her voice.

The man continued toward her, but that was when Denise started to realize that there was something well and truly wrong. It wasn't just that the man was obviously suffering from extreme frostbite. There were other signs.

For the first time, she noticed a large, dried splash of red on the man's jacket. Then, the wind whipped his hood fully away from his head. The extra light allowed her to see deeper into his mouth.

It looked like someone had worked on the back of his throat with power tools. The once pink flesh, since turned black, was shredded apart. It almost looked like the man had placed a pistol under his chin and pulled the trigger. The massive damage could have simply been a further effect of the frostbite, but Denise had never even heard of anything remotely like this. If the cold had penetrated so far into the man's body, how was it even possible that he was still alive?

"Fletch, hold on a minute," she said, throwing up an arm.

Fletch either didn't hear her above the wind or he was too engrossed with the broken thing in front of them to pay any attention to her. He took another few steps forward, his arms outstretched and ready to lead the man back to their plane.

The man swiveled his head around and fixed his unblinking gaze on Fletch. Denise realized that the man's eyelids had frozen and fallen off somewhere, giving him a look of perpetual surprise. His pace quickened, the herky-jerky movements carrying him straight toward Fletch.

For a second, but only for a second, Denise thought she saw something poke out from the shredded remains of the man's throat. All she saw was a glimpse of something pale, something that moved and pulsed, and then it was gone. The man pitched toward Fletch and then crashed straight into him.

The impact caught Fletch off guard, knocking him over backward onto his butt. Continuing forward, the frostbitten man crashed down on top of Fletch. His teeth gnashed at the air, making loud clicking noises as they chomped and bit.

Shouting in surprise, Fletch tried to push himself back up onto his feet, but the man in the yellow jacket kneeled down on top of him, slithering over his body. The frostbitten man pinned Fletch on the ice, trying to bite him.

What teeth remained in the man's jaws sank into the Fletch's outmost jacket and tore out a layer of stuffing. The man swallowed the hunk of white insulating padding without chewing, and then he went in for another bite. Fletch squirmed and struggled, shouting at the man to stop, but he couldn't free himself from the blackened ghoul's grip.

Denise fired her revolver in the air as a warning shot. The man didn't even flinch. He ripped off another patch of Fletch's jacket, devouring the entire wad of fabric in a gulp. Pieces of insulation stuck to his teeth like fuzzy, white mold.

She didn't want to fire directly at the man, not when he was right on top of Fletch. She could accidentally hit them both. This behavior wasn't just the result of frostbite. There was something truly wrong here. The cold and his own deterioration could have driven the man mad. But this seemed much worse than even a total mental breakdown. This seemed like something else entirely...

Her feet crunching on the ice, she ran over and kicked the man in the side. Her boot crashed into the man's side, partially knocking him off Fletch. Even through multiple layers of protective clothing, Denise could feel that the man's body didn't feel right. It was reedy, and it felt like his bones were made out of charred sticks that had been hastily bundled together. Something snapped where her foot made contact with his body.

The man rolled partly off Fletch, but one hand still had a grip on Fletch's jacket. The hand clinging to Fletch had lost its glove sometime in the past. It wasn't much more than a gnarled claw. A couple of the fingers had fallen off, and the remaining digits were all black and crooked, like something salvaged off a burnt mannequin.

Fletch scooted backward, trying to break the man's grip, but the frostbitten thing clung on. The man looked like nothing so much as a charred revenant coughed up from hell, desperately trying to grab onto something corporeal so he wasn't dragged back. Fletch shoved the man away, trying to push himself free.

The man tumbled backward, but his hand remained attached to Fletch's jacket. It snapped off with a crunching noise not so very different from the sound of their boots on the ice. Fletch rolled over and clambered to his feet before he noticed the hand still stuck to the front of his jacket. He plucked it off. Apparently still unsure about what to make of this new situation, he tossed it back to his assailant.

The hand bounced off the man's chest and plopped to the ground. He made no attempt to catch it. At first, he didn't even seem to register the hand at all, but then he bent down and scooped it up with his other hand, which still had a glove attached. He lifted the hand up and started chewing on it, biting off blackened hunks and swallowing them in great, choking gobs.

"What the hell is wrong with him?" Fletch turned to Denise.

"I don't know," she said. That was technically true. She was no medical expert. Cornelia might be able to explain what was going on from a medical and physiological perspective, at least to some extent.

Denise might not be able to explain it, but she could recognize some basic facts. The man in front of them was almost certainly dead. He'd been out here for long enough that he looked like a project Dr. Frankenstein had given up on in despair. Yet he was still up and moving about. Not only was he moving about, but he was actively trying to eat them.

Score one for St. George's Squires. There was something deeply unnatural happening down here.

The man gulped down the last remains of his own hand, swallowing the bones and everything else. Denise and Fletch backed up as he continued to move toward them. Nothing seemed to faze him. Denise had already probably broken one of his ribs, and his hand had just ripped right off.

She was already sure that it wouldn't do any good, but Denise fired another warning shot. This time, she planted the round right between the man's shuffling feet. "Stay back," she yelled.

As expected, the shot didn't provoke any sort of reaction. The man continued toward them with hitching movements that reminded Denise of a steam shovel encumbered with rust.

"Let's get out of here," she said to Fletch. He touched the holes in his jacket and nodded.

The dead man apparently had other ideas, though. He kept shambling after them. Denise didn't bother firing at him again. He didn't seem to be able to move very fast. His joints and tendons were probably just as frozen as the rest of him.

They retreated back toward the plane, putting distance between themselves and the ghastly figure stumbling along after them. He almost looked like he was following them to try to beg for help. From further away, with the details less clear, it almost made her want to try to stop and double back. But then the image of the man eating his own hand came back to her. She already knew that was a scene that would be replaying itself in her nightmares over and over again in the future.

Reaching the plane, they scrambled up into their respective seats. Fletch took the controls and toggled a couple of switches. Denise looked back. The man was still following them across the ice. She suspected that he'd probably follow them for as long as he could sense them.

"Hold on a minute," Fletch said.

"We don't have a minute. We need to get moving."

"The propeller is starting to freeze. I have to clear that off. The ice on there could create a strain on the equipment. It might tear itself apart while we were in the air." He hopped out of the plane and dashed around to try to clear some of the icy buildup.

Denise jumped out, too. "How can I help?"

"If you start scraping along here, we should be able to…" Fletch looked up. "Actually, on second thought, even working together, we won't be fast enough. You chip the ice off everything. I'll try to lead that thing away. Gimme your gun."

Denise looked back. The man kept moving toward them at a steady clip. "No. I'll keep him away. You know best which parts of the plane need to be de-iced. I know more about how to deal with things like that."

"But you're a lady."

"Shut up and get the ice off the plane." She stepped away and trudged in the general direction of the thing pursuing them. Waving her arms, she made sure to get the man's attention. He started angling away from the plane and more in her direction.

Now that he was closer again, Denise could tell that the man was no longer among the living. Something horrible had happened to him. And if he had his way, it seemed that he would be happy to do something horrible to Denise and Fletch.

Denise raised her revolver and levelled it at the approaching figure. She squinted her eyes, focusing on the gun's sight rather than on the shape it was pointed at. Reminding herself that she wasn't pointing the gun at a human being, just something that used to be one, she pulled the trigger.

The revolver kicked in her hands. The sound of the report washed over her before the wind whipped it away. She saw the bullet's impact on the man's chest. His yellow jacket rippled for a second almost like a pond after a large rock was thrown into it. The bullet punched a hole through the material and burrowed inward. Instead of a spurt of blood, there was just a neat little hole rimmed by fluffy, white padding.

Staggering, the man took an involuntary step backward. Denise watched as he recovered and immediately took another step toward her again.

She'd heard of stories where a bible or a deck of cards or a flask tucked away in a pocket had stopped a bullet. Anybody who stopped by a Cape Town general store could probably hear a couple of old-timers in the back telling similar stories about incredible escapes and lucky misses during the Boer Wars. Even if the stories grew more fantastical every year, at least a couple of them were probably true. Well, true-ish.

However, she didn't think there was any way in hell that just the padding from a few layers of cold weather gear could stop a bullet, not from the kind of revolver she was using. This thing was meant to blow the back of a lion's skull off in the last couple of seconds before it mauled a person to death. A couple of high-quality parkas weren't going to do a thing against that kind of power.

The man drew closer. Denise now knew beyond a shadow of a doubt that the man was dead. Some unknown force was keeping his legs under him and his jaws gnashing, but he was as dead as dead got. Just in case he did have something under his layers that had partially deflected her last shot, Denise adjusted her aim slightly and punched another round into the man's gut.

Instead of sending him down on the ground in a hunched ball like any living thing would have down, the man kept right on coming. If anything, he actually seemed to be coming a little quicker, as if he was close enough to lock onto Denise now.

She checked the revolver. It held six shots, and she'd already fired off four of them. Two warning shots. Two direct hits. She had more ammo stuffed in her pocket, but now she was wondering just how many shots it would take to actually bring the man down. He was already falling apart, and that didn't seem to be stopping him. The bullets didn't seem to be having much of an affect. Hell, they weren't even dissuading him.

This time, she aimed directly at the man's head. She pulled the trigger, and the man dropped to the ground in a tangle of limbs.

Denise stood where she was for a moment. She had seen people shot before. It was never pleasant business, but she knew what it looked like. They didn't clutch themselves and fall over dramatically the way they did in the movies.

Nobody ever really expected to get shot. It just wasn't something the human brain had evolved to deal with very well. Upon discovering a large brass pellet inside itself, the body's initial reaction wasn't really that different from an unexpected goosing. Usually, they jumped like they'd just sat on a hornets' nest. There was a big jolt as the body sprang into action.

Most people found themselves on the ground right after that. That was some ancient survival instinct telling them not to get hit again. The body tried to react the same way it would to a surprise insect sting, but with torn muscles and damaged ligaments, everything usually just collapsed on itself. People usually went down and stayed down, because the pain would set in shortly after that.

This man hadn't done any of that. The first couple of shots she'd fired into him hadn't affected him in the slightest. The last one did the trick, though. Well, maybe. Denise didn't want to assume anything at this point.

She pulled some extra ammunition out of her pocket and filled the revolver's five empty chambers. With her thick gloves, the process was slow and laborious. She never took her eyes off the figure sprawled on the ice, replaying what she'd seen over and over again in her mind. By all rights, the man should have been dead just from the cold. It shouldn't have taken three bullets to settle the matter.

"Is he dead?" Fletch called.

Denise didn't bother to answer. The man had been dead the whole time. The real question was whether or not his body had finally accepted that fact.

Taking one careful step at a time, Denise approached the body. It wasn't moving at all anymore, and that was a good sign. She came up to within a few feet of the corpse and stopped. She didn't want to stay out here too much longer. There was the omnipresent cold to consider, though her heart was racing fast enough to pump some feeling back into her limbs. There was also the idea that there might be more ghouls like this out here somewhere.

Still, she wanted to make sure the man was actually dead and also give a quick examination. Ideally, she would have turned the body over to Cornelia, who had the skills to say a lot more about its condition, but there was no way to bring the dead man back to Delambre Station, and even if there was a way, it would be impossible to examine him there. There wasn't really a good way to hide a blackened, bullet-ridden body from the French researchers in their own facility.

She shot the body in the pelvis to test out whether the man was down permanently or not. The body rocked back and forth a little, but there was no other reaction. She mentally marked that experiment down as a success, and then she scooted a little closer. Keeping her revolver aimed at the body, she reached out a foot and tapped the dead man's legs a couple of times in quick succession before leaping back.

No reaction. Finally confident that the man was as dead as he was going to get, Denise stepped up next to the corpse. The man had a small hole in his forehead, a couple of inches off center. There wasn't any blood around the rim of the hole. Most likely, all the blood in the man's body had congealed a while ago.

Even though the bullet hole going in wasn't particularly dramatic, the exit wound was a godawful mess. The interior of the man's skull was spread across the ice behind him. Bits of pulverized bone and rubbery-looking grey chunks had left streaks across the ground. Denise assumed that the rubbery-looking bits were pieces of spoiled brain matter. Again, there wasn't much blood. That only confirmed to Denise that the man had been dead for a while. There had been damn little liquid blood inside his body. It was all coagulated or frozen.

There was something amid the organic wreckage that she couldn't identify, though. Most of the debris looked about like what anyone would expect to come out of a corpse's head if the contents had been exploded like an old pumpkin dropped from a great height. It wasn't pleasant, but it wasn't unexpected, either.

Some of the chunks didn't really make sense to Denise, though. There were curious fleshy bits that didn't seem to be brain matter at all. Some of them had a smooth outer surface, but the interior was a mess of different parts. To Denise's untrained eye, it looked like there were guts and organs and blobs of unknown purpose. Again, she wished she had Cornelia around to tell her what she might be looking at with those chunks. Hell, she wished she even had Metrodora. Maybe St. George's Squires had some experience with this kind of thing.

She debated picking one of the larger mystery chunks up and taking it with her back to the station. That seemed like a bad idea, though. She didn't have any sort of baggie to transport it in, and she sure as hell didn't want to carry it around in her pocket. That thing had just been riding around in a deranged dead man's head. Aside from the indisputable scientific fact that it was super icky, there was a better than average chance that it was dangerous in some capacity. Maybe it was ridden with some uncategorized disease.

And then there was the problem that she'd have to try to hide it from the researchers back at the station. She didn't want them knowing she'd been out here.

Now she realized why Benoit had told her not to try to help anyone she found out here. They couldn't be helped, and they might try to eat her face off. Benoit knew that something had gone horribly wrong out here.

Instead of sifting through the contents of the dead man's skull, she patted him down instead, looking for any useful information. After a minute of shifting through multiple jacket pockets, she found an identification card.

The picture on the card was completely unrecognizable from the face in front of her. The picture showed a smiling man with thinning hair and ruddy cheeks. Denise assumed it was the same man as the husk in front of her, but there was no way to tell just by looking. Going through the rest of the man's pockets only yielded a couple of coins and some lint. She looked at the identification card again and noted the name. Leon Villiers. Then she slipped the card into the same pocket where she'd folded the map she'd found earlier.

A quick scan of the area around the overturned motor sledge didn't yield anything of interest, either. She assumed Mr. Villiers had been the original driver, but maybe whoever was piloting the vehicle was dead in a crevice somewhere nearby after encountering Villiers.

The supplies scattered around were mostly cans of food and some basic survival equipment. They were the sort of thing someone might bring with them if they were fleeing into the wilderness from something. Then again, they might just be standard equipment for any significant trek across the ice out here.

Denise had learned that there was definitely something terribly wrong down here, but she knew precious little other than that. Something like this had to be connected to the meteorite somehow. She didn't know how else to explain the scene out here.

"I've gotten the ice off the plane. We're ready to take off," Fletch said, trudging over to her.

"Good. Let's get back to Delambre Station. They're going to start to wonder what happened to us if we stay out here for too much longer."

"What was that...thing over there?" Fletch tilted his head in the direction of the thankfully still form sprawled out on the ice.

"Frankly, I don't really know."

"And why did you bring a gun out here? The last I knew, you were just out here as some sort of vacation trip. I'm glad you brought it, but you should have told me."

"It's kind of a long story. I've been investigating, looking for something out here. Maybe something like him." Denise looked over at the dead body again. The wind was rustling its jackets, trying to rip them away.

"I think you owe me one hell of an explanation."

"Yes. Yes, I do."

SEVEN
FLY ON THE WALL

"It would have been ideal if you brought some samples back," Metrodora said.

"I didn't have anything to pick them up with or carry them in. And what would we say if the French found our little collection? That stuff would start to smell sooner or later."

"It still would give us a better chance to identify what you've just described if you had brought us some samples."

"She's right about that," Cornelia said. "I can't really tell you anything about what you saw just from your description. There was something weird inside the man's head, and you're right; he was probably stone dead the whole time. That being said, I'm glad you didn't try to bring anything back with you. There could be disease or something equally dangerous. Best not to poke that bear." Cornelia absently reached down and rubbed her artificial leg.

They were all crammed into Metrodora's quarters. Trying to fit three people into one of the rooms was difficult. Trying to fit four was nearly impossible. Denise, Cornelia, and Metrodora were all sitting on the cot. Fletch leaned against the dresser. None of them could move their feet without kicking each other.

But the mess hall was in use. The French researchers didn't seem to stick to any particular schedule for eating or even sleeping. The constant, unending sunlight and the toils of their uneven work schedule meant that the French team ate in staggered schedules whenever they wanted. Plus, most of the crew of the *Sulaco* was at the station to stretch their legs, and a lot of them were also eating or relaxing in the more spacious public spaces. That made it difficult to discuss anything in any sort of privacy.

"So, let me get this straight," Fletch said. "You three all work for this Squires group...and you hunt monsters?"

"I'm the only member of St. George's Squires here," Metrodora interrupted. "These two are independent contractors." She had her notebook open, and she'd taken a series of shorthand notes.

"And that's the way it's doing to stay," Denise said.

"Most likely," Metrodora said. "You seem temperamentally unfit for the organization."

Fletch barked at both of them. "First of all, I almost had a chunk taken out of me by some dead guy. I don't really care about who's pissed at who right now. I just want to know what you people have roped me into."

"The long and short of it is that there was some sort of meteorite strike down here. After that, the French sent down a large contingent of biologists. My organization wanted to know what they were up to down here," Metrodora said.

"And they sent you and the farm team? There was a dead guy trying to kill me. That seems like a pretty serious matter to me."

"We've seen worse," Metrodora said.

"You weren't the one in danger of having your face torn off."

"Obviously, we didn't know exactly what was happening down here. We would have sent a larger team if we had known. Most of the biologists that were sent down here aren't at Delambre Station. I can only assume that they're at this Merovée point on the map Denise recovered."

"Or dead," Cornelia added.

"Or dead," Metrodora agreed.

"Alright, yesterday I would have just assumed that you were all crazy. Who works as a monster hunter?"

"There are nearly five thousand Squires around the world, counting support personnel. Plus a smaller number of independent contractors. That just covers the British Empire and its dominions, colonies, and protectorates. France has the Bureau de Gévaudan, though it's been a shadow of its former self since the war. The Russians had a similar organization, but it went underground when the Soviets took power. They might not exist anymore. Japan is developing a contingent of professionalized kaiju hunters, although they're being integrated as part of the military. And then there's the Americans," Metrodora said, ticking off countries on her fingers.

"Forget I asked. Fine. You're monster hunters. It sounds a lot less preposterous after being attacked by a walking corpse. Either way, give me one good reason why I shouldn't go up to Dr. Benoit and tell him what you're up to. I don't want to get caught up in whatever this is. You're poking around something seriously unpleasant, and I'd prefer to stay well clear of it."

"Benoit told you to stay away from anyone you met outside, too. The researchers don't know the real reason we're here, and they probably wouldn't be thrilled if they did know. They built this station in record time, and there's apparently something else that we haven't see at this Merovée, too. They've invested a lot of time, money, and manpower down here. Do you think they'll be happy if they find out that you've met this Villiers character? The three of us might get brought up on some sort of espionage charges, but you probably would, too," Metrodora said.

"Sorry, Fletch. This was never the intent, but you know too much now," Denise said.

"And what is that supposed to mean?" Fletch was obviously agitated, and Denise didn't blame him. He'd been hired just to help show them around, and that was all Denise really thought they'd need him for.

"It means you're in just as deep as we are, unfortunately. And we're in just deep enough to know that we've found something big, but not so deep that we've found the bottom," Metrodora continued.

"What if we just left?" Cornelia asked. "We found out that there's something going on down here. There's some sort of plague of the damned or something. Mission accomplished. The Squires wanted to know what was going on with that meteorite, and we put them on track to find out. There's no reason things have to go any further than that." Cornelia crossed her arms.

Metrodora sighed. "There's plenty of reason to continue on from here. We've only just discovered the very edge of whatever's happening here. We know something is happening, but we don't know what or why. I still think we should break into the research wing of the station. We could do it tonight, after most everyone has gone to sleep. That seems like the surest way for us to find any answers here."

Denise looked at the three other people in the room. "Alright, I'm the one who's in charge of this expedition. Cornelia, you know I always value your input. But this could turn into something bad. I think we should at least keep an eye on it. That being said, we are absolutely not going to break into the research wing unless we have to. We'll hold the course and see what we turn up through normal means. We're not going to take any stupid risks about this, even if it means we have to leave a couple of stones unturned, capisce?"

"This is acceptable for now," Metrodora said.

"I can stick with it," Cornelia agreed.

Denise nodded. "Okay. That settles it then. Fletch, sorry we misled you about the reason we're actually here. You did a good thing when you landed the plane so we could help that man. If I had known things were as dangerous as they are around here, I wouldn't have asked you to do it. We'll stay through our scheduled time here, but now that we know how far gone things can get out there, we won't ask you to do anything else like that."

"Thanks. I guess I probably would have landed anyway, even knowing what might be out there. I wouldn't want to leave anyone out there. The cold is bad enough. Being stuck out there knowing that those things were around too would be a lot worse."

"I appreciate it. Hopefully, once we've reported back, the Squires will send people out, and those things won't be a problem much longer. Who knows? Maybe we were lucky, and we got the only one. What exactly will the Squires do about this, Metrodora?"

"Once we let the French know that we have a pretty good idea of what's going on here, it'll be easier to pressure them into sharing any data and specimens. They won't be able to deny what they have anymore. That's one of the reasons I want to catalogue what they're working on as completely as possible. The more we have, the easier it will be to get the rest."

"And once you have the data?"

"We'll study it and determine the best way to either isolate or stop things like the man you killed. We'll figure out if it's a disease or if it's something else, and we'll keep it in our libraries. In the event that it becomes a problem that we can't deal with on our own, we'll find a way to get our recommendations into the hands of the military or medical professionals. Whoever can make the best use of it, really."

Fletch looked unhappy. "Your group, the Squires, they aren't top secret or something, right? This isn't the sort of situation where somebody from the intelligence services is going to throw a bag over my head and whisk me off to some dungeon somewhere, is it?"

"No. We're not that sort of organization. We keep a low profile, but no one is going to force you to sign a secrecy oath under threat of death just because you've met me. Some other groups around the world that have similar missions are much more aggressive about enforcing secrecy though, so I wouldn't recommend you go seek any of them out after all this."

"I'll keep that in mind. I don't think I'd want to tell too many people about this, anyway. I'd get some odd looks if I told them a dead man tried to kill me."

Denise smiled to herself. She'd opened up her business with Cornelia in part because they both had stories that they couldn't tell in polite company without sounding like they'd lost their minds. This was almost tame by comparison.

"Alright," she said. "I think we all know what to do. Keep looking around, and keep your wits about you. Don't take any unnecessary risks, and I'd recommend you keep a gun hidden on you, if you need to go outside. If something dead attacks you, pop it in the head. That seems to work pretty well. Oh, and don't freeze to death."

"Just another day in paradise," Cornelia said.

There was a knock on the door. Denise whipped her head around. She hadn't heard any footsteps outside in the hallway. Whoever was out there had approached very quietly.

"Yes?"

The door swung open and revealed Dr. Benoit. Cripes, how long had he been out there? Could he hear them through the door?

"My, but it is crowded in here. How are you all doing, hmm? I and a couple of my men were going to take the snow tractor out to the penguin rookery. It would be a good time to see the birds now." Benoit's voice had lost some of the easy-going charm of when he'd first met them.

"Yeah, I suppose that's a good idea," Denise said. She didn't really want to go visit a bunch of penguins, as fun as that sounded. Now that she knew there were undead freaks prowling the ice, she wanted to check a few other things out around the station.

"Good. There's only so much room on the tractor at a time. You and you, come with me." Benoit pointed at Denise and Metrodora.

He was onto them.

EIGHT
UNIDENTIFIED FLYING OBJECT

Denise sat on the snow tractor as the great mechanical beast trundled up the short hill toward the penguin rookery. The cold cinched around them and squeezed, penetrating every layer of clothing when the wind picked up.

Benoit and three other researchers rode on the tractor with Denise and Metrodora, but no one said anything. Benoit sat in the front next to the driver, Louvain. The other two researchers sat in the rear. Denise felt like she was riding around in a prison van.

The mood had completely shifted since the *Sulaco* first arrived at Delambre Station. Yesterday, the men at the research station had been cautiously pleasant. Even if they were clearly absorbed in their work, they'd been interested in seeing new faces after weeks of isolation.

She didn't know how much of their earlier conversation Benoit had heard, but there was a tension in the air now. Everyone was playing a dangerous game, pretending everything was normal but sizing each other up.

When they set out for the penguin rookery, all the researchers who weren't leaving had been gathered around the radio room. There'd been hurried communication in French back and forth between the researchers and whoever was on the other end of the transmission. Denise didn't even know who they would be talking to out there. The last she had heard, some whaling vessel was the only thing within receiving range. Maybe they were talking to Merovée?

The researchers on the snow tractor were speaking in rapid-fire French, and every once in a while, one of them would glance at her or Metrodora. Most of the conversation went completely over Denise's head. French was not a commonly spoken language in South Africa. She'd never bothered to learn it.

She could pick out one thing that they seemed to be saying again and again. "*Dagenais.*" It sort of sounded like a name, but none of the researchers were named Dagenais. For all Denise knew, they could be talking about what they wanted for lunch, though.

Benoit and Louvain were arguing over something. She didn't need to speak any French to know that. Their voices were growing louder and louder as they talked, and their gesticulations grew more frenzied. Finally, Benoit made a slicing gesture with one hand and said something in a firm tone. Louvain went back to driving, but Denise could see that his shoulders were stiff with tension. Evidently, the matter had been put to rest.

Benoit turned around and looked at Denise and Metrodora. "So, how are you enjoying your stay so far? Is Antarctica everything that you hoped it would be?"

"Yes, it's thrilling. Maybe I'll hit the beach for some tanning later," Denise said.

Benoit gave a big, fake laugh and smiled. The smile didn't get anywhere close to his eyes. "Good. I'm glad you two are enjoying yourselves. I trust the weather wasn't too rough when you and the pilot flew out?"

"No. It wasn't too bad. Beautiful landscape but the trip was uneventful," Denise said, playing the game. Benoit was trying to feel her out. He'd obviously heard at least some of her earlier conversation, and now he was fishing for anything else. He just wasn't sure if Denise knew if he knew yet.

Denise was going to keep playing it straight. Just in case things took a turn for the worse, it was better that Benoit assumed he had the upper hand in who knew what. At least then, maybe she could keep a few surprises up her sleeve. In case things went really wrong, she had her revolver tucked into her pocket again, too. She didn't think it would come to that, but it was better to be prepared. For all she knew, they could run into more frostbitten dead men while they were outside.

"I hope you don't mind if I pry," Benoit said, shifting his attention, "but Metrodora is an unusual name. It doesn't sound African."

"It's Greek," Metrodora said. "I picked it out myself, actually. I was raised by a philanthropic group after my parents died. They were very interested in collecting and preserving knowledge. It rubbed off on me. The original Metrodora is the first known woman to write a medical textbook. She was very influential in the Greek and Roman world because of it. I liked the sound of it, and I liked the story behind it."

Denise had never bothered to ask. Maybe South Africa's shitty politics were rubbing off on her. Or maybe she just didn't like Metrodora enough to think about it too much. That was one point in favor of the Squires, though. For an organization interested in studying monsters, it was smarter to hire someone local, especially someone who would have better access to the regions folktales and legends.

Some tweedy type shipped in from London would have to start from scratch, and people didn't always like to tell outsiders about the things people claimed to see in the darkness. In South Africa, the black population had been there for thousands of years longer than the

Europeans. They'd know more about local conditions and other things the Squires wanted to know. It was a good call to bring someone like Metrodora on board.

For the first time since they'd arrived at Delambre Station, Dr. Benoit seemed to run out of pleasantries. The snow tractor fell into a protracted silence. The wind lashed at them through the open cab, whirling past them with howls and moans.

The snow tractor itself was basically just a bulldozer built for transporting people. It had a wide, slanted blade at the front to push through Antarctica's rare snowstorms. The oversized treads allowed them to rumble over the ice and the rocks. Black, oily smoke belched out of the machine and wafted up into the brittle air.

They chugged up the low ridge that separated the penguin rookery from the station grounds. The low hill was a mixture of ice, rock, and stony debris. Trying to walk up on foot would be a surefire way to break an ankle or lodge a leg in some narrow stretch of rock. Fortunately, the snow tractor was able to trundle upwards like a tank. It wasn't especially fast, but it could fight its way through rough terrain just fine.

Cresting the ridge, Denise looked down the other side. There was a gently sloped icy surface leading down toward the water. It was rimmed on several sides by more rocky outcroppings, creating a sort of protected bowl. A few hundred penguins were out on the ice.

"This is where we get out," Benoit said. "The penguins like to nest in the rocky portions here. If we try to go down in the tractor, we risk disturbing them or crushing a nest. Just stay where we can see you."

Just stay where we can see you. Yeah, Benoit was definitely onto them.

Denise hopped out of the snow tractor with Metrodora and stepped out into the full force of the wind again. She hugged herself tight, which had the benefit of keeping her a little warmer and also allowing her hand to rest closer to her revolver.

She didn't think she would need the weapon to deal with Benoit. She prayed she didn't need the weapon to deal with Benoit and his men. They were just trying to make sure they could keep watch on her now that they suspected she knew too much. She didn't think they'd taken her out to summarily execute her. Benoit had been fishing for more information about what she knew just a minute ago. She was pretty sure that they just wanted to keep an eye on them from here on out to prevent any further incidents. Or anything like the shakedown Metrodora had planned for their laboratory. She hoped so, at least.

Still, things had moved into potentially dangerous territory. Well, they'd been in dangerous territory the entire time, given that something about that meteorite had caused a dead man to get up and start trying to kill them. But now, they all had to deal with the fact that the researchers would be keeping a much more vigorous eye on them from here on out. There was probably some sort of law on the books that could get them all in a lot of trouble if a government lawyer decided they were a menace to the interests of France. False pretenses. Industrial espionage. Trespassing. They'd think of something if they really wanted to throw the book at her.

She started to pick her way down the side of the slope one step at a time while she plotted how to ditch their chaperones at some point. Or at least learn something useful from them. So far, she had a lot more questions than answers.

What was at the point on the map labelled Merovée? What on earth had happened to Villiers, the man she'd been forced to put down? How did the meteorite fit in? St. George's Squires would want to know the answers to all those questions, and her own curiosity wasn't satisfied, either. Staring at some penguins would be a pleasant diversion, but it paled in comparison to the other things she wanted to know about.

She noticed the smell about halfway down the side of the slope. The air was painful to breathe. Each intake of air was like swallowing a handful of tiny knives. They cut all the way down. Each exhale sent out a little white puff. The air was completely pure, too. Except for that odor.

That was why she noticed the smell so quickly. She tried to pay attention to odors when she was out in the field. The scent of rotting meat could indicate that there was a carcass nearby, maybe just starting to get picked over by the vultures. It could also indicate that a large predator was nearby, though. There were few things quite as frightening as suddenly getting a whiff of old viscera and musk while walking through the tall grass. Once you smelled that, it was an open question over who was stalking who.

This odor was sort of similar. There was a rotten component to it, but there was also something else, something acrid. It wasn't a pleasant smell at all. Something like leftover bacon mixed with hot vomit. Meaty yet sharp. It was the smell after a summer hot dog eating contest gone horribly awry.

She looked up and tried to pinpoint the source of the smell. With the wind moving the way it was, the odor had to be coming from somewhere off to her left. She veered off the route she had been taking and angled around, still searching for wherever that smell was coming from.

She was almost to the bottom when she found the source. She'd found it, but she still wasn't sure what she was looking at.

Near the base of the rocks was a puddle of some kind of semi-congealed sludge. It was a vaguely yellowish color and chunky. To Denise's eye, it looked like something that had been poured out of a witch's cauldron after a serious potion bender.

There were bits of brown fur sticking out of the morass in irregular clumps. In addition, there were a few meaty bits strewn around, but only near the edges. She stared at some nubby bits for a moment before deciding that they had probably been bones before they'd been rendered down like a tooth left in a saucer of cola.

This had been an animal of some sort, but then something awful happened to it. Denise circled around to get a better look at some of the few relatively intact pieces. She found a mostly unscathed flipper, but the rest of the animal looked like someone had poured lye on it. Judging from the flipper, it had been a seal once. The flipper was the only thing that gave it away, though. Even the basic skeletal structure was almost completely unrecognizable after what had been done to it. The corpse was mostly dissolved.

Well, this raised a brand-new set of questions for her to wonder about. Could the researchers have done this? It clearly wasn't the work of anything like the dead man she'd encountered before. He'd been trying to take a bite out of her and Fletch. This was a different kind of mess altogether.

"What are you doing?" Benoit noticed that she'd stopped at the base of the incline and scrambled over. He really didn't want her wandering off.

"There's something over here," she said. Maybe there was some sort of natural phenomena down here that melted the occasional seal. She didn't know all the secrets of the Antarctic. There could always be dangerous geological hot springs or something. She didn't want to jump to any conclusions.

But she also had no idea what sort of conclusions she could even jump to just by looking at the ex-seal. She needed a mental ladder to get to the elevator that would take her to the stairs that would get her within jumping height of any conclusions here.

Benoit and Louvain crunched over. The other two researchers stayed near Metrodora as she approached. The French team stayed clumped around them like a team of bodyguards.

"What have you found?" Benoit asked. He came up behind her and looked over her shoulder.

"I think it used to be a seal, but you tell me. See the flipper?"

"I see..." Benoit took another step closer and bent down on his knees to get a better look.

From up close, the smell of the thing was truly revolting. The mélange of material wasn't rotting. It was too cold for it to decay very easily. The entire continent was basically one giant ice box. Nor did it look like the corpse had been eaten. Denise was used to looking at the carcasses of downed antelopes and zebras. They were always torn open and covered with claw marks and gashes. There was no sign of any sort of conventional attack here. She didn't see any indication of tearing fangs or slashing talons. This almost looked like some sort of chemical accident, as if the seal had dissolved.

The smell only seemed to confirm that idea. There was an odd, vaguely acidic tinge to the scent. The odor wasn't so much rotten as it was unwholesome. Somehow, the meat had been rendered down to a semi-liquid state rather than being left to spoil.

Denise grimaced. The idea that maybe the French were working on a new generation of chemical weapons flitted across her mind. That was not a business she was eager to stick her nose into. She was here to see if anything living had arrived on that meteorite. Maybe the Squires had interpreted their data incorrectly, though. Maybe the French biologists sent down here hadn't travelled to study something living but rather the effects of a new compound on other living things.

That was a possibility. She had no idea. Maybe that answer could explain why she and Fletch had been attacked by a seemingly dead man, or it could help explain what could melt a seal. But it couldn't explain both, could it? Those incidents seemed far too different to be so neatly explained with one answer. Denise shook her head, trying to clear her thoughts. There were still far too many pieces of the puzzle for her to say anything definitive about anything she'd seen. For all she knew, she was adding pieces to the puzzle that didn't fit at all.

Benoit stood up and started speaking in French to Louvain again. She picked out that name, *Dagenais*, again, but the rest of what they said was completely opaque. Their emotions were clear, though. This time, they didn't seem to be in disagreement. They both just seemed perplexed. Whatever had happened to that seal, it was apparently news to them, too.

Turning around, Benoit issued an order to one of the men guarding Metrodora. Then he turned back to his guests. "I'm afraid we have run into a problem here."

"What happened here?"

"I have no... I'll explain later," Benoit said, meaning that he needed time to come up with some sort of logical explanation for what they were looking at. "Moreau will take you back to the station with the ice tractor. Louvain, Ferrand, and I will stay behind to deal with this." Benoit issued another stream of French to the man tasked with guiding Denise and Metrodora back to the station.

Moreau took Denise's arm in one hand and Metrodora's in the other, brokering no argument about coming with him. He started off up the slope toward the parked snow tractor.

Denise didn't try to resist. She wasn't going to learn anything new just by staring at the dead seal for any longer, and they weren't about to let her go get Cornelia and the proper tools for poking and prodding at the dead creature. She wasn't even sure that any sort of autopsy would do her much good in figuring out what had happened here. It would be like sorting through a tub of cold grits.

They started up the craggy slope, finding their footing one step at a time. The slope wasn't quite as rough on this side, and Denise managed to pick her way up without too many problems. She did twist around to get one more good look before she continued on, though. The whole scene was so bizarre that she wanted to gather a final impression before leaving it behind.

Benoit was still standing near the outcropping, looking down at the mess in front of him. Louvain had scooted closer, getting ready to prod at the swamp of ruined flesh with a pen. Suddenly, there was a little spurt of movement among the ruined mass.

Louvain jerked backward, but it was already too late. Something leapt out of the mass and attached itself to his outstretched arm. At first glance, Denise thought it was a tentacle of some sort. Then, she realized that the strange mass of lumpy flesh that had jumped out at Louvain wasn't attached to anything except for a clinging trail of goopy ooze.

The thing was some sort of segmented slug, maybe eight inches long. It had a pale, squishy-looking body.

Louvain batted at the creature with his free hand as it squirmed up his arm. It opened up its mouth and unsheathed some sort of pincers. The pincers crunched down on Louvain's fingers like a pair of stubby hedge clippers. There was a squirt of blood, and a couple of Louvain's fingers sheared off.

Benoit was trying to help, swatting at the slug while trying to avoid its mouthparts. Louvain's finger disappeared down its maw with a crunching and grinding noise. Bloody drool dripped from the slug's mouth as it continued up Louvain's arm.

The slug, Denise really didn't know what else to call the creature even though it clearly wasn't like any mere garden slug, surged up Louvain's arm. The creature moved surprisingly fast, flailing and flagellating its body to propel itself along. A trail of mucus remained in its wake after it had finished squirming across an area.

Denise had already broken free of her guide's grip and rushed down the incline to try to help. Louvain kept reaching around with his injured hand to try to peel the slug off again, and he flailed with his other arm. The flailing only made it harder for Benoit to aid him, though.

The screaming and cursing carried over the sound of the wind as Denise ran up. She didn't need to speak French to understand the gist of it. The slug took another chunk out of Louvain's hand and gobbled it down, including the pieces of shredded glove. Blood squirted down the front of his parka and dribbled onto the ice. The man's flapping, flailing attempts to grab the slug sent little crimson droplets through the air with each motion.

A few drops splashed onto Denise as she ran up. She grabbed a fist-sized rock off the outcropping to squash the strange creature. Trying to grab it clearly wasn't working. It was surprisingly savage for something its size, and it was covered in a thick sheen of mucus. Even if someone could wrap their hands around it, the slug would be a nightmare to actually try to hang onto. The bulbous body would twist and slither and knot itself around in anyone's gloves, and then those pincers would start seeking out more fingers.

She was too slow, though. The slug reached Louvain's shoulder and surged forward. Those hungry mouthparts latched onto the side of Louvain's neck and gnawed through the delicate flesh in an instant. Squirming and thrashing, the slug stuck its head in the hole it had excavated and tried to stuff itself all the way into Louvain's body. First, just the head fit through, but then the slug managed to cram half its length through the red slit.

Louvain gasped and spat a gob of blood. He collapsed to his knees, more blood welling out of his mouth.

Denise dropped her rock as she reached Louvain and tried to pinch the slug's rapidly disappearing tail before it could completely disappear inside the man. Her fingers scrabbled at the creature's slimy skin, but she couldn't get any purchase.

They had to rip the slug out. She knew that it was normally a bad idea to remove something caught inside someone, like a piece of metal after a car accident. The foreign object could actually help staunch the bleeding to some degree, and removing it could cause even more damage if it wasn't done properly. They didn't have that luxury right now, though. There was at least the chance that it hadn't torn through any of Louvain's major veins or arteries. He might be able to survive a grisly hole in his neck long enough to drag him back to the station's medical facilities. He surely wouldn't survive for very long with that little buzz saw inside him, though. The slug would only burrow further in and cause even more damage the longer it was in there.

Her gloves were too bulky and unwieldy to get a good grip on the slug. She threw them off and tried to grab the worm directly. The cold that slapped her bare skin was physically painful, like dipping her hand in a bucket of angry ants. It stung and tingled. She clamped down on the slug with her fingers, and she could feel its body wriggling to try to get free. Blood and oozing ichor sprayed across her fingers.

Louvain gave a coughing sound and shuddered. He collapsed down onto his knees, and Denise lost her grip on the slug's tail. There was more blood now. It was welling out of Louvain's nose and dripping into his beard. It came out of his ears and dribbled out of his tear ducts. More blood jetted out of the hole in Louvain's throat.

Denise realized that the slug was climbing upward inside Louvain's head, hacking and chopping its way through his skull. The man had probably been mortally wounded when the creature tore open his neck, but maybe they could have saved him. Cornelia might have been able to sew everything shut before he died of blood loss. Now, they were completely out of options, though. The creature was burrowing upward and inward, rupturing everything in its path.

Involuntary jerks and spasms ran through Louvain's body. He collapsed onto his back, quaking and twitching. His limbs leapt and shook, jolting like they were trying to separate from the rest of his body. He moved around on the ice as his body arched and flexed. Trails of blood pooled out on the ice wherever he moved, dribbling out of his throat wound or draining out of his hand. The blood smeared across the white like some sort of avant-garde painting.

Denise backed up a couple of steps, unsure what to do. It didn't seem right to let the man bleed out in a tangle of limbs right there on the ice, but she had no idea what else she could do for him. The slug was all the way inside his body and working its way deeper into his skull. There was no way to get it out, and even trying would only cause more damage to Louvain's body and risk losing some fingers to the creature's mandibles.

She jumped at the sound of the gunshot. The noise blasted out and echoed against the nearby rocks. Louvain's head burst open, and he went mercifully still. Off in the distance, some of the penguins panicked at the loud noise and waddled away toward the waves in terror. After a second, the only noise was the sound of the wind and the disturbed birds.

Benoit looked at the gun in his hand for a moment before tucking it back into his pocket. He crossed himself. Noticing that some blood was on his parka, he tried to wipe it away but only succeeded in smearing it around.

"I'm sorry you had to see that," he finally said. "Let's get back to the station. We'll come back for Dr. Louvain's body after you've been put away."

Denise had already seen what she needed to know, though. Louvain's brains sat steaming on the ice, but the pulped remains of the slug were mixed in. She'd seen a nearly identical scene when she shot the dead man out at the overturned motor sledge just a few hours ago. Out here, the blood and brains were fresher, but that was the main difference. Judging from the amount of bloody debris left on the ground, Denise thought the slug in the first man's skull was probably larger. Maybe double the size. It had also been in its cozy little den a lot longer, with more time to get fat and comfortable.

She felt like she understood what had happened now. The slugs had probably arrived on the meteorite. Or maybe they'd been living underground, and the meteorite punched through the ice to where they were living. She didn't know, and it wasn't important for her purposes. The thing that really mattered from her perspective was that they were real sons of bitches.

One of them had gotten into Dr. Louvain, and it was obvious that we wouldn't have survived much longer even if Benoit hadn't intervened. It didn't take too many mental gymnastics to figure out that one of the slugs had somehow gotten inside Leon Villiers.

The next part required a little speculation but didn't seem too radical, given the circumstances. When the circumstances were killer death slugs from space, a lot of conclusions seemed a lot more reasonable for that matter. This one seemed downright conservative.

Once the slugs managed to burrow their way into someone's brain, they were obviously able to hotwire the motor functions to some degree. Even after the victim died, the slugs could still force the body to walk around and attack.

She hadn't actually seen Dr. Louvain's body rise up from the ice and come after them, but it seemed like the logical next step that connected Louvain and Villiers. Plus, Benoit seemed to know what was about to happen next. He shot Louvain in the head straight off, presumably because he knew what was about to happen and wanted to prevent his colleague from scrambling back to his feet with the sudden urge to devour human flesh.

Denise still didn't know where some things fit in, like the melted seal, but it seemed like things were finally coming together in her mind. She had enough information to give St George's Squires a decent picture of what was going on down here. The French research station was studying slugs, quite possibly slugs from outer space, that could kill a person and then hijack their nervous system. Presumably, they could attack other animals too, so it was a blessing that the meteorite had landed in one of the most desolate and remote areas of the planet. That would help keep the worms isolated at least.

If Benoit hadn't been sure how much Denise knew before, he sure as hell knew now. Entirely too much. That was what she knew. Now the question was, what was he going to do about it?

"Back to the station," Benoit said, his hands trembling so badly that he was having trouble adjusting his parka about himself.

Everyone started climbing the incline to reach the snow tractor again. No one bothered to speak as they all thought about what they'd just seen.

"Are you alright?" Metrodora asked in a quiet tone.

"Yeah. I just need to clean up a bit." Denise looked down at her hands. Both the inside and the outside of her gloves were tacky with blood. She could also feel the slug's slime drying on her fingers. She needed to make sure she washed that off as soon as she could, especially before she rubbed her eyes or anything. There was no telling if the ooze was dangerous or not.

"Are you okay?" She noticed that Metrodora looked a lot more drawn than she had even a few minutes ago.

"I am. I just don't normally do field work. I've never seen anyone die right in front of me like that."

"I don't want to say you get used to it, because you don't, but you get better at dealing with it."

The wind was loud in Denise's ears as she moved. She mostly kept her head down. It allowed her to watch her step better, and it helped protect her face a little from the harsh gusts of cold. Some of them were like a blast of sandpaper against the skin, trying to rub it raw every time they kicked up.

There was some other noise, though. At first, she just thought it was the wind blowing over some surface in an odd way. Maybe rushing over a sinkhole like a kid blowing over an open soda bottle. It was an odd, moaning drone.

She was barely aware of it at first, but then it grew louder and louder. After a few seconds of increasing volume, she realized that it wasn't just the wind, it was something else. The loud thrum almost sounded like an airplane engine.

Halfway up the incline, Denise stopped and looked up. She expected to maybe see one of the research station's little biplanes, like the one she and Fletch had taken out a few hours before. Instead, she saw a huge, black shape plunging downward.

She ducked, pulling Metrodora down with her, just as the shadow swept over them. They both hit the rocky ground, scrabbling at the icy earth. The thrumming sound grew into the roar of a hurricane. Amid the flurry of ice and grit that blew into her face, all she could see of the two scientists were two sets of legs. Before Denise could even press herself all the way flat, a massive downdraft hit them, and there was a scream.

One of the pairs of legs in front of her suddenly lifted upward into the air and zipped away. The downdraft subsided, and the loud thrumming noise faded slightly. Denise pushed herself up onto her knees and looked up.

Benoit and Moreau were still standing on the outcroppings nearby. The third researcher, Ferrand, was gone, though. Denise looked to the sky and saw a gigantic shape zooming away from them. It had to be at least forty feet long, counting the tail. The distance between them and the flying thing grew rapidly, making it hard to determine the details of what she was looking at.

The thing could have been a flying vehicle, or it could have been some sort of freakish animal. Denise really couldn't tell. She had some sense of scale though, because Ferrand was caught on what were either the thing's legs or its landing struts. He flailed wildly in the thing's grip, but he couldn't fee himself.

A few minutes ago, Denise thought she'd figured everything out. The slugs seemed like the threat that the Squires were worried might be down here. Now there was…whatever the hell this ungodly terror was. The thing soared inland at remarkable speed, soon disappearing into a little black speck on the horizon. Maybe a plane could outrace it, but not by much.

Benoit had an expression on his face like he was just as surprised as Denise and Metrodora. He had his gun in his hand again, pointed vaguely in the direction the flying threat had disappeared to.

Denise didn't bother with her revolver. It stayed in her pocket. She wished she had her elephant gun. A sidearm wouldn't do much good against something that size. She wasn't even sure the .577 Nitro Express would take out anything that big, at least not very easily. They needed a howitzer to deal with something like that.

She didn't wait for Benoit. Grabbing Metrodora, she started moving up the incline as fast as she could without twisting an ankle. "Get to the snow tractor," she yelled as she passed the stunned researchers.

At least the vehicle would offer them some kind of cover. It would put some steel between them and whatever had just flown off with

Ferrand. Benoit and Moreau took off behind her, navigating the ice-slicked rocks as best they could.

Denise's mind raced. What was that thing? She'd heard stories about flying saucers disgorging little green men before, but she'd always chalked such tales up as the work of crackpots, weirdos, and attention seekers. Surely, she hadn't just seen some sort of alien craft pluck a man up off the ground and whisk him away toward whatever fate awaited him? Or maybe the huge black shape had been a living creature? She didn't know, and she didn't want to find herself close enough again to find out.

She reached the crest of the incline and darted over to the snow tractor. They'd left the keys in the ignition and the engine idling to avoid any chance that it would freeze up on them away from the station. Denise thought about hopping in the driver's seat and charging pell-mell for the station herself once everyone was inside. The controls were unfamiliar though, and Benoit and Moreau weren't far behind. She clambered up into one of the rear seats, Metrodora right behind her.

Looking around, they didn't have far to go to reach the research station. It was less than two miles away. With the air so crisp and clear in the eternal sunlight, it looked even closer. The heavy-duty concrete structure would offer them even better protection than the snow tractor. Denise and Cornelia could hunker down with their elephant rifles amid the bunker-like construction and create a fairly formidable defense.

Of course, if the pulp magazines were right, and that thing really was an alien spaceship full of little green men, they might also have a death ray of some sort aboard. Jesus. Spaceships. Death rays. Giant flying creatures. Denise wasn't even sure what she was dealing with, she just knew she wanted to get off this blasted continent at the first safe opportunity. She'd seen enough to know she wanted nothing to do with whatever snatched Ferrand up into the air. That was a problem for somebody else, preferably somebody with an army at their disposal. St. George's Squires were going to get their report in full detail, but it could be summed up easily enough. Things had gone to hell down here.

Benoit and Moreau climbed up onto the snow tractor a few seconds later and climbed behind the controls, steering the machine down the opposite slope toward Delambre Station. The tractor snorted and burped out some black soot, and then, with agonizing slowness, it started its bumpy rumble toward the promise of safety.

The snow tractor lurched down the far side of the incline and made its way back toward the station. Denise sat and fidgeted. The journey out to the rookery hadn't seemed very long at all. Just making it back down the incline seemed to take an eternity. The snow tractor simply was not a fast vehicle. She debated hopping out and just running for it, but that would leave her out in the open for too long, an easy target.

Denise peered out from under the metal roof as they made their way back, looking in the direction that the strange flying thing had gone with Ferrand. Aside from the snow tractor itself, they didn't have any cover. She and Benoit had handguns, but that wasn't likely to do anybody much good if the thing came back for them.

The thing came back for them. It came from further inland, the same direction it had disappeared to. At first, it was just a little black granule on the horizon, but it was moving low and fast, occasionally switching paths but basically zigzagging in their general direction.

They'd only closed about half the distance to the station. If the flying thing zeroed in on them, there was no way they'd make it all the way back in time.

"It's coming back," Denise said.

"I see it." Benoit had his pistol out again, but his hands were trembling so badly now that he'd be lucky if he could hit the ground if he aimed at it.

"What is that thing?" Metrodora asked, her own voice scratchy with tension.

"I have no idea. We've never seen it before. It's nothing like the others," Benoit said.

Denise believed him. He seemed as shaken as anyone else by the thing's sudden appearance. She noticed his choice of words, though.

She could have asked more questions. Were the "others" he mentioned the slugs? Something else entirely? She would have liked to ask, but that horrible black shape was bearing down on them again.

There was no more time for questions. The next couple of minutes would be entirely about survival.

NINE
INCOMING

That loud thrumming noise filled the air again, overtaking even the sound of the howling wind and the sputtering tractor engine. Denise could feel the noise in her bones as a steady vibration. In a second, even the air around them beat with that awful juddering sound.

The huge black shape descended on them with surprising speed for anything so large, dropping out of the air like a bird of prey. Denise took out her own revolver. She knew she was blowing whatever shred of a cover story she might have left, but now wasn't the time to worry about that. Her revolver didn't really increase the odds of surviving, but it at least made her feel like she was doing something.

She caught a glimpse of the thing above as it swept down on them. There was just enough time to make out a few details. It had some sort of black armor that glistened in the sunlight, sending out iridescent green and blue reflections. It was tapered at the front and the back, much of the rear portion apparently being some sort of lengthy tail section. The middle portion of the body was fat and swollen, though.

Then it was upon them.

The entire snow tractor rocked as the massive thing alighted on the rear of the vehicle. The roof caved downward, crumpling and shrieking under the huge weight above it.

For the first time, Denise managed to get a clear look at part of the thing's body, and she could tell that it was organic rather than a spaceship. She couldn't see very much of the creature, but she could tell that it had large, powerful rear legs and a body completely encased in some sort of black carapace. Its head was somewhere up above her, where she couldn't see due to the tractor's partially collapsed roof.

A long, spindly leg shot down from above and grasped at them. Thick, greasy-looking bristles stuck off the leg at irregular intervals. Some of the hairs were almost two feet long. One of them whipped past Denise and struck her face as the leg probed the inside of the vehicle. She felt blood trickle down her cheek where the razor-sharp bristle had sliced her.

Two gigantic tarsal claws grasped from the end of the leg. The claws were the size of Gurkha swords, and they were just as sharp.

Everyone screamed and tried to avoid the massive claws as they explored the snow tractor's interior.

Denise and Benoit both fired their weapons at the gigantic creature attacking them. The muzzle flashes lit up the vehicle's interior in staccato bursts of light and fury. Despite everything, the bullets didn't even seem to affect the creature attacking them. It didn't flinch or back down. Denise didn't see anywhere that their bullets had actually penetrated its armor. To the behemoth attacking them, the bullets were probably nothing more than noise and an annoying tapping on its carapace.

Sitting at the snow tractor's controls, Moreau had less room to try to avoid the huge claws. The monster's leg wedged itself further inside and tried to grasp anyone it could. They shot past Denise and latched onto Moreau, tearing through his jacket and slicing into his arm.

Moreau screamed as blood burst out in every direction. He struggled with the huge leg as the entire snow tractor rocked from side to side like a child's toy. Denise saw a brief glimpse of torn flesh and raw bone as Moreau tried to free himself from the giant beast's clutches.

It was too late, though. The claws hooked more firmly into Moreau's flesh. Securing their crushing grip, the claws tried to wrench Moreau out of the tractor, banging him around the inside of the vehicle in the process. Blood sprayed everywhere as if from an overhead sprinkler system.

The claw ripped Moreau out of the snow tractor and tossed him on the ground nearby. The researcher tried to claw his way back to the vehicle, but he didn't make it more than a few inches before a huge globule of ichor sprayed down and splashed over him.

Moreau's parka sizzled and puckered, the material seemingly melting wherever the strange goop touched. An awful smell assaulted Denise's nostrils. It was similar to the odor around the seal remains they'd found earlier, but it was much stronger and all the worse because she knew it was human flesh she was smelling this time.

After only a couple of seconds, Moreau was completely unrecognizable. His face was just a dribbling red slurry, and that boiling vomit smell was almost overwhelming. Moreau's flesh and clothing were both sloughing off his form like hot tallow. The monster had sprayed him with some sort of acid, and it was chewing through flesh and cloth alike.

The same claw that had scooped Moreau out of the snow tractor reached down again and plucked the man's dribbling form up off the ice. A second later, the creature had lifted off again, flying in the same direction that it took Ferrand.

Denise let out the breath she hadn't realized she was holding. Her revolver was hot in her hands. She reached into her pocket with her bloody gloves and fished out more ammo for it, opening the cylinder and shoving each bullet inside. The gun hadn't done them a damn bit of good, but she still wanted it loaded and ready. It at least made her feel like she was something other than prey. She dropped a couple of bullets on the floor of the snow tractor as she gave a shiver that had nothing to do with the cold.

Benoit slid across the blood-soaked front seat and took over the vehicle's controls. They shuddered forward, still not moving half as fast as Denise would have liked.

She looked back in the direction the creature had flown off to. It seemed fair to assume that it had a nest or some other kind of home base in that direction. That was also the direction where Denise had encountered Villiers by the overturned motor sledge. And it was the same direction as whatever Merovée was.

Looking in the opposite direction, she could see activity around Delambre Station. People were moving about outside. They must have seen the creature attack the snow tractor and carry Moreau away. A group of people were moving toward the docks. That was probably whatever members of the *Sulaco*'s crew had been ashore at the time.

As far as Denise was concerned, they all had the right idea. The thing that attacked the snow tractor and carried the two Frenchmen away was the size of a damn dinosaur. At least to some extent, it was built somewhat like one too, maybe a tyrannosaurus or one of the other big carnivores. When it attacked the tractor, it had balanced itself on two girthy rear legs and its tail. She'd never gotten a good look at the head, but it seemed safe to assume that it was something gruesome and toothy.

Of course, a tyrannosaurus couldn't fly. This thing was more like some sort of dragon, with its wings and thick armor. Maybe it couldn't breathe fire, but the ability to spray acid was just as bad.

They managed to reach the edge of the station without being attacked again. Maybe the creature was full. Denise hopped out of the beaten snow tractor and headed for the relative safety of the main building. It was fortified, and she could get her Nitro Express.

One of the researchers who'd stayed behind pushed the door closed and shouted at them in French. Benoit trotted past Denise and Metrodora. A short but agitated conversation in French commenced.

Denise tried to push past them to get inside. She was cold and wanted to put some concrete walls between herself and everything else out here. Giant monsters. Ravenous dead men with slugs in their skulls.

No thank you. She was checking out. Time to blow this popsicle stand for good.

Benoit grabbed her by the arm as she tried to slip past him. "I'm going to need you to come with me," he said.

"I don't think so. I'm leaving." Denise didn't consider herself a coward. She'd been in some tough spots in the past, and she'd pushed through. She'd opened a business that specialized in hunting man-eaters and things that lurked in the darkness. However, she didn't have the equipment to deal with something like this. They needed tanks and flamethrowers for a problem of this magnitude, and those weren't available here. Not even her trusty elephant gun could guarantee a quick takedown. Time to cut her losses and head back to Cape Town.

"Unfortunately, you will not be leaving yet." Benoit said something to the other man. The second man pulled out a pistol as Benoit reached over and fished Denise's revolver out of her pocket. "You are not who you say you are. You are certainly not here simply as a tourist. Colonel Dagenais will be here soon. He will decide what to do with you. Until then, you and your associates are being detained."

"Wait, you can't do this."

"I can and I will."

"We should be leaving on the *Sulaco*. We all should. You too."

"Colonel Dagenais will decide that. We're in radio contact with him now. Until then, we should all be safe here at Delambre Station. Dagenais and his men will be able to secure the area. The *Sulaco* will be impounded temporarily until this matter is resolved, though."

"It looks like they have different ideas about that notion." Denise nodded in the direction of the shore. The *Sulaco* had pulled up its skiff and was churning away from the station, picking up steam. A couple of sailors stood on the docks, frantically waving after the departing ship. Evidently, the captain saw what happened on shore and decided, quite reasonably, that he didn't want anything to do with that heinous fuckery.

The Squires had chartered the ship without mentioning that there might be monsters involved. Denise was starting to think that this cloak and dagger business was just going to come back and bite them all on the ass more often than not. Now she was marooned here, probably the single worst location to be marooned on the entire planet right now.

"Dagenais will convince them to come back," Benoit said. The tone was certain enough that Denise knew that he had something up his sleeve. She hadn't met this Dagenais. She had no idea where he would be travelling in from that he could get here with any reasonable speed. She just knew that if she were the captain of the *Sulaco*, it would take one heck of an offer to get her to turn around and come straight back to this godforsaken stretch of ice and rock.

"You'll be staying in here until the colonel arrives," Benoit said, gesturing to the storage shed. "There's food on the shelves and heating. You'll be fine for the amount of time you'll have to be in there. We don't want you wandering around the facility until then."

"And just how long will we be in here? What about bathrooms and the like?"

"It won't be long." Benoit shuffled them into the storage room and shut the door behind them.

Denise looked at Metrodora. Metrodora looked at Denise. "Well, this is bad," Metrodora said.

"Yes. Yes, it is," Denise agreed. She was inclined to add something snippy to Metrodora about it being her boss's fault for sending them down here in the first place, but she held her tongue. The last thing either of them needed right now was a protracted hissy fit.

A few minutes later, Cornelia, Fletch, and the remaining crew of the *Sulaco* who hadn't been lucky enough to make it on board were tossed into the makeshift brig, too. Poole was there along with a Filipino engine room worker named Valdez and an engineer called Hobart.

There was a window on the far side of the storage room. It wasn't big enough to bash open and crawl through, though. That would only let the cold inside. Denise could see a little bit, though. Most of the view was obscured by a shed that sheltered a small fleet of motor sledges.

However, she also had a view of a corner of the coastline. The *Sulaco* was picking up speed as it made for open water. Navigating around the large chunks of ice near the shore meant it hadn't gotten terribly far yet, but Denise hoped they'd be able to open up the throttle soon. Hopefully, they were already transmitting out to anything in the Southern Sea and asking for backup of some sort. With a little luck, the Squires would hear that their team was stranded down here and send in the diplomatic cavalry. And then maybe some real cavalry to deal with the gigantic beast that apparently lived somewhere around the inland mountains.

"You two had the best look at it. What was that thing that attacked the snow tractor?" Cornelia asked.

"Honestly, I don't know," Denise said.

"I've never seen anything like it in our records," Metrodora said.

"We came down here because of a meteorite, originally. Do you think it was, you know, alien?" Cornelia glanced between Denise and Metrodora.

"Wait, what?" Poole asked.

Denise quickly filled Poole and everyone else on what they'd seen, including the slug slithering its way into Louvain's body, which was news to Cornelia, too. Fletch had already known the real reason for this whole expedition. The other crew members didn't look happy about this revelation. For that matter, Fletch looked unhappy all over again.

Denise felt a pang of conscience over dragging everyone out here again. At the time, it seemed to make the most sense. The French wouldn't have let them stay here if they knew that her team just wanted to poke around and see what they were studying, and it seemed unlikely that anyone from the ship would need to know about any of that. Now, people like Poole, Valdez, and Hobart were stuck here and only just finding out the full story why. That wasn't how Denise wanted to operate.

Things had just gotten out of hand. Neither she nor the Squires had expected a problem quite so voracious. That was her fault as much as theirs, though. She'd started her business with Cornelia because she wanted to use her skills to help people in need. Now, she'd only helped put people in danger. She and Cornelia had known the risks. They hadn't.

Denise barely knew Valdez and Hobart apart from seeing them around the ship a couple of times. Poole seemed like an alright sort from the little she'd talked to him. She liked Fletch, though. He'd acquitted himself well when they were investigating that overturned motor sledge earlier. Now they were in trouble right alongside her. The buck needed to stop somewhere. It was cold comfort, but she got them all up to date with what she knew. If nothing else, they deserved to know what was happening and why.

"The group that sent us calls themselves St. George's Squires. They're responsible for investigating—" She got as far as explaining who had sent them when Metrodora interrupted her.

"They don't need to know that."

"Maybe they don't need to, but we owe it to them at this point."

"The details aren't important on that part," Metrodora said. "Just know that we're a group that seeks to investigate and secure unusually dangerous biological specimens for the public good."

"I don't really care if you're elves working for Santa Claus," Fletch said. "Just fill us in on what you know about that thing that attacked you and the slugs. I'll worry about who you work for once our butts are out of the fire. So, you said you came here because of a meteorite. Are these things alien, or what?"

"Hard to say," Denise said. "I don't see how the big beast can be. It seems like it would burn up if it tried to ride through the atmosphere with the meteor. The slugs, maybe. They could ride inside the heart of the meteorite and possibly survive. Maybe. It's all speculation at this point."

"So, if the big critter isn't some sort of space monster, where did it come from then? You bozos are supposed to be the experts," Hobart said. "It looks like a damn alien to me."

"It could be some sort of throwback. Something prehistoric that was locked in the ice for eons and only thawed out because of the meteor impact. The same for the slugs. We just don't know," Denise said. That answer clearly satisfied no one. What else could she say, though? Maybe giant monsters just lived in Antarctica all the time, and no one had met them before because there were so few expeditions to down here. She had no idea. Maybe the French researchers new some things she didn't, but even Benoit seemed surprised by the arrival of the space-dragon or whatever it was.

She was saved from further questions when the station's PA system blared to life and a stream of French spilled out. Denise went to the tiny window and looked around just to make sure that the flying monster wasn't attacking again. There was no sign of it, though. All she could see was the *Sulaco* growing smaller in the distance.

Then she looked a little closer. There was something else in the distance, out past the *Sulaco*. It was another ship. The second ship was still too far away to see clearly, but it seemed to be rapidly approaching.

Denise remembered that there was supposed to be a whaling ship somewhere in the area. The *Sulaco* had been in radio contact with it a couple of times, even if they'd never actually run across each other. Someone must have sent out a distress signal. This must be the whaling ship coming to answer.

The litany of French ceased. A moment later, the voice switched to English. "Good day. This is Colonel Ozias Dagenais. I understand there are several of you there who do not speak French. I will be brief, but I owe you a brief explanation for what is about to happen."

As Denise watched, Benoit and the other remaining researchers charged out of the main building and ran to the parked motor sledges. They leapt on and started the motors. Each one of them was in an almighty hurry.

Denise felt her mouth grow suddenly dry. The researchers weren't just in a hurry. They looked absolutely terrified. Colonel Dagenais had also just said that he owed them an explanation for what was coming. She'd just used the same reasoning for explaining to Fletch and the crew how they'd found themselves so suddenly screwed.

"Unfortunately, the reports from Delambre Station tell me that the situation has gotten out of control. I have made a decision. It has become apparent that further research cannot be conducted safely, even after new safety measures were put in place. The mission has thus shifted from one of research to one of containment. It is of utmost importance for the people of France and the world at large that this be transferred from civilian control to a matter for the military. As such, and under the authority granted to me by my command, I have made a decision. My apologies."

Outside, Denise saw several bursts of light from the second ship that was approaching. For a second, she thought that maybe they were signaling lights, trying to communicate with the *Sulaco*. Then she realized what they really were.

That was the ship the *Sulaco* had been in radio contact with earlier, alright. The problem was, it wasn't a whaling ship. It was a military cruiser.

The first shell the military ship had fired crashed down next to the *Sulaco*, sending a geyser of water up into the air. The next shell hit a nearby sheet of ice, sending flames and massive hailstones careening through the air. They had the range.

The next shell landed squarely on the *Sulaco*. The ice-breaker wasn't a warship. All its armor was dedicated to protecting it from ice beneath the waterline. It didn't have any armor at all on its upper decks. The shell plunged right through, like it was punching through tissue paper. A massive explosion shook the ship, sending parts of its superstructure tumbling down to the deck.

A second later, the ship started to crunch inward on itself, creating a gigantic "V" shape like a giant pair of scissors closing. The explosion had broken the vessel's spine. Even if it had been fast enough to escape before, now it was crippled. From the shore, Denise couldn't hear the metal grinding against itself, but she knew the ice-breaker wasn't structurally stable anymore. It wasn't built to take weapons fire.

With a final shriek, the ship lost all structural stability and snapped completely in half. Pieces of equipment, burning metal, and human beings all tumbled into the freezing water as the French cruiser steamed closer.

A massive explosion annihilated the rear half of the ship before it could slip below the waves. The shell must have started a fire in the coal and fuel reserves, and it finally reached a critical mass. The light from the explosion lit up the day like a second sun. It took another split second for the sound of the blast to reach the mainland.

Their little window imploded inward in a shower of shattered glass. What heat they had disappeared as the freezing air rushed in. Inside their little structure, they were mostly protected from the blast itself, but the noise was still like having angry rioters trying to attack her tympanic membranes.

There wasn't much left of the *Sulaco* out on the water. The entire rear portion of the ship had simply disappeared in the explosion. There would be individual rivets and scraps of metal falling from the sky out over the sea like red-hot hail, but the rest of the debris and human crew had simply disintegrated in that savage orange bloom.

What was left of the other half of the ship slid beneath the water in a tortured, burning ball of scalded metal. Flaming oil spread across the surface of the water where the ship had been. Only a few pieces of debris still floated on the surface, and they were soon engulfed in flame.

Outside the station, Benoit and his team had hopped on the motor sledges and taken off as fast as they could. That only meant one thing. The cruiser was about to start shelling the station. When Dagenais said that the situation had switched to one of containment, he meant that it was too dangerous to leave any survivors behind.

Denise saw another series of flashes out beyond the burning wreckage, just like the ones she'd seen before the *Sulaco* exploded. Colonel Dagenais had ordered the ship to start firing on Delambre Station.

TEN
INHUMAN

Denise bashed herself against the heavy steel door, but it didn't even rattle in its frame. The doors here were meant to handle the stress of a severe environment while limiting the amount of cold air that could seep inside. They weren't supposed to warp or buckle under even extreme conditions. They also made a dandy prison.

Fletch and Poole joined her in trying to slam the door open, but even the three of them together couldn't force any give in the lock. Denise might have been able to shoot it open if she still had her revolver, but Benoit had taken it.

She could hear revving engines outside and then the roar of several motor sledges tearing past them all at once. Denise screamed at them through the door, but the first couple of them tore off without slowing down.

The first blast hit a few seconds later. Denise stumbled as the ground shook beneath her feet. Shelves collapsed in their storage room, and supplies rolled across the floor. Cans of food and spare parts rattled off the shelves that stayed up. The shell must have landed some distance away, or Denise knew she never would have felt the earth shake. She'd either be unconscious under a pile of heavy rubble, or she would have been blown out of existence. Dagenais and his men hadn't quite found the range yet on the big guns. It wouldn't take them long, though.

She banged on the door with her fist one last time, already knowing it was pointless. Then, Denise turned and looked around the floor for something, anything, they could use to get out. They needed a crowbar or something they could use to get some leverage. But there was nothing but nonperishable foodstuffs and some miscellaneous small equipment. None of it would do them a damn bit of good.

The window was too small to crawl out through. The fact that the glass was missing didn't change that fact. They were stuck, completely trapped in here.

Another blast rocked the research station. Some fuel pumps near the docks went up in a series of secondary explosions, painting the ice red with dancing fire. Burning oil and gasoline sloughed across the ice like an avalanche of flame and slid toward the water.

The inside of the storage shed was a bundle of anarchy. There was shouting and more attempts to bash the door down. No one was having any success, though.

Denise's ears were so stunned, she never heard the sound of the lock clicking. Nonetheless, the door suddenly flew open. Dr. Benoit stood on the other side next to an idling motor sledge. He didn't say anything before hopping back onto the sledge and zooming away.

Evidently, he wasn't any more pleased about suddenly finding himself expendable than Denise was. He was already speeding away, heading inland with the other remaining researchers. They were no doubt headed toward Merovée, that mysterious point on the map she'd found before.

Good God. She'd found that map and Villiers less than a day ago. She'd thought things looked bad before, but everything had gone to absolute hell in only the last few hours. If the researchers had been updating Dagenais about what was going on here on a consistent basis, it was no wonder the military decided to step in and take over the operation.

Apparently, the research team didn't realize just what that would entail, though. No one told them that the contingency plan was to blow everything up, themselves included. They obviously weren't interested in falling on their swords over this.

Of course, being forced inland was probably just as much of a death sentence as staying here. The elements. Dead men with slugs in their skulls and a hunger for human flesh. Some sort of goddamn dragon monster. And those were just the threats they'd face trying to reach anywhere else. Once they got to relative safety, there would be the problem of supplies and other essentials. Even if the French military didn't send anyone after them, they couldn't hide out in any one place forever.

Benoit had evidently opened the door to the storage shed for the same reason someone would unlock the cage doors at a burning animal shelter. There was no guarantee that the escapees could find a way to survive on their own, but anyone's conscience would be bothered by just leaving them to their fate.

Denise glanced in the opposite direction of the fleeing motor sledges, toward the shore. There were still a number of motor sledges parked and ready. There were also some smaller shapes fanning out from the French cruiser, clipping across the water toward the coastline.

Those were landing craft. The French were indeed sending in a team to clear out anything that survived the shelling. Even if there was some safe haven near the station, Denise knew she didn't want to be around when those troops arrived. Maybe Benoit had let them out simply to serve as a distraction and speed bump for the soldiers coming to clear the area.

"Get those sledges running," Denise yelled, pointing to the remaining vehicles. "I need to get something."

"No, we need to leave right now," Cornelia shouted at her. Off in the distance, Denise saw more giant muzzle flashes. Dagenais was firing another set of shells at the station.

Cornelia was right. They needed to leave right now. But Denise also needed something from inside the research facility. There was a good chance that they were all only delaying the inevitable if she didn't get it.

"You go. Take everyone inland, out of the range of the guns. Just leave a sledge running for me."

Cornelia tried to grab her, but Denise dodged out of the way and ran into the main science facility. Behind her, she could hear the sound of engines humming to life.

Delambre Station was abandoned. There were some papers on the floor where they'd been hastily dropped, and Denise stepped over them. To her left was the science wing of the facility. There were still gurneys and other medical equipment parked near the door.

She ignored all that and took off for the crew quarters, sliding past the mess hall. Outside, she could hear the scream of incoming shells growing louder and louder. Denise ducked back inside the mess hall and threw herself under one of the tables as the sound grew into a banshee shriek.

A second later, the shells hit the far side of the structure. The blast picked Denise up off the ground and threw her back down. A concussive shockwave of air swept through the facility. Denise lay still for a second as the air settled inside the building. Cornelia was the one who knew all about explosives and artillery from her stint as a wartime nurse, but Denise knew a little too.

Namely, she knew that she didn't have to be that close to the actual explosion for it to kill her. Fire and shrapnel would do the job just fine, but with naval artillery, that probably wasn't even the biggest threat. The shockwaves from the burst could kill her just as dead. When the shells exploded, the force of the blast pushed all the air out of the way very suddenly.

In a way, it wasn't so very different from the katabatic winds that blew over Antarctica all the time anyway. The wave of extra dense air could move so fast that it was like smacking into a brick wall with a car. It could pulverize organs, break bones, and hurl a person through the air.

Probably the only reason Denise was still alive at all was because of the station's heavy construction methods. The same techniques that helped it withstand the elements meant it could block some of the shockwave from the blasts, sort of like a bunker. If the rounds had landed much closer though, she wouldn't have survived.

She could hear crumbling cement and shifting rubble back in the direction of the science quarters. A few seconds later, the dull roar of a fire overtook the other sounds.

Denise crawled out from under the table. She didn't have much time. Dagenais and his ship were going to raze this place around her in short order. The ship's crew was no doubt already reloading the guns and preparing to send more shells toward the facility.

The floor around her was now littered with shattered dishes and scattered utensils. The shockwave had blown open cabinets and spewed the contents onto the floor. There were large cracks in the concrete walls from where the blast sent reverberations through the entire structure. With a couple more well-placed shells, there wouldn't be much left of the research station's main structure. The increasingly loud crackle of fire reminded her that there wouldn't be much left soon regardless of whether the French ship kept firing. Soon, it would be a race between the flames and the military to see who could reduce the building to rubble faster.

She debated scampering back outside and leaping onto one of the motor sledges. She could retreat inland and hope for the best. Trying to traipse through the facility while it was being bombarded by naval artillery was a cosmically stupid idea on almost every level.

Instead of turning around, she plunged deeper into the facility, though. Rounding a corner, she reached the cramped room that had been her quarters. Denise ran through the door and wrenched her luggage out from underneath her cot. She yanked clothes out and threw them on the floor. Then, she lifted the false bottom out of the trunk. Her .577 Nitro Express gleamed up at her.

If they were about to head inland, deeper into the territory of that flying monstrosity that attacked the snow tractor, she wanted something that would up their chances of survival. Wandering into the wasteland unarmed would be just as deadly as staying here. It would just be a colder death.

Just as she slung the gun over her shoulder, the sound of more incoming shells reached her ears. The little room didn't offer anything solid to hide under. Denise did the only thing she could. She dove under the cot.

The roar of the shells grew and grew under it mushroomed into the deadly bellow of an explosion. This one had been farther away, striking near some of the more distant outbuildings. It wasn't as if the French knew where she was. From that far out, they couldn't even tell if anyone was still in the facility. They were just working to level the place. But still, Denise was playing a dangerous game by staying here any longer. It was only a matter of time until a shell landed too close. With the size of the cruiser's guns, there wouldn't be anything left of her except a puff of blood and a burnt and shredded parka.

She could still feel the reverberations of the blast in her entire body from the last impact. Scrambling to her feet, Denise picked up the elephant gun and a sack of ammunition boxes. She dashed back out into the hallway.

Should she get Cornelia's elephant gun, too? It would take less than a minute to grab it, and it would double the firepower available to them. No, there just wasn't time. She was already going to have trouble making it out of the building before the next set of shells crashed to earth. Better to get out safely with one weapon than get killed trying for two. A bird in the hand and all that.

Weaving back the way she'd come, she did her best to navigate the cramped corridor while holding the large rifle. She vaulted over some overturned equipment that kept spitting out sparks and made her way down the hallway. It was like trying to move through a crippled submarine. The blasts had knocked debris loose, and the narrow space was quickly filling with smoke and dust.

Denise made it past the mess hall when she realized that the hallway ahead had partially collapsed. She was going to have to go around to the other side of the building and use the other exit. She darted down the next cross-section of hallway, skirting around the wall that separated the laboratories from the rest of the facility.

The wall was cracked and crumbling, and Denise could feel intense heat building on the other side. The roar of the fire was loud now. Despite the cold air seeping into the building from every shattered window and collapsed wall, Denise started to sweat as she ran past the wall. It was like standing next to a bakery oven.

Rounding another corner, she took cover as the scream of more incoming shells built up again. She laid herself flat on the floor and cringed as the roar of the shells grew louder and louder. A moment later, they landed at the far edge of the station, sending an angry rumble through the main building.

Coughing on the smoke, Denise hauled herself back to her feet. She tried to wave away the soot billowing through the air, but that only seemed to sir it up even more. Her eyes burned and streamed tears as she fought her way through the acrid cloud.

She came to a section where the wall to the laboratories had collapsed. Most of the science facility was engulfed in dancing flames, casting the room into stark shades of light and flickering shadow.

But what caught Denise's attention were the bodies. There were maybe ten of them strapped to gurneys around the room, and they were moving, thrashing at their bonds. Some of them were already on fire. Others soon would be.

The artillery rounds had hit this portion of the building. Some gurneys were tipped on their sides or blown apart. Bodies and pieces of bodies lay burning on the floor in a scene straight out of hell.

Denise stepped forward to help when she realized what she was actually looking at. The people strapped to those gurneys were already dead. Several of them were black with frostbite, just like Villiers. Others looked relatively fresh, and some were rotting slightly. Some of the moving corpses wore button-up shirts. Some wore a jumpsuit of some kind.

Benoit and his men had kept this part of the facility secret because they were experimenting on the undead. This was where they kept their specimens. They'd known about the slugs and what they could do this whole time.

As Denise looked at some of the empty gurneys that had been flipped over, the restraints snapped. She paused and fished out a box of ammo. Cracking open the Nitro Express, she loaded in a couple of oversized bullets.

There was more equipment to the rear of the laboratory, but it was hard to make out through all the smoke. It looked like there were autopsy tables and a sort of morgue.

But there were also big, cylindrical tubes. Most of the tube was metal, like a big trash can, but they had large glass windows in front. The stainless-steel tubes were dented and punctured by shrapnel. One of them was completely snapped in half. The glass observation windows on all of them were shattered.

There was something inside each tube. They were all roughly man-sized. They were even vaguely man-shaped. But they weren't human. The outlines were all wrong. The things inside the tubes were apparently still alive. Or maybe they were like the people strapped to the gurneys and they were dead but moving. They flailed in their containment cells as the flames lapped around them, cooking them like lobsters in a pot.

Denise couldn't get a good look at them, and she wasn't sure she wanted to. All she could make out were spindly limbs and the glint of what appeared to be segmented eyes. Those things must have come from the same place as the slugs and the huge, flying monster. Maybe they were aliens. Maybe they were just horrifically mutated human beings.

Whatever they were, there was no way for Denise to help them. The flames were already too high, and they were surrounded by undead trying to break free of their restraints. Denise coughed again. There were a dozen different ways to end up dead from trying to venture into the science facility, even without more naval artillery inbound.

Nearby, she saw the entrance to the *radiographie* room that she'd first seen when she walked into Delambre Station for the first time. This time, the door hung from its hinges, and she could see what lay inside. There was some unwieldy equipment that Denise recognized as an X-ray machine. There were also individual X-ray sheets of a multitude of different heads. Each skull had an angry, blotted mass in the middle of the brain matter. There were several dozen pictures hung up on the walls, and each one showed a different human skull with a slug ensconced inside.

She pushed down the hallway, and a figure lurched out of the smoke ahead. It was a man holding a severed leg. He stopped midway through ripping a strip of sinew away from the leg with his teeth and looked at Denise. The man was wearing one of those jumpsuits. He dropped the leg. It hit the ground with a meaty splat as he stumbled toward her.

Denise leveled the Nitro Express at the ghoul and pulled the trigger. Inside the enclosed space of the hallway, the roar of the elephant gun was almost as loud as any of the peals of artillery Denise had heard. The man's head disappeared in a burst of red. Shattered chunks of skull clattered off the wall, and bits of brain matter plopped onto the floor alongside shredded lumps of slug. His body flipped backward like he was trying to perform some particularly difficult gymnastics move. Denise skirted around the twitching body and continued down the hall.

Pushing through the smoke, she saw that the door outside had been blasted off its hinges by the explosions. She lunged outside and took a great, rasping breath of outside air. The cold clawed at her raw throat, but she didn't care. It was relatively free of smoke, and that was all that mattered to her right now. She bent over and dry heaved. Her lungs felt like they'd been used to sponge up grime at a steel mill, and she'd just seen a human head pop like a soap bubble. It wasn't a good combination.

She glanced backward through the open doorway. Smoked puffed out of the opening, swirling up into the otherwise perfectly clear air. There was so little precipitation in Antarctica that there would probably be a giant black smear in this location for years from the soot. The debris might very well sit here for longer than she was alive.

Denise started to straighten herself back up when she saw something move amid the smoke inside the facility. It was a flicker of light in the swirling darkness. Then the flaming corpses started to pour through the doorway.

Several of the ghouls had managed to free themselves from their confinement in the science laboratory. Either they'd broken loose on their own, or the fire had eaten through the restraints for them. All of them were on fire to varying degrees.

The first one through the door wore the remains of a bloody parka. Only his sleeve was on fire. The second one out the door was a walking pillar of flame. Bits of burning clothing and charred flesh crumbled off with each step, leaving a macabre trail of ashes and hot grease in his wake. Obviously, the dead body didn't feel any pain. It simply continued forward toward Denise, arms outstretched to grab her.

Denise didn't bother to waste her bullets. She took off running around the side of the building. She only had so much ammunition, and she had even less time. The next round of shelling would start at any moment.

She rounded the corner only to see that more of the undead had actually beaten her outside. They must have gotten free from their restraints right after the shelling struck the science labs. Hobart and Valdez lay dead on the ground near several idling motor sledges, and the ghouls now had Cornelia surrounded in the alcove where the vehicles were parked.

Cornelia had a lead pipe, and she was swinging it at the dead men every time they reached for her. The metal club struck grasping arms, breaking fingers and snapping bones in the process. The ghouls coming after her didn't seem to care one way or the other, though.

The dead men must have taken her and the others by surprise while they were warming the motor sledges up. She'd probably been watching for Denise to come out through the same door she entered in. Instead, the dead had come around from the other side and killed the two sailors and trapped Cornelia.

Denise raised her Nitro Express again and aimed at the monster closest to Cornelia. She was too far away to guarantee a headshot, so she simply swiveled the gun over and fired. The man tore in half like a wet piñata. Guts and viscera spooled out in an explosion of red confetti.

Cornelia looked up in surprise and saw Denise. Then she immediately had to push another dead man away with her pipe.

There were a couple of ghouls gnawing on the sailors' corpses. Denise broke open the Nitro Express and jammed in a couple more rounds. She lifted the gun up and fired twice more in quick succession.

The .577 Nitro Express was a big, mean weapon. The kickback could seriously injure a person's shoulder if they were handling the elephant gun improperly. Even though Denise had plenty of experience with the weapon, she knew she'd have a sore arm tomorrow from the repeated donkey kick recoil. The weapon was meant to not only kill but bring down large, enraged or panicked animals. It was designed to have stopping power through sheer, massive bodily trauma and penetration. You could destroy a lightly armored tank with a Nitro Express. Using it on something as small and puny as a human being was almost a waste.

She stepped over the four motionless bodies now in front of her. The creatures from the laboratory lay next to the men they'd been eating. The ghouls were both missing everything above the shoulders. There was very little liquid blood, though. It had all coagulated inside their bodies some time ago. The pulped remains of their heads were more like dried pet kibble spread across the ice than the soupy mass that occurred when an elephant gun struck living flesh.

Denise slapped a couple more rounds into the Nitro Express and blew the last of the things attacking Cornelia way. Going back for the weapon had been the right choice. They could have just as easily all been trapped by the undead while waiting for the motor sledge engines to warm up. Now, she only regretted not grabbing Cornelia's elephant gun, too.

"Thanks," Cornelia said, tossing her pipe to the side. Her blonde hair lay scattered around her face, and she was breathing hard. "We need to get out of here."

"I know. Where are the others?"

"Metrodora, Fletch, and Poole were able to hop on their sledges and get out before those things surrounded us. The rest of us got cut off. They were on top of us before we could do anything about it."

Denise looked at the bodies of Hobart and Valdez. In a couple of minutes, a shell would probably land in the vicinity and spread the two men over the landscape in a fine mist. She already felt guilty about bringing everyone straight into the heart of the storm here. Now, the *Sulaco* was destroyed, nearly all of its crew was dead, and Colonel Dagenais and his men were actively trying to obliterate any sign that any of them had ever been here.

She hadn't known things would be so bad. She hadn't known, dammit. But she knew that wasn't an excuse. She'd done things the way the Squires wanted them done, not the way that she thought was right.

The blame wasn't entirely hers. Not even mostly hers. There was a lot of blame to go around. The research teams had clearly been tampering with things that never should have seen the light of day, and it had come back to bite them. Colonel Ozias Dagenais was the one who had actually given the orders to destroy the *Sulaco* and murder its crew.

But Denise had still played a role in the way things turned out. That brought a sour taste to her mouth.

"Let's get out of here. There are going to be more of these things coming out of that building any minute," Denise said, gesturing at the dead men on the ground. She didn't bother to mention the additional shells that were no doubt coming their way.

"Where can we even go?" Cornelia asked. It was a good question. They couldn't stay near the coast. They cruiser out there would destroy them. Even if they could follow the shoreline out of French Territory, there wasn't another outpost of any sort for thousands of miles. Antarctica was double the size of Australia, but there were probably no more than a hundred people walking its surface right now.

That number was about to increase substantially. Denise looked back out toward the coast and saw the troop transport ships steadily approaching, bringing men and equipment to clean up and contain this mess. Unfortunately, they considered Denise and Cornelia to be part of that mess.

Denise looked at Cornelia. "We go to the only place we can. Merovée." They both got on the humming vehicles and took off before the next round of shelling could start. The great white expanse opened up in front of them as they accelerated away, and Denise just hoped there was actually something out there for them to go to.

ELEVEN
SPOILED FOR CHOICES

Denise couldn't really feel the wind rushing past her face anymore. She'd been outside long enough that her skin was numb anywhere that she wasn't wearing several layers of clothing. She hadn't grabbed any extra gloves or anything else from Delambre Station before she left, and she regretted that now.

Even though the continent wasn't locked in winter anymore, it was only a few degrees above freezing. The wind robbed them of any warmth they might have been able to find, though. The constant dry wind bombarded them like it was trying to push them back in the direction of the coast, like it was frantically trying to convince them not to go any deeper into the interior. Denise's face felt like a sheet of chipped porcelain, as if the skin would shatter if anyone tapped on it too hard.

She didn't have frostbite yet. The operative word was "yet," though. They were all going to need shelter and a heat source in the not-too-distant future if they didn't want to start losing fingers and toes.

The problem out here was that there was no way to live off the land, even for a short time. There was no fuel to start a fire. Away from the coast, there was no animal life to hunt for food. They could get water from the ice, if they had to, but that only served to remind everyone how much they needed heat more than anything else. Surviving down here took vigorous planning and attention to supplies. And that was without monsters to contend with.

None of them had done any planning, and they didn't have any supplies except for an elephant gun and some ammunition. Denise didn't even know for sure what they were steering toward. She'd just seen the point on the map, and she'd seen the trail from the air. For all she knew, there was nothing out here but an impact crater from a meteorite.

The French researchers had taken off in this direction, though. She had to assume they would travel toward shelter and supplies, if there were any to be had.

Given that Dagenais was trying to contain the outbreak of monsters, he couldn't have asked for an environment that was more favorable to him. Destroying Delambre Station meant that there were only so many options for someone who didn't want to be blown up. They could go to

Merovée, or they could freeze to death. Or they could freeze to death on the way to Merovée. That was an option, too.

Dagenais seemed to have been dispatched down here by the French as a contingency plan. The research team had clearly been in communication with him. However, Benoit and his men had apparently expected the colonel to help them if things got out of hand. Dagenais, on the other hand, had obviously decided that the safest course of action was to destroy anything having to do with the monsters. That included the research itself and anyone who knew about it, apparently.

It wasn't even a wholly unreasonable decision. Denise had seen what those slugs could do to a person. She'd seen the slug-infested corpses attack the living. If the meteorite had released the slugs into a populated area, it would have been a disaster.

As far as she knew, the slugs didn't spread or reproduce by killing people. They just seemed to need a human body to control, and then everyone else was food. Just being bitten didn't seem like it would spread the slugs to a new host. Maybe if the little slime balls were happy and well-fed for long enough, they would lay eggs or something and spread that way. Denise couldn't tell much about their life cycle from the little she had seen of them.

The best plan was probably just to steer clear of anything that might be of alien origin. That meant a growing list of threats, though. As far as Denise could tell, there were at least three different types of organisms loose down here.

First, and probably the most dangerous, was the giant dragon creature. It could sweep in and carry them off or lob deadly acid at them. Denise kept her eyes on the sky as she rode the motor sledge across the bleak landscape. Even with her Nitro Express, she wasn't at all confident that any of them would survive an encounter with that monster. Maybe the elephant gun could punch through its armor. Maybe the elephant gun couldn't. She didn't care to test the idea out, if it could be avoided.

The next biggest threat was the slugs. Or rather the human corpses the slugs used as surrogate bodies. Denise wasn't too worried about them right at the moment, though. Her group had already passed the overturned motor sledge she and Fletch found before. Villiers was still sprawled out dead. They might run into more of the walking corpses in due course, but they could move faster than the dead mean with their motor sledges. And Denise knew perfectly well that her Nitro Express could deal with a few of the ghouls at a time. Besides, the open spaces out here were so vast that the odds of running into a group of the dead men were actually pretty small. One problem at a time.

There was one last problem that they might have to deal with, though. Denise thought back to the weird, inhuman shapes she'd seen in observation pods back at Delambre Station's science quarters. She didn't even know what those were. For all she knew, they weren't even dangerous. They could be not-particularly-little green men here to offer the people of earth peace and prosperity. Or they could be here to harvest human brains for lunch.

The creatures were shaped a bit like people. That made Denise think that maybe they were different from the slugs or the dragon. Maybe they had some intelligence and understandable motivation. Or maybe they were just dumb, hungry brutes. Just because they had a vaguely familiar shape didn't mean it was safe to assume anything about them. It was speculation to try to guess either way.

It might have been a moot point to begin with. As far as she knew, the only specimens of that species had burned up with the rest of Delambre Station. Anything that made it out had presumably been riddled with bullets courtesy of the French military shortly after that. The creatures' intentions didn't matter much one way or the other if they were dead.

Denise rode at the front of their little convoy because she had the elephant gun. Fletch and Cornelia rode behind her, and Metrodora and Poole took up the rear. They'd been travelling what seemed like forever over the ice, picking their way forward a little at a time.

Strictly speaking, their destination wasn't that far. The motor sledges could make the journey fairly quickly if they opened up the throttle and went at full speed. However, their journey was punctuated by fits and starts as they darted between the landscape's rare pieces of cover to check the skies for approaching monsters.

The trail that led to Merovée was easy enough to follow. The ruts and chewed ice mostly just continued in a straight line across the landscape, occasionally weaving around the rare ridge or dip in the ice.

However, Denise was having a difficult time figuring out how far they'd come. The route to their destination was mostly flat and featureless. It made gauging distances harder than it should have been. She thought that they'd reach the mountains visible from the research station half an hour ago. Instead, they were only just beginning to reach the craggy foothills.

The ground was becoming less flat, and the route they were following took more twists and turns to avoid eruptions of stone or crevasses. Right now, they were in a shallow valley that tilted gradually upward.

With everyone lined up as they were, it was impossible to hold any sort of conversation. That just left Denise alone with her thoughts. She tried to steer clear of thinking about what she could have done differently over the previous few days. The simple answer was, she wasn't sure. Instead, she focused on trying to gather up what she knew and what she could surmise about the situation they were in.

Unfortunately, she was coming to a pretty simple conclusion. They were screwed. Behind them lay Colonel Dagenais, who wanted them dead if it helped contain this incident. She didn't know exactly what lay ahead of her. For all she knew, they had managed to pick up some arms of their own and would shoot on sight.

There was death behind and uncertainty ahead. It was more death off to the sides, too. Either from the cold or from monsters. They could press onward and maybe die, or they could go in some other direction and definitely die.

Spoiled for choices.

The icy gorge's walls were riddled with thick cracks and crevices. In places, frozen boulders had collapsed down to the floor of the canyon. In other places, raw stone managed to poke up through the ice from below, and the walls of the valley gave way almost completely to rock. There were more cracks and even some caves carved into the ice.

Denise kept her eyes pointed toward the sky whenever she could. The gorge they were moving up was shallow but only modestly wide. If something dropped in on them from above, there would only be so much room to maneuver.

She hadn't seen any sign of the dragon creature since it attacked the snow tractor, but she knew it still had to be out there somewhere. Denise didn't think they could outrun the creature with their motor sledges. The beast moved fast through the air. An airplane might be able to outrace it, but not by much.

She wondered what Colonel Dagenais knew about the creature. Benoit and his team seemed surprised about the monster. If Dagenais had been keeping abreast of the situation through the researchers here, he might know even less than Denise. Did he even have the equipment to kill the monster? One surefire weapon would be the cruiser's big guns, but the creature moved too fast to have much chance of hitting it with those. If Dagenais only knew that something large had attacked the snow tractor and killed a couple of the researchers, he probably had no idea what he was actually up against.

As if summoned by her thoughts, a black dot appeared in the sky behind them. Denise swiveled her head around and cursed. The dot grew into a larger speck. It was heading their way.

Denise spotted a particularly large cave opening in the rock wall ahead of them. She signaled with her hand and pulled her motor sledge over to the side of the rock. Dismounting, she pointed skyward.

"I see it," Cornelia said.

Denise peered into the darkness inside the cave. She couldn't see much more than a few feet inside, but the cavern seemed relatively deep. Certainly deep enough for five people to huddle up inside for a little while.

"It's dark," Poole said.

"I don't think we have any other options," Denise said. "Our best shot is to get inside." She gestured toward the cave entrance.

Everyone parked their motor sledges along the wall of the gorge and scrambled inside the cavern entrance. Denise took her elephant gun with her as she abandoned the sledge. If she could get a good shot at the dragon, she intended to take it. Maybe she was wrong and the creature's armor wasn't as durable as it appeared. Striking the monstrosity down would make the rest of their journey a lot safer. Eat your heart out, St. George.

Denise crouched down just inside the cavern entrance, deep enough that something would have to reach in to paw for her and give her time to scurry away, but not so far back that she didn't have a good view of the sky. Inside the cave, she could actually see her breath misting in the cold air. Outside, the wind whipped it away too quickly to see most of the time. She held the Nitro Express on her knees and rubbed her hands together, trying to keep the numbness at bay. The rubbing produced an unpleasant tingle in her fingers.

She knew they couldn't stay outside too much longer. If any of them knew they were going to be travelling for miles outside, they would have bundled up in extra layers. What they had now was good for short jaunts outside but inadequate for the sort of journey they were on now.

Metrodora crawled up close to Denise. "Where is it?"

"Can't see it just at the moment, but I think we'll be able to spot it just over those rocks there in a minute, assuming it keeps following its course."

"Good. I want to get a good look at this thing."

"I do too. But so I can get a clear shot at it."

"Don't let me stop you. If you have a shot, take it. I still want to do what research I can on this thing, though."

"Research? Now?"

"It's what the Squires were set up to do. The more we know about something, the better we can understand it and how to mitigate the risks. In theory, people are safer when we better understand these things. If we ever encounter another one of these creatures someday, any data points we can call on will be invaluable."

"You said people are safer in theory? Why in theory?"

"The Squires are a very old group. The world is a lot different from when they were first established. It's a lot different even from when are current leadership was a bunch of young biologists and monster wranglers. There's a lot of people pushing into areas where they never lived before. There's a lot of forests and jungles being cleared for cities and farmland. It's flushing some creatures out into the edges of society. There's things that are living off the refuse at landfills that previously only lived in the uncharted corners of the earth. The Squires were set up intending to help out with once in a generation monster attacks. Some of our leadership is still in the mindset that we only share our information when people are under siege behind the castle ramparts. Things have changed, though."

"What would you do?"

"Publish our materials. Make them public. There'd be a lot of benefit for people who are living in the territory of very aggressive and rare creatures. A lot of them don't even realize it until it's too late. Then you read in the paper that a family disappeared from a farmstead here. Backpackers were mauled by something there. Work crews building a road through some stretch of forest were killed in a freak accident somewhere else. If people were aware of the risks, they might stay out of those areas, and we wouldn't need as many people like you."

"Stop trying to put me out of business, Metrodora." Denise forced her face into a smile to show she was joking.

"I meant it as a compliment. I called you unprofessional before, but I think I might owe you an apology. I still think you're a little slapdash here and there, but you've kept us alive so far. The teams the Squires use are very regimented. They're disciplined, but they do things in a particular way. I don't think we'd still be alive if they'd sent one of our dedicated hunt and capture teams on this trip."

"I appreciate it. Maybe I misjudged you a little myself. You've handled yourself well out here. Don't thank me too much yet, though. We're alive now. We'll see how we're doing in an hour."

Denise could hear the steady hum of the thing approaching them, now. She steadied herself and raised the Nitro Express. The sound of the creature's approach was different than before somehow. The acoustics of the gorge maybe? Something about the distance between them and the creature this time? A trick of the wind? Denise squinted over her sights and waited.

The black speck she'd spotted a couple of minutes before glided over the rocks right where she thought it would. It wasn't a black speck anymore, though. It was an airplane.

It was a small, single person seaplane, a scout. The plane flew in low. It had French markings on the side, leaving no question as to who had sent it. When the pilot saw the motor sledges parked near the cave entrance, he pulled up and went out of sight for a moment. The buzzing sound of his engine continued overhead, though. He was circling, inspecting the area. From up there, he probably couldn't tell if it was Denise and her group or if it was the French research team.

Either way, the pilot would report back to Dagenais and confirm which direction they went, as if the colonel didn't already know. There was really only one place to go.

Denise debated firing her Nitro Express at the plane when it wheeled back around for another pass at the gorge. She didn't bother. The plane was flying relatively low, but it was also fast. She'd almost certainly be wasting her ammo on the scout plane. Even if she managed to bring it down, Dagenais would still have a good idea where they were headed.

Denise let the gun drop. She didn't gain anything by firing at the airplane. She didn't lose much of anything if she let it go, either. She also didn't really want to fire the gun at another living, breathing human being. She wasn't a pacifist by any means, but she didn't like the idea of blowing somebody out of the sky when it didn't do her one bit of good, either.

The others further back in the cave had seen the scout plane, too. They crept forward to get a better look. All but Cornelia, who stayed back in the shadows for another minute.

"Well, that's just great," Poole said.

"Could be worse. It could be armed. He could be strafing our transport with machine guns right now."

"Think they've got more planes? Ones with guns, I mean?"

Fletch scratched his chin. "Probably not. There's not a lot of spare room on a cruiser. They probably had to keep that plane in parts under a tarp the whole time they weren't using it. Keeping fuel and parts for it takes up even more room, and they have to keep the pilot somewhere. Then, they have to reassemble the thing and lower it into the sea to use it. Having just the one would be a royal pain in the ass for everyone involved. More would be even worse. I'm guessing they only brought the one plane."

"Do you think they'd allow us to surrender to them?" Poole asked. "They can test us. We're alright. We're not infected with those bugs.

We're totally clean. Those no reason for them to try to off us after they know that."

"I don't think they care if we're clean or not," Denise said. "I think they already know that. I mean, how many people with slugs in their brains can drive motor sledges? Dagenais is being intentionally over inclusive in his purge here. He wouldn't have risked shelling his own researchers if he had any interest in our health and safety. He didn't have to blow up the *Sulaco*, either. An order to stop probably would have worked. He wants to make sure this thing gets put to bed for good, and we're loose ends. Just like the research team. Just like the *Sulaco* crew."

"That's crazy," Poole said.

"I'd probably err on the side of caution too, if somebody told me there was a weird alien infection taking over the dead down here," Metrodora said.

Denise had to admit that she had a point. Blowing up a civilian ship and shelling a settlement so its inhabitants were forced into the wasteland was a championship-level dick move, but it wasn't totally illogical in this context. Overzealous and heartless, sure. Illogical, no.

"There's something back here," Cornelia said from behind them.

Denise looked backward into the darkness. She couldn't see very far into the cold shadows. Cornelia was only a vague shape in the gloom.

Above them, the French scout plane wheeled off and continued following the trail inland, looking for traces of Benoit and his research team. Denise backed away from the cavern entrance and picked her way down the short, rocky descent toward the back of the cavern.

"What's back there?"

"Bodies."

"On a scale from dead to dead-but-trying-to-kill-us, just how dead are they?"

"Regular dead. One of them is weird, though."

"Weird how?"

"It's kind of hard to explain. Just get back here."

"I have something that might help," Fletch said. He dug around in his pockets and pulled out a lighter. He tossed it to Denise, and she flicked the little flame to life.

The tiny spark of fire didn't do much to dispel the shadows all around them, but she could at least see Cornelia better now. She could also see some lumpy shapes amid the rocks. There were indeed bodies back there. Three of them, by her count. Fortunately, none of them were moving around.

As Denise moved closer, she had a better view. It was pretty obvious what had happened to two of the corpses. They'd been eaten.

Their clothes were shredded, and the meat had been torn off their bones. Bits of partially mummified flesh clung to exposed rib cages, and pieces of gnawed organs lay on the cave floor. The weather was so cold and dry that nothing had really rotted.

Denise couldn't say exactly how they died. Maybe they'd frozen to death in here, and then something ate them. Maybe they'd gotten trapped in here by one of the ghouls, and they'd been devoured alive. For their sake, Denise hoped it was the former rather than the latter. Hypothermia would have been like falling into a deep slumber. Being eaten alive would have been a slow and foul business.

Most of her attention was focused on the third body, though. Cornelia, in her learned medical opinion, had called it "weird." Denise didn't have a better phrase to describe what she was looking at. The body was clearly human, but something very bizarre had happened to it.

It was like a husk. The entire body was split up the middle, as if someone who didn't really know what they were doing had tried to perform an autopsy while armed with only a shovel. From forehead to groin, the man had been torn open in a gigantic gash. All of his insides had been scooped out, too. The body was just an empty shell.

It didn't look like the man had been chewed on too much. There were some marks on the body where it had suffered some damage, but he hadn't been pulled apart and consumed like the others. This was an entirely different kind of damage. The corpse had been *harvested*.

Denise couldn't figure out how it had been done, though. There was a certain amount of precision to what had happened. Nearly everything had been removed, leaving mostly a frozen layer of skin and some subdermal tissue. Without most of its internal mass, the body looked almost deflated. It reminded Denise of a sports mascot costume that had been hung up to dry after a game.

At the same time, it had been done fairly crudely. The tears in the skin were jagged and rough. The incisions hadn't been done with any sort of sharp instrument. It looked more like the flesh had been torn open like the bottom ripping out of a paper grocery bag. She just hoped that whoever the man was, he had been dead when that happened to him.

"Well, then. We've seen some weird shit over the years. We're actually pretty good at identifying weird shit by now, I'd say," Denise said, scratching her chin.

"We pretty much have honorary doctorates in the field of weird shit," Cornelia agreed.

"And that is some weird shit."

"Metrodora, you ever see anything like this?"

"This is something I'm unfamiliar with."

"Any ideas what could have done something like this?" Denise asked Cornelia.

"It's like everything, pretty much everything, has been removed. What's left is just a shell. I don't know how that happened, let alone why."

"Can you tell what killed him? I mean, was he alive when this happened or had the slugs gotten to him?"

"I'd need better conditions and a lot more light to give a proper opinion. I'm not a medical examiner, either."

"Best guess?"

"Well, he wasn't chewed up like these other guys. That much is obvious. That means he either wasn't alive when these gentlemen were attacked, or he arrived later. There's no skull left to examine, so I can't say if there was anything inside there when any of this went down."

"Think he was the one responsible for doing the others over?" Denise pointed to the skeletal bodies sprawled on the floor of the cave.

"I wouldn't have any way of knowing that. Not at this point. No stomach contents to examine because there's no stomach. Can't compare tooth marks from the jaw to the bodies because there isn't a jaw anymore. There's not much of anything anymore, really."

"Fair enough. Is there anything you can tell us just from what you've seen?"

"Yes. These three men are very dead."

"Ah, yes. I see it now. Very astute. This is why I pay you the big bucks."

"All in a day's work."

Denise tossed the lighter back to Fletch. They weren't going to learn anything else here. The whole situation was screwed up six ways to Sunday, and they weren't going to unravel it holed up in this cave. They needed to get moving again before the motor sledge engines died.

"So, where did these people come from?" Fletch asked. He pointed his lighter at the dead bodies and frowned.

"I'm pretty sure they came from Merovée, where we're going," Denise said. "There's nothing else out here. The first dead man we found, Villiers, was probably coming from there, too."

"And that's where we're headed?" Poole asked. "Right into the middle of where all the dead bodies seem to be originating from?"

"You got a better idea?" Denise asked.

Poole started to sputter something, but Fletch cut him off. "Stow it. We don't have any other options right now.

Denise had been thinking about some things, though. Delambre Station had a large number of corpses in its laboratory. The building was also large enough to house a lot more people, too.

She was pretty sure that Benoit and his team were actually the second wave of researchers. Metrodora said that the Squires first noticed this area in part because so many biologists had been dispatched down here all at once. Where were all those people now?

The three of them had asked themselves that question at one point earlier. The answer seemed painfully obvious, now. All the dead people they'd seen wandering around had come from somewhere. The initial team that was sent down here had succumbed to the slugs and been wiped out. Benoit and his men had come down and managed to impose some order on the situation. Or at least they'd been able to keep the coastal station safe from the plague of monsters. They thought they had everything under control again, but the French military also sent Dagenais and his cruiser as a final contingency. Now things had escalated with the arrival of the huge, flying creature, and the situation had spiraled out of control all over again. The dead people they kept encountering were the original research team, plus any construction or security crews stationed down here.

Benoit and his men were building off the ruins of what came before. But they hadn't been able to clean up the mess completely. Things had been festering in the shadows, and Dagenais had been sent to make sure the same mistake wasn't committed twice.

Denise slithered out of the cave and into the sunlight, like a cockroach checking if the coast was clear to scurry out from under the oven. The scout plane was gone, and she didn't see any other threats on the horizon yet.

There would be, though. There would be. Sooner or later, troops with orders to shoot to kill would hear from the plane pilot that Denise and everyone else had followed the expected route. And there was always that damn flying monster to worry about.

She wasn't sure what she was going to do about any of those problems yet. All she knew right now was that they needed to reach some modicum of warmth and safety soon, or the cold would moot all those other problems for them in due course. Once she had that threat to their lives settled, maybe she could work on solving some of the others. Hopefully.

Throwing her Nitro Express back over her shoulder, Denise hopped on her motor sledge. Everyone else followed her out of the cave, and their bedraggled band beat its way further into the wasteland.

TWELVE
MEROVÉE

Denise unslung her elephant rifle as she stepped away from the motor sledge and crept forward. She'd had the Nitro Express and similar weapons in her hands for thousands of hours over the course of her lifetime. She knew its contours and mechanisms.

But the gun still felt strange in her hands. Her thick gloves padded everything and made it hard for her to stick her finger inside the trigger guard. The numbness in her hands reduced her familiar grip on the stock to a vague sense of pressure. She kept her finger away from the trigger because it was difficult to tell how much pressure she was applying to it. Accidently firing the weapon could send the elephant gun flying out of her hands and twenty feet behind her, her finger possibly still stuck in the trigger guard.

She kept the weapon at the ready, though. Ahead of her, she could see what they'd been travelling toward all this time. Merovée Station was constructed much like its cousin near the shore. Blocky outbuildings and a main structure made up the bulk of the station. If anything, this station was even bigger than Delambre.

The main difference between the two research stations appeared to be that Merovée was built on the edge of a large pit. Or rather, an impact crater.

Jagged cracks ran through the ice leading away from the crater. The ice at the edge of the impact site itself appeared to be melted, though. The edges were dull and smooth rather than rough and splintered, the way the ice was around the cracks. From the air, it almost would have looked like someone punched a hole through a gigantic spider web.

Denise hadn't stopped and pulled her weapon around simply because they'd arrived, though. There were already several motor sledges parked near the station's entrance.

That had to be Benoit and his men. Denise didn't actually see any of the French research team, though. She did see signs that something had gone wrong with their arrival, though.

The motor sledges were scattered. Several of them faced the entrance of the station. A couple more were some distance away, facing in the opposite direction. It looked like those two had been turned around and started back the way they had come before coming to haphazard and crooked halts.

The last Denise knew, Benoit had four other men with him, too. She only counted four motor sledges. There were a few more parked in orderly rows next to the buildings, but they were all covered in a fine gilding of frost. No one had used those any time recently. Maybe the last of Benoit's team had been waylaid or otherwise prevented from reaching Merovée Station. Out here in this climate, that meant he was dead.

Denise approached the vehicles. The first was left so it was facing her head on. She signaled for everyone else to stay back.

"What is it?" Poole yelled.

She didn't bother to answer. Denise focused on watching the area ahead of her for movement of any sort. If Benoit and his men were here, that could be good or bad. Maybe Benoit would recognize that there was safety in numbers, and they could help each other find a way to get out of this jam. Then again, the researchers might not be in the mood to throw a welcome party. Benoit still had her revolver, too.

If Benoit and his team weren't here, that was even worse. That could mean they'd taken anything useful and moved on to a location she didn't know about, stranding everyone here. And that was probably the *good* explanation for them not being there. The other alternatives mostly involved Benoit and his team being very dead.

Denise walked up next to the motor sledge, looking it over. She wanted to take her glove off and feel the engine for heat, but that would leave her with only one hand to hold the Nitro Express. Until she knew what had happened, she wanted both hands firmly on the elephant gun.

The motor sledge had been left next to a small concrete hut. A narrow window ran across the length of the hut's front. Frost had pebbled the glass, making it impossible to see inside. There were official-looking statements painted on the side of the building, but they were all in French, so Denise couldn't read any of them.

Moving forward another few feet, Denise saw that the door to the hut had been bashed inward. There some old, dried blood on the floor. None of it was recent enough to have come from Benoit or any of his team.

She realized that the hut was a guard post of some sort. The words painted on the side probably warned visitors to have their identification ready and to submit to a search. Or something along those lines. It didn't matter anymore. Someone had been stuck with the truly unfortunate job of manning this freezing little hut in the middle of nowhere and checking in scientists. That someone and those scientists were probably all dead by now, judging from the smeared red stain on the floor.

The problem was that they might still be walking around here somewhere, dead or not. Denise had no idea how many people were originally stationed here. The facility had room for plenty, though. That could potentially mean dozens of the undead prowling around in the various buildings.

Her boots crunched on the ice as she moved toward the next motor sledge. That was when she smelled it. It was the same odor she'd noticed at the penguin rookery. It was like a big, bubbling cauldron of pig vomit.

She skirted around the second motor sledge and moved toward the third. On the other side of the next vehicle was a thick, yellowish puddle. There were human remains in the center. There were a few scraps of cloth floating in the foul broth. They were the same color as the jacket Benoit had been wearing when he left Delambre Station.

Glancing over, she saw the remains of the fifth motor sledge that she had been looking for. The vehicle had been flattened and crushed. Bits of metal lay strewn around the sledge's crumpled form. Not only had it been crushed and mangled, but it looked like it had been thrown against the edge of the nearest building. There were cracks and bits of metal spall stuck in the side of the wall. There was also quite a bit of blood, much fresher than the stuff in the guard hut.

The structure itself was a small hangar, with a two-seater airplane inside. It looked just like the one she and Fletch had taken out from Delambre Station. She was more concerned about the smashed motor sledge at the moment, though. There was only one implication.

The dragon had been here. Denise didn't know what that thing was, but it had been here. An awful thought suddenly occurred to her. What if there was more than one of the beasts? She had only seen the one, but that didn't necessarily preclude the possibility that there were more of them. Hopefully not.

At least the sky leviathan didn't seem to be around right at the moment. Hopefully, it was off terrorizing Dagenais and his troops, slowing their approach here. Maybe they could even find a way to kill it. Denise would rather deal with Dagenais than the dragon, even if it just meant picking her poison.

Human beings she understood. At least, as well as anyone understood other human beings. She didn't even know what the dragon thing was, let alone if she could kill it.

Hopefully, the creature was off giving Dagenais unholy hell, but she wasn't counting on it. When she first saw the creature on the snow tractor, it took the man it carried off in this direction. And now it had killed Benoit and his men when they arrived here at Merovée Station. This was its territory. It might be out at the moment, at least she hoped so, but she doubted that a few researchers had permanently scared it off just by intruding. This thing wasn't some rare bird that would abandon its nest just because human beings had traipsed too close. It would probably be back more frequently now to see if more food had blundered into its territory. Benoit had just been unlucky enough to be around right when the creature happened to be here, too.

The safest place would be inside. Well, maybe. That might not be strictly true if she opened the door and dozens of ghouls came pouring out.

The nearest door to the main building was a large, metal sliding set up, a bit like a barn door. Denise let the Nitro Express rest from the strap over her shoulder for a minute and pushed the door open and inch. The door issued an awful, squeaking racket as it moved, making Denise cringe.

She pressed her eye to the gap and looked inside. The area beyond was bifurcated. There was another large, sliding door where sizable equipment could be wheeled in and out of the building, and then there was a normal-sized entrance for people to move in and out of. There were more motor sledges parked along the near wall. This was apparently a transition area and garage of sorts.

Denise checked the sky above them. Still clear. She waved everyone forward. Cornelia, Metrodora, Fletch, and Poole scurried up. They all swerved well clear of the goopy remains that used to be Dr. Benoit.

"We can get it through here," Denise said. "We'll be safest inside."

"Doesn't look like they have any power. We're going to need to get warm at some point," Cornelia said. She had her arms wrapped around herself. Denise could feel the cold sapping her strength as well. The lot of them wouldn't be able to go on too much longer.

"They'll have a generator of some sort in there," Fletch said. "So long as we can toss some fuel in it, it shouldn't be too hard to start some heat up. If we have to, we can burn a mattress out here or something and get a quick bit of warmth, too."

"A place like this probably has a long-range radio," Metrodora said. "Once we get some power flowing, we need to see if we can get word out to anyone. If I can get in contact with the Squires, they can send another ship down here."

"What and get them all killed, too?" Poole asked.

"We would warn them and arrange someplace for them to rendezvous with us. Someplace far away from Delambre Station and this Colonel Dagenais. We need to contact somebody eventually. We're just treading water here if we don't have any means of escaping."

"Good thinking. The first order of business should be to find that generator and get it up and running," Denise said. "We'll get the heat running again. We won't freeze to death in the time it takes to dispatch a rescue ship that way. While we're looking for that, keep your eyes peeled for communications equipment and supplies. We might have to live here for a little while. If you see food or guns, we're probably going to need those. Ready?"

Everyone nodded, and Denise twisted the doorknob. She swung her Nitro Express around, ready to blow away anything that lunged out at them. There was nothing but a barricade made out of desks and chairs.

Only darkness lay beyond. Denise squinted and tried to see deeper into the station. Most of it was too deep in shadow to make much out. Nothing was moving back there. She was sure of that, at least. The rest was simply murky shadows, though.

She shut the door and walked over to the sliding door meant for supplies. Pushing it open a few feet, she backed up and peered inside. Someone had started building a barricade at this entrance, too. More desks and lab equipment were piled up, but only to about waist height.

There was a chaotic scattering of more materials just on the other side of the makeshift barricade. Denise climbed on top of a desk and saw why. There was a chewed skeleton on the ground nearby. The man had been trying to disassemble the barricade in order to get out when he was killed. He hadn't toppled enough of the construction to make it to the door before his pursuers caught up with him, obviously.

The macabre scene told a little story. Denise was used to looking at animal carcasses and determining information from them. The age of the body. What predators and scavengers had been at it. Whether it had been brought down by carnivores, natural causes, or even an aggressive rival during the mating season. Examining a dead human being wasn't so entirely different, even if it made Denise's stomach churn in a way that a chewed-up antelope never would.

The outbreak had begun inside the facility. The staff here had tried to protect themselves by blocking the entrances. Unfortunately for them, the problem had found its way to them eventually. What followed was probably an outright massacre. Frostbite or monsters apparently claimed most or all of the poor souls who fled. Other people never even made it out of the station.

The chewed body also meant there might very well be more of the undead haunting these halls. Denise kept the Nitro Express locked tight in her grip as she continued forward. She could see her breath coming in white puffs again. The interior of the station wasn't much warmer than the outside.

110

Fletch flicked his lighter on and held it over his head as they moved forward. It wasn't much, but with the power off inside the building, it was dark as Satan's thoughts. Denise padded forward, shuffling her feet a little to avoid pitching forward over some obstacle or another.

They were in a large, mostly open area. It seemed to be a warehouse of some sort. She was hoping that meant there would be plenty of supplies to scavenge. The French had built this place with the intention of staying. There had to be cans of food and the other essentials for survival lying about.

Now wasn't the time to search, though. She strained her ears, trying to listen for any sounds that didn't belong. It wasn't easy, though. There was a lot of debris on the floor. Her boots kept coming down on bits of broken glass or crumpled papers. Everyone else was doing the same, creating a little beacon of sound in the darkness. Every time something tinkled or scuffed immediately behind her, it sent her heart skittering up her throat like a skittish animal ducking back into its burrow. Anything in here with them might very well be zeroing in on their location as they moved. The howling wind outside obscured any sound that wasn't more than a few feet away, making it impossible to tell if there was anything coming toward them.

Denise hoped the generator was somewhere in the warehouse. It probably wouldn't be right in the living quarters or the science laboratories. The sooner they found it, the sooner they could get not only the heat but the lights working again. Trying to creep through the entire facility in the dark seemed like a surefire way of being taken by surprise.

The size of the warehouse section was disorienting in the darkness. Denise tried to stick to the wall. With only a little circle of light to work with, it would be easy to get turned around or start moving in circles through the middle of the building. There were stacks of crates and equipment under tarps filling the center of the warehouse, creating a network of passageways in between them.

Something crashed down in the darkness. Denise swung her rifle around, looking for the source of the sound. It sounded like a wooden crate smashing down to the concrete floor from somewhere deeper in the structure.

Denise froze for a minute, shuffling around in a tight semi-circle, her back against the wall. She pointed the Nitro Express into the darkness, waiting for something to come toward them. Was there any possibility that part of Benoit's team had survived and made it in here? She hadn't seen enough bodies to be one hundred percent positive, and she didn't want to blow away another survivor.

She wasn't betting that whatever made that noise was alive, though. Her money was on a shambling body bumbling through the darkness, looking for human prey. Denise felt like she was trapped in the Minotaur's labyrinth, stuck in the dark with something that intended to tear them all apart.

After a minute, there weren't any more noises. There was just the omnipresent howling of the wind. Denise would have preferred that the noises continued. At least then, she'd have some idea where the room's other occupant was. With only the sounds of the gale outside, sounds that muffled any approaching footsteps, it was impossible to tell if anything was coming toward them. On the African plains, she could watch the tall grass and tell if there was something stalking toward her or not. She might not be able to see the predator coming to investigate them, but at least she knew where it was. In here, she was deaf and blind.

Without anything else to go on about which direction a threat might come from, Denise continued forward, slinking along the wall. They passed a couple of doors that led deeper into the facility. They were labeled in French, which didn't help Denise in the least. She didn't want to open any of them just yet. That could risk allowing something else in here. There was no way to know who or what might be behind any given corner.

Passing another door, she spotted something along the far wall. It was a generator. The oversized generator wasn't running. It had no doubt run out of juice shortly after the people here lost control of the station. But Denise saw a manual fuel pump nearby. If they could just get everything primed and working again, there would be heat and lights in the facility again.

There was also a body sprawled out in front of the generator, as if in warning. It was another one like the corpse they'd found in the cave. As Denise drew closer, she could see that the body had been hollowed out until there was only a dried-out crust of skin left in a vaguely human shape.

The body was directly in front of the generator. Denise tried to push it out of the way a little with the toe of her boot, but the part she touched just crumbled in on itself. Bits of skin clung to her boot like oversized flakes of dandruff. She didn't know what kind of creature could do that to a human being, and she'd be perfectly happy to never find out.

"We have to get this thing working again," Denise said, gesturing at the generator.

"The fuel pump is right there. They must have some underground tanks," Fletch said.

"They aren't dry, are they?"

"Probably not. This system was designed so it had to be manually fueled every so often. It didn't draw directly from the storage tanks. If they had to leave the facility due to a particularly harsh winter or some other problem, it would be easier to restart everything when they came back this way."

"Yeah, I don't think this is exactly what they had in mind, but it works to our advantage, either way," Cornelia said.

"Fletch, you and Cornelia work on the pump. Poole and Metrodora, make sure everything is alright with the generator itself. We don't need it shorting out when we try to turn it on again. I'll keep watch while you're working," Denise said.

Everyone started in on their tasks. Denise turned around to watch the darkness behind them.

There was a figure in the shadows not ten feet away. It wasn't human. Denise started to shout a warning and raise her elephant gun, but it was already too late. The thing was coming at them on long, spindly legs, moving freakishly fast.

It was one of the creatures that Denise had seen in the burning laboratories at Delambre Station. The creature was as tall as a person, but it was built *wrong*. The limbs didn't fold the right way, and each appendage ended in a set of gnarled claws. The head was a misshapen mass studded with a pair of oversized, bulbous eyes that glittered in the darkness. Every square inch of its flesh looked like a fresh scab. It looked like if, instead of robbing graves and stealing full body parts, Dr. Frankenstein had tried to build his creature entirely out of discarded medical waste.

A great, sizzling gob of foul liquid shot past Denise's head, and Poole screamed. Denise raised her rifle and tried to bring it to bear on the creature. The thing moved with curious, quick hopping movements, skipping this way and that way. It was much faster than the dead men with the slugs in their brains, much faster than anything human.

It was on top of them in the blink of an eye. The creature slashed out at Denise. She felt the material of her outermost jacket slice open. There was just a small tugging sensation and a loud noise. If those claws had extended a little further and reached her actual flesh, they would have unspooled her guts like party streamers.

Denise fired off a snap-shot with the elephant rifle. In the enclosed space of the warehouse, the sound was like the end of the world. The muzzle flash lit up the space around them in a brilliant flashbulb moment, scorching the scene onto Denise's corneas. The muzzle flash disappeared as quickly as it appeared, and Denise was blind for a second.

She lunged backward, unsure if she'd actually hit the creature. There was a loud thud directly in front of her, the sound of something fleshy collapsing onto the concrete floor. Poole was still screaming, but his shrieks were turning into strangled gurgles. Denise tuned the awful noises out for a moment and focused on whether the creature in front of her was dead or not.

Fletch rushed over to help Poole, and he brought the glow of his lighter with him. The flickering light revealed the shape in front of her. The Nitro Express had excavated a hole in its chest region, blowing one of the creature's arms off in the process. Pulped innards lay strewn around.

She turned around. Poole was in bad shape. He was flat on his back, his hands clawing at what was left of his face. Most of the flesh had dribbled off like melting chocolate. There was just runny sludge, dripping onto the floor. The bone was starting to sizzle and pit, too. Nearby, Metrodora turned around and threw up.

The creature that had just attacked them had the ability to spew acid, just like the dragon. Maybe the two were distant relatives. If these things really had come from some distant corner of the cosmos, maybe the entire ecology was based around that little trick. Maybe big grazing herbivores spat acid on the rocks, slurped the nutrients out, and were in turn sprayed with acid by hungry carnivores like these things. She didn't know how the rules of evolution worked on whatever hell-planet these things came from.

Cornelia straddled Poole, trying to prevent him from clawing what skin he had left off and working to keep the stuff at bay. There wasn't much she could do, even with her medical experience. They needed an operating room and a staff of doctors and equipment and adequate lighting. They had none of that. Cornelia had ripped the sleeve off her jacket and was using it to try to shovel the caustic gunk off Poole's face. The vile ooze was eating through the jacket material as fast as Cornelia could work. She yelped as a drop ate through her gloves.

Some of the burning slime had landed on Poole's neck. The stuff was bubbling and eating its way through the flesh. Poole's gibbering screams changed timbre as the walls of his esophagus started to melt away. Blood and liquid flesh spread away from Poole in a growing pool. After a minute, the man went still at last. The soft tissues below his eyes and above his Adam's apple were mostly gone. What was left looked like it had been sent through a blender.

Denise rubbed her face with the back of her hand. There were only four of them left now. Four people against an unknown number of monsters and the French military. Those weren't good odds.

"Is everyone alright?" Denise asked.

Cornelia nodded. She'd taken her gloves off. There were a couple of angry raw spots on her hands, but most of the acid had been blunted after chewing through a few layers of clothing.

Fletch ran his fingers through his hair. "Yeah. I'm fine. I just had a really strong memory from back during the war, but I'm okay. Wouldn't mind a drink or twelve right about now, though."

"No injuries," Metrodora said, hunched over with her hands on her knees. She was still turned around so she couldn't see Poole.

"Right," Denise said. Everyone had been pushed too far, but they were still holding it together. They needed some sort of reprieve, even if it was only temporary. "Okay, get the generator up and running. Let's try to get it done quick."

She didn't bother to mention that there could be more of the creatures in here with them right now. If there were more monsters in the warehouse, the noise and bright flash of light from firing the elephant gun had just given away exactly where they were. Everyone turned around and started working. They didn't need to be told that they were still in danger. It was as apparent as the darkness all around them.

Denise crouched down to make herself a smaller target in case anything else started lobbing acid in her direction. She moved forward a little bit and looked at the body of the creature in front of her. It looked the part of something that conspiracy theorists would believe was on ice in a secret government facility somewhere. Most biologists would probably give their eyeteeth to be able to examine this cadaver on a slab.

The head was the strangest feature. It had two large, compound eyes, like an insect. The bulging, lidless eyeballs were both a bit bigger than Denise's fists. It didn't have any nose to speak of, just a couple of pits in the middle of its head. Denise assumed they were nostrils of some sort, but they could be mating orifices for all she knew.

From what she could see, the creature didn't have a jaw. Instead, its mouth was just a gaping hole. A thick, runny fluid dribbled from the creature's mouth. Denise didn't dare touch anything. That seemed like a good way to get her fingers melted off. There were some sort of parts inside the creature's mouth. It almost looked like baleen, the material whales used to filter tiny organisms out of the seawater.

This thing couldn't bite anyone. Instead, it spat acid and reduced its prey to a slurry, kind of like a spider. Then it slurped up the resulting mess and filtered everything through its mouthparts. Once it had killed, it probably lapped its meal up.

There was a series of whirrs followed by a sort of rapid clicking. A second later, the lights snapped on overhead. Denise blinked in the sudden light, squinting against the fluorescent brilliance. Somewhere out amid the field of crates and tarp-covered equipment, something skittered across the floor in surprise.

Denise swiveled her Nitro Express in that direction, but she couldn't see anything. "Let's get to a location we can secure and then work on gathering supplies," she said as she backed toward the closest door. If they could fortify a large office or someplace, they'd be able to rest and warm up a little bit without the constant fear that something was about to sneak up on them. Then they could grab some equipment and evaluate their options.

She turned the knob the nearest door until it was ready to swing open, then she let it open just an inch. Both hands firmly on the Nitro Express again, she pushed the door the rest of the way open with her foot. She stuck the rifle's barrels through the open doorway first and swiveled them around, taking in the large room beyond.

Denise looked down the sights, but her vision soon drifted upward. There, standing on a pedestal in the middle of the room, was the meteor.

THIRTEEN
THE SOURCE

The meteor was a gigantic, potato-shaped hunk of blackened rock. Almost the entire surface was covered in dark scorch marks from its entry into the atmosphere. The only exceptions were some places where pieces had obviously been chipped off by the scientists here for further study. Overall, the giant hunk of space debris was perhaps the length of two transport trucks and as tall as a two-story building. The entire meteor had been placed in a giant glass structure, separating it from the rest of the building.

There were workstations and equipment lining the walls. Overturned chairs and binders swept from desks lay on the floor. More papers lay on the desks themselves, along with black and white photographs of wives and families. There were various knickknacks and diplomas hanging on the walls. This place had been the heart of the station before everything went to hell.

Denise wondered what the French government had told all those wives and children in the various photos. Their loved ones fell down a frozen crevasse? Gas leak at the science quarters? Transport ship sank in icy waters with no survivors? She was guessing that they hadn't been told their loved ones had been devoured by undead colleagues and bug-eyed monsters from outer space. Maybe they hadn't been told anything at all yet. As far as anyone in the outside world knew, the French research stations down here were humming along just fine.

Denise could now report that things were, in fact, not fine.

"They must have winched the meteor out of its impact site and then built the facility around it," Metrodora said. "I don't see any other way they could have gotten it in here."

"Most of its mass probably burned up when it hit the atmosphere. It was a lot bigger when it was just floating along in space. This is just what's left," Cornelia said.

"So, this is what the monsters hitched a ride on?" Fletch asked.

Denise looked the meteor over. It was big, but it wasn't enormous. There was no way that the dragon creature that attacked the snow tractor could have ridden around inside this thing. Nor could it have simply attached itself to the outside and surfed through the atmosphere. As

Cornelia pointed out, the temperatures would have been immense. Anything on the outside would be charcoal in a matter of seconds.

"I don't see how," Cornelia said. "I mean, the only safe place on this thing when it entered the atmosphere would have been the interior, deep toward the center. Maybe the slugs could make the journey safely in there. I don't think the creatures that killed Poole would fit, though."

"Do you have another explanation about where they came from?" Metrodora asked.

"Hell," Fletch suggested.

"Maybe the meteor opened up a subterranean cave system or something. Maybe they're not from space at all. I have no idea, and I'm not about to ask them," Cornelia said.

"I think they probably have to be from space," Denise said. "Otherwise, why bother dragging the meteor up here in the first place? They were obviously studying it before everything went wrong. This whole facility was a costly endeavor. They wouldn't build it just to study a single meteorite, even if it is a sizable specimen. There had to be something special about it. I'm guessing it's because they found life on this one."

"So where does that leave us? Fast-tracked evolution? These things started out as microbes and diverged into giant flying monsters, slugs, and bug men in the span of a couple of months?" Metrodora asked. She pulled out her notebook and jotted something down inside.

Denise hadn't even noticed that Metrodora still had the little book. "Maybe. Could be. Could be something completely different. I'll bet good money that's the source right there, though."

The air was starting to warm up a little as the heating system kicked in. It wasn't very dramatic, but it still sent a painful tingle across Denise's skin as she started to thaw out. A few more hours outside, and she would have been in real trouble.

"Let's focus on doing what we can to keep this area safe. Now that we've got the power back on, this is our chance to get what supplies we need and try to contact the outside world. There were a lot of supplies in the warehouse back there, but I think we should try to find some weapons," Denise said.

"Right. They had a guard hut at the front entrance. There was probably some sort of security team located here. If we can find their offices, they probably had an armory or at least a gun locker," Cornelia said.

"We shouldn't split up to look. Not until we're all armed to the teeth, at least," Denise said. "Stick with me. We'll see what we can scrounge up." Everyone nodded. They liked the idea of getting their mitts on some guns of their own.

There were several doors leading off in various directions from the meteor laboratory. This seemed to be the central hub for the entire facility, which confirmed in Denise's mind that the researchers here had been interested in the hunk of rock because it harbored some traces of life. A couple of the nearby entrances were barricaded up.

Denise didn't want to go through the effort of pulling the desks and equipment away only to discover that they had been piled there for good reasons in the first place. Instead, she chose one of the doors on the opposite side of the room and started toward it.

Walking past the glass enclosure the meteor had been placed in, Denise noticed that one of the glass panels had been shattered. The shards sat glittering on the floor nearby, drops of blood glistening from some of them. From the way the glass had landed, she could tell that whatever had broken the glass had come from the inside and burst *out* rather than in. Maybe that represented the exact moment the researchers here lost control. It was impossible to say.

She opened the door she'd chosen and poked her rifle through. This was not the door they wanted. That much was obvious at a glance. What lay beyond was mostly just a single long hallway without any doors leading off it. There appeared to be the entrance to an industrial-sized cable car at the far end of the hallway. The hallway stretched far enough that it probably reached the melted rim of the crater, and the cable car allowed people to descend down and retrieve anything of interest.

There was a gate near their position, though. A sign hung from the metal grating. The sign was in French of course, and most of it appeared to consist of warnings and admonitions. There was a lot of red lettering marked with exclamation points.

A smaller sign seemed to be a directory of sorts, though. Denise could puzzle out a few pieces of French on that one. One line in particular caught her eye. *Espace de stockage: équipement d'urgence.* She didn't need to be a linguistic savant to figure that one out. Space of stocking: equipment of urgency. Or less cumbersomely, "storage area: emergency equipment." Something like that, anyway.

That option intrigued her. Emergency equipment might include all kinds of goodies in a place like this, maybe everything they needed. She wasn't sure she wanted to travel straight into the belly of the beast yet, though. There'd be only one way in or out of that pit. With only one weapon between all of them, things could get really ugly if something went wrong down there. Maybe there were easier pickings up here on the surface.

She backed out into the meteorite observation chamber again and picked another door. Once again, she stuck her gun barrels through first, just in case something was in the mood to jump out at them. So far, the interior of the base itself was relatively quiet.

Denise thought back to the bodies she'd seen outside and in the science laboratory at Delambre Station. A lot of people had fled from this place. Maybe some of them made it back to the coast and were rescued. The dead had followed them out and killed or infected a lot of them, though. Apparently, the exodus had left the original site relatively abandoned. Benoit and his team had probably wrangled a lot of their specimens from here and the surrounding environment too, further reducing the local monster population. Denise was thankful for the service. Too bad Benoit and his crew apparently knew nothing about the dragon creature and how to get rid of it, though. Everything might have stayed under control if they had been able to capture or kill that particular beastie. Its arrival had brought Colonel Dagenais into the game and gotten Benoit and his team killed at the front door to this station.

The hallway ahead was empty, but it had several doorways leading off of it. Offices of some kind. The first door led to something unexpected.

It was a cellblock. There were about twenty cells, all lined up next to each other like a prison. Concrete walls separated each cell, but the front of each was simply made of cold iron bars. Each cell had two cots and a couple of basic amenities. The space was small enough that prisoners could have laid on their respective cots and held hands if they wanted to.

Most of the cells were empty. A few weren't though. The one nearest to Denise held two emaciated bodies. The prisoners wore matching jumpsuits that practically fell off their skeletal frames. Denise thought back to some of the dead men she'd seen in the burning science wing of Delambre Station. They'd been wearing jumpsuits identical to the two bodies in the cage.

"Looks like they starved to death," Cornelia said.

"They were protected from the creatures that took over the station, but there was no one left to feed them," Metrodora said.

Denise shuddered at the thought of being trapped in a place like this, left to slowly die. There wouldn't have been anything the men in there could do about any of it. Maybe that wasn't even the worst way to go around here, though.

Another cell also contained two dead bodies. The difference was, one of the men was moving around. The corpse stuck its arms through the bars and grasped at them. It banged its head against the metal over and over again, trying to reach them. The steady beat of the man's skull against the iron set Denise's teeth on edge as the sound rattled out over and over again. Another body sat on the floor of the cell, the flesh chewed off its bones. At some point, a slug had made it in here and infected one of the men, with unfortunate results for his cellmate.

"Who were these poor suckers?" Fletch looked the occupied cells over.

"Test subjects, I would guess," Denise said, thinking again about what she'd seen at Delambre Station. There had been a disproportionate number of ghouls in jumpsuits locked in the laboratory out there. She was guessing they'd been deliberately infected.

"Probably condemned criminals," Cornelia said. "Easy to get ahold of, and most people won't miss them."

Denise looked around the room. The cells were of a different construction than the rest of the facility. The concrete walls were painted a different color, and the room was in an odd location within the facility for holding prisoners. She was guessing that this area was only turned into a makeshift prison after the researchers studying the meteorite met the slugs and bug men. It didn't look like it was part of the original plans for the place but something that had been set up later, like a bad home renovation.

Delambre Station had been a relatively unsecured complex. It was built in such a way that even visiting scientists could walk into certain parts of it. It had probably only been co-opted for studying the dead after this place fell.

Merovée Station on the other hand, was clearly never meant to be seen by anyone from the outside. The place had been guarded, and the cellblock reeked of unethical experiments and human guinea pigs. She had no doubt that Dagenais had orders to raze this place to the ground in due course, too. Not only would it help contain the monsters, but it would also eliminate evidence of complicity in such conditions.

Whoever was in charge here would probably be hanged by some secret military court if the evidence of human experimentation came to light. That, or quietly shuffled off to some new position and given a medal. The same people who originally approved of this place might not be too concerned with the excesses if they gained something valuable out of it. There'd still be hell to pay for the government, trying to explain just what had been going on here, though. Yes, this place was going to be demolished and the rubble burnt and bulldozed into the crater as soon as the military got the chance.

There was another door at the far end of the miniature prison. Denise moved toward it. They seemed to be on the right track here. The main security annex was almost certainly somewhere near the prisoners.

The inside of the room led to what was obviously a senior military administrator's office, with smaller rooms for other personnel nearby. There was both a French flag and a flag for the French Antarctic territories. The territorial flag had a small French flag in the upper left, and the rest was primarily plain blue with a few stars and some lettering that was probably an acronym in French.

There were also pictures on the wall. A young man in an officer's uniform standing in a muddy trench, one hand holding a scruffy little mutt dog under an arm, the other resting on the breach of a piece of heavy artillery. Another showed a slightly older version of the same man standing in front of a row of tanks. The little dog in his arm had been replaced with a woman in a bridal veil. A third picture showed two young boys in playtime soldier outfits. The pictures told a little story about a man dedicated to his craft.

The nameplate that still sat on the desk added context to that story. *Col. Ozias Dagenais.* He had been in charge of security on the station. Obviously, he'd failed. Based on what she'd seen, only he and a few others, probably mostly from the armed security team, had survived the collapse of the station's defenses.

Aside from a layer of dust, the desk looked like it was ready for use. A typewriter sat off to the side. Forms sat in neat little piles, ready to be read or carried off to the appropriate recipient. Most of the room was almost pristine.

One of the few things that had been disturbed was a large vault that took up part of the sidewall. It was the station's armory. There were maybe a dozen racks for rifles, all of them empty. A half-empty box of rifle ammunition sat on the floor, brass spilling out and rolling onto the room's carpet.

There was exactly one weapon left in the armory, a standard-issue pistol. There were a couple of boxes of ammunition for it. Everything else had been pillaged in the original defense of the station. Denise reached in and tossed the pistol to Cornelia, handing the extra ammo boxes over next.

"That's it?" Fletch asked.

"There's some rifle rounds. Maybe if we run really fast when can shove them into anything that attacks us," Cornelia said, scowling.

"We can probably find a couple more guns around the station, but they're almost certainly locked in somebody's cold, dead hands," Denise said. "We'll keep looking, but this is a start. Eventually, I want to start working on securing the area and finding some sort of communications system."

She looked back at the desk that used to belong to Dagenais. She felt like she understood the man a little bit better now that she knew he'd been the head of security here. A man of his obvious military pride probably felt a stain of shame and dishonor from being forced out of his own headquarters. Neither ambition nor honor were well-served by such a situation, and Denise had the suspicion that Dagenais was the type who had a lot of the former and paid a lot of lip service to the latter.

He'd probably been looking for an excuse to either destroy or retake this place. Either option would ensure that there was never any public evidence of what transpired here. Human experimentation and a monstrous invasion from outer space wouldn't look good on anyone's service record. If there were no survivors, there wouldn't be anyone to dispute his account of things, though.

And that meant there would be no negotiating with him. In all likelihood, no quarter would be given, even if asked for. The twin forces of pride and fear of censure were hard to overcome, especially given that Dagenais clearly had the upper hand. If his troops showed up outside the station right now, the four of them only had two guns to defend themselves.

Denise and the others checked the extra rooms that branched off of the main security office. There were some personal items left behind but nothing that was especially useful to them. Moving back out through the cell block, they returned to the central chamber and the meteor. The giant rock loomed over them, as if sitting in judgement.

They tried another passageway and found the station's communication center. Radio equipment sat on tables, unused but activated again after the power had been restored.

"Jackpot," Cornelia said.

"Does anybody know how to work this equipment?" Denise asked.

"I can figure it out," Fletch said.

"Perfect. At some point, we're going to need to get out of here. We need to get on the horn with anybody we can. Anybody who isn't Dagenais. A passing ship is probably our best shot. They can pass on word to somebody else that we need help getting away from here. If we can arrange to be picked up at some stretch of coast far away from whatever's left of Delambre Station and Dagenais, maybe we can trek out there and escape. With food, fuel, and tents, we can keep going for days. That'll give us a chance."

Denise knew it wasn't a perfect plan. Even if they could arrange a secret extraction at some anonymous stretch of shore, there were still threats from the air. The dragon creature was the most obvious. If it found them out in the open, it would make short work of them. That French scout plane could be just as dangerous, though. If it spotted them, it would report their position right back to Dagenais. And if Dagenais knew where they were, he would no doubt try to stop them, even if it meant sinking another civilian ship.

A voice squawked to life over the radio. There was a jabber of French. Another voice responded, also in French. Then, the voices cut off.

The system must still be tuned in to the French military signals it had been using when the station's population was killed. They could listen in on the French military here. Not that it did them any good. They could be listening to French commandos sneak up on the outside of the building right this very instant, and none of them would be able to understand the conversation or orders.

Then a voice came through the radio in English. Denise recognized the voice's controlled, dulcet tones in a second.

"This is Colonel Ozias Dagenais. I am addressing the people who have fled inland to Merovée Station. I see your transmitter has reactivated. Our equipment has been picking up your signal for several minutes. Are you there?"

Denise was tempted to pick up the receiver and tell Dagenais that they had seen the cells and the starved bodies. They knew about the experiments that must have been conducted here. Nobody took a step forward, though. The thought that this might be some sort of trick must have crossed all their minds at some point.

"I will repeat this message every fifteen minutes for the next two hours. After that, I will assume you are all dead. Surrender now. We know you are there. Even now, my men are preparing to retake the station. They have been warned about the extremely dangerous situation inside and its infectious nature. I'm sure you have seen the noxious nature of this threat by now, too. It must be contained at all costs, and your presence is only complicating matters and putting lives at risk. Agree to turn yourselves in to my men, and we will see to it that you are given medical testing to ensure you are not infected, and then we will allow you to leave. I will issue this message again in another fifteen minutes. This offer will expire after the end of two hours."

"Do you believe any of that? About letting us go?" Metrodora asked.

"Not for a minute," Denise said. "He just wants to get us out of here, so he can be done with us faster. He blew up a civilian ship without warning, and he shelled French citizens. He wants this contained, and I don't think he cares how he goes about that. He's not going to let us surrender. Not after all he's already done. He just wants us to make things easy for him."

"So what's the plan?"

"This part of the facility is relatively free of monsters. Most of them don't seem to have stuck around since they took over the station. Makes sense. Not much prey around here at this point. That's too our advantage, though. We can secure this area and stay safe for a little while."

"A few barricades won't hold off Dagenais for very long," Cornelia said.

"No. No, they won't. That's why we're going to do what we can to get out of here. This is just a layover. We take what we can, and then we move on. Fletch, you said you can work the radio?"

"Yeah, it's not too complicated."

"Alright, good. I want you to do everything you can to contact the outside world. There might be a British or Norwegian basecamp within a few hundred miles. Nothing as advanced as this place, but if you can contact them, that would be a start. A passing ship would do. We just need to get word out that we need rescue. And don't talk to Dagenais. He doesn't know what we're working on. He doesn't even know how many of us are left. Let's keep him guessing as much as possible. Leave him in the dark. If we can call in a rescue ship, make sure they know to stay far away from whatever's left of Delambre Station. We don't need that cruiser sinking our rescuers, too. We can hike out to some remote anchorage and meet them there. Hopefully, we can be on board and sailing toward civilization by the time Dagenais realizes where we are."

"What are you going to do?" Cornelia asked.

"Apparently, the cable car into the crater can take us to some sort of emergency supply cache. I want to get my hands on it. Maybe there will be more guns. If not, hopefully there's fuel and canned food for us to take when we make a break for it."

"I'll go with you," Cornelia said.

"No. After me, you're best with a gun. We'd be better off if you stay up here and protect Fletch while he's on the radio. More of those bug men might try to break in while I'm down there, and it would be good to have someone topside who can handle a weapon."

"I know my way around a gun," Fletch said.

"I'm sure you do, but you're going to be holed up in the radio room for a good chunk of the time while I'm away. You won't be able to see what's happening elsewhere in the facility while you're in there. Besides, I want Cornelia to do something else while she's topside."

"What do you need?"

125

"You've got some training in geology. Put that degree to good work. See what you can learn about the meteor. Maybe there's something that will prove useful. If we can learn something from it about any of the monsters, that might be able to give us the upper hand."

"I mostly studied paleontology. You'd want a team of specialists and a lot of time to learn anything about that rock. Mineralogists. Exogeologists. The works. The French brought those guys in, and they're all dead. I can't promise you I'll come up with anything helpful."

"I know. But try. We're going to have to claw for any little advantage we can get here."

As if to underscore Denise's point, a loud thrumming noise came in low over the building. Denise gripped her Nitro Express a little tighter. After a moment, the noise faded off into the distance.

The giant monster had just buzzed past them. They were firmly in its territory right now. Even if Fletch did manage to contact a rescue ship, they were still going to have to contend with that big son of a bitch. Hopefully, they could find a way to avoid the creature. If they couldn't, they'd all end up as melted stains on the ice.

"What can I help with?" Metrodora asked.

"I could do with an extra set of hands and eyes when I look for those emergency supplies. Think you can handle some field studies?"

FOURTEEN
AND CLOSE YOUR EYES WITH HOLY DREAD

The cable car shuddered and swayed as it moved. The movement made Denise yearn for the journey of the *Sulaco* through the ice fields or Fletch's plane rattling through the sky. They were almost as far from the floor of the crater as she had been from the ground in Fletch's plane.

The meteor had punched a hole a couple of hundred feet deep into the ice. Denise did her best to avoid looking down. She did once, and it was a mistake. There were still bits and pieces of the meteor down in the bottom of the hole. Those were the parts that had broken off on impact. They were embedded in a flat layer of ice at the bottom of the hole.

Most of the water locked up in the ice had probably just evaporated on impact. The meteor strike would have been like a giant bomb hitting the area. What ice had merely melted dribbled down to the bottom of the crater and refroze in a perfectly flat surface. For a few short hours, it had been a bubbling, boiling lake. Now it was just a stretch of fresh ice among layers upon layers of ancient frost.

There was a giant rectangular section cut out of the frozen lake near the middle, though. That must have been where the French researchers and engineers sawed through the ice to fish out their prize. From up above, it almost looked like a gigantic key slot. Unfortunately, it had apparently unlocked one of the gates of hell.

The cable car didn't lead straight down, though. It wasn't an elevator. Rather, it led across to midway down the other side of the crater. The teams that built this place had excavated out part of the wall of the crater, apparently as a place to store supplies early on in the construction process. It sheltered everything from the constant wind, and it had provided a platform to start carving a path down along the side of the crater.

Denise could see the path from here. It rimmed the side of the impact site, starting with the area that had been excavated for storage. The path swept downward almost like an oversized spiral staircase. It would have allowed small vehicles and foot traffic down to the bottom of the crater.

The excavated portion of the wall was massive in and of itself, though. Denise could see the cable car wires leading down into a slit in the ice, but she couldn't tell exactly where they stopped. All she could see was a large space beyond.

Metrodora had her notebook out, and she was drawing in it. It appeared to be a sort of sketched out portrait of one of the bug men, with notes off to the side. She seemed fairly absorbed in the task, despite the swaying and creaking of the cable car.

That swaying and creaking made Denise want to claw her skin off, though. She felt like a rabbit being dangled over a pit of wolves. Locked in here, she was completely helpless and only too aware of how thin the cables supporting them were. Had the cold weakened them at all? Just how precarious was their position, really? She knew what to do when she had a gun and a threat in her sights. This was just a big crap sandwich, though. She needed to think about something else. Anything else.

"So...you, uh draw?" Denise asked.

"Yes," Metrodora said, without bothering to look up.

"I noticed you take that notebook everywhere with you. Do the Squires require you to take field notes, or is it just for your own personal satisfaction?"

"It's not for the Squires. I'll have to file a full field report when we make it back to South Africa. The notes can help a bit with that. I'd get in trouble if they found me with this, though."

"What kind of trouble? If it helps with your field report, I don't see why they would care if you do some drawings. You're pretty good at it from what I can see."

"Remember how I said St. George's Squires have been a little slow to adapt to the twentieth century? Even though more and more people are encountering aberrant zoological specimens, sometimes discovering new ones we've never even heard of, we don't release our data. There are dozens of deaths every year across the globe due to creatures that we know about. We have some idea of how far their territory stretches and how aggressive they are and a dozen other data points. Are they predators, or are they primarily scavengers? Do they prefer to ambush their prey, or do they lay elaborate traps? Things like that. Aside from some tribal elders and a few others, most people these days have never heard of these animals. They've been relegated to myth, if they haven't been forgotten entirely. With the way populations in South Africa have been forced to move around in the past hundred years, a lot of people don't live anywhere near where their ancestors did. They have no idea what's out there."

"That's one of the things Cornelia and I try to help with."

"And that's a valuable service in its own right. I'd like to work on the problem from a different angle, though. The Squires are sitting on huge troves of data, carefully collected ever since Europeans started carving colonies out of Africa. What has been released only goes to carefully selected groups of researchers. None of it's available to the general public. I'd like to change that."

"You're going to publish your notes?"

"A spruced-up version of them anyway. I've been working in their archives for years. I know the habits and territories of half the creatures in our data collection by heart. The ones I don't know are mostly because we only encounter them so rarely that we don't have very good data on them. Some of them we've only encountered once, maybe only to have them wipe out a hunting team. We have good information on lots of the other creatures, though. I want to publish a field guide to biological anomalies. It would help people steer clear of the creature's habitats and save lives."

"Will the Squires be able to figure out who is responsible for publishing all their secrets?"

"They'll probably know it was someone in the South African division, but they won't be able to pin it on me. There's plenty of other people who have access to the same information I do. Any of them could publish their own bestiary. I'm going to use a false name on the book. Hendrik Meltebeke. I'm not interested in credit for this. I'd be kicked out of the Squires if they found out about my little project."

"Will any publisher actually want to pick up something like that?"

"I'm hoping that one of the specialty presses that puts out hunting guides, travelogues, and bird watching books will think it's interesting enough to pick it up as a curio item. Even if they think its fiction, a few copies here and there could save lives."

"That's...not a bad idea, actually." Denise thought it over for a minute. "The maps of the creatures' territory, though. How precise are they?"

"Good enough to keep people out of certain areas. There's not much I can do about the range some of the creatures cover. They might have a territory of hundreds or thousands of square miles, and they meander across that entire area. It's very hard to pin them down at any given time. Others have their entire populations limited to particular rivers or isolated valleys and swamps. I can provide pretty precise instructions for avoiding them."

"May I make a suggestion?"

"Shoot."

"Leave the maps and other locations out entirely. Stick to the broadest possible descriptions of the environment."

"Why? I think it's better to give people as precise a warning as possible to they know if they're in a particular creature's territory or not. If something only lives on the banks of the Orange River, the people in that area should know that they might have to contend with that."

"And that's a fair point. I think you might create some unintended consequences, though. Tell people that they can eat any fruit in the garden except for the apples, and some nitwit is going to get in their head that they simply must try the apples. Tell people that they can go wherever they want except for a dangerous area, and a couple of folks will beeline straight for the dangerous area to see what the big fuss is about. Somebody always has to poke the badger. More people might end up going to those areas just to see if they could see what they'd read about."

"I suppose curiosity might cause some people to investigate, but I still think the average person would be better off knowing if they were about to head through a particular stretch of wilderness where they were at increased risk of attack."

"If you could give very broad descriptions of the types of environment a particular creature likes, it might be just as useful. But consider this. Some of these creatures are incredibly rare, yes?"

"A few of them might very well be one of a kind."

"I used to run a regular big game hunting business before I started specializing in man-eaters and things that go bump in the night. I met all sorts of people, including a good share of pompous twerps who didn't give two goddamns about anything other than themselves. They weren't all like that by any means, but there were a few. There was a type. They're the art collectors who don't like art. They just like having something rare that will make other people jealous and they can pat themselves on the back for their exquisite taste. If you provide a map to finding some of these animals, there would have been somebody in my office asking me to lead him out to gun them all down. My client would have them all on his wall so visitors could fawn over him and tell him how brave he was to hunt anything so dangerous. The Squires evaluate these things rather than exterminate them, correct?"

"You're one to talk. You run a business to hunt things like this."

Denise could see that she'd trammeled on Metrodora's toes. This was obviously important to her, and she thought Denise was trying to crap on her parade.

"Look, if somebody told me that they wanted to kill one of these things because they thought it would be a gas, I'd kick them out of my office. I don't do pleasure hunts anymore. We're not on opposite sides of this argument. I try to help people, the same as you and the Squires. It sounds to me like the Squires do a lot of research but don't take a lot of direct action. Fine. I hope they learn something valuable. You and I are both trying to fill the void when the Squires fail to act. You're trying to educate people. My methods are a little more…direct."

"Alright, fair enough. I helped vet you before we hired you to come down here. I know you're not some wild woman with a rifle. And you've managed to help keep me alive so far, which I appreciate."

"I accept tips and gratuities. Just saying for when we make it back to civilization."

"Do you really think people would try to seek these creatures out, even if they knew how dangerous they were?"

"I think that if you told everyone the sun was about to explode and destroy the earth, some people would get up on their roofs to watch. With a guidebook, you might be saving some lives. It would also be an open invitation to a certain number of yahoos, though. Depending on just how dangerous any given creature really was, more people might end up dead, and the creatures might be driven extinct, too. Any time you introduce the human element to a problem, things get messy in a hurry. I'm not saying you should quit working on your guidebook. I just think it's important to be circumspect about some of the particulars. If Hendrik Metlebeke's bestiary manages to save even one life, then you're owed a toast."

"I'll think about it."

"Just feel free to ask if you want me to impart any more of my infallible wisdom. The first one's free."

They were nearly to the other side of the crater now. A few seconds later, and they slid through the gap in the ice wall. Denise felt better knowing that they were only a few feet up in case anything went wrong. Now, she only had to worry about the threat of the living dead ripping the flesh from her bones. Or alien slugs crawling into her brain. Or inhuman bug men spewing acid at her. What a relief.

Denise watched the white-blue ice slide by on either side, the edges rough where the opening had been blasted open. The ice continued to slide past for several seconds as the car creaked and groaned on its overhead cables. The construction crews had blasted deep into the ice wall, isolating the chamber beyond from the worst of the exterior conditions.

A moment later, the ice around them fell away to either side. The space beyond was a large room, almost the size of a sports stadium. Pillars of ice led up to the ceiling, helping to support the giant cavity. The walls and roof were all rough and blocky, barely touched after the cavernous space was excavated. The floor had been smoothed over to hockey rink perfection, though. Rubber traction matting covered the floor in discrete paths so people could move about without slipping and sliding all over the place.

The cable car came to a halt at a little platform, and Denise shoved the doors open. Inside the subterranean space, the air was just a little below freezing. Not having to contend with the constant wind made the chamber feel much warmer than the rest of the outside.

Denise looked around, taking the area in. The first thing she saw was a huge stack of bags for cement mix. There was more construction gear spread around the area near the cable car. As far as Denise could tell, this area had been carved out before Merovée Station was built. It would have given the work crews somewhere to shelter during the harshest weather, and it also provided storage for supplies and equipment so not everything lay exposed to the open air. Compared to the scouring wind on the surface, it was downright cozy down here.

Merovée Station had its own warehouse, but this area had apparently been converted into additional storage after construction was finished. This was probably where they kept the stuff that they didn't necessarily need every day that wouldn't have been harmed by a little cold.

Apparently, they also kept the stuff they didn't want at all anymore down here. It looked like the far end of the chamber now served as the station's refuse heap. All manner of debris lay on the floor in a giant pile that was twice as tall as Denise. Everything from bald tires to fruit rinds lay on the heap. It wasn't a very tidy pile. Pieces of garbage lay strewn in every direction nearby. Some of it even spread into the rest of the chamber, the areas that were obviously meant for storage.

With the way everything was tossed around, it looked like a small bomb had gone off in the trash heap. Denise wondered if that was a sign that the people here had simply been messy, or if it meant that they had come here and tried to scavenge what they could before the station's security completely failed. If they'd been desperate enough to root through their own trash, Denise didn't hold out much hope that that emergency supplies were still down here. Still, she had to check. If there was anything useful at all still down here, they needed to drag it back to the main station.

Denise didn't see anything that could be construed as emergency supplies near the cable car platform. That meant they were going to have to wade out there into the construction equipment and look.

There was a sound from deeper in the chamber. Something under the trash heap moved a little bit then went still. Neither Denise nor

Metrodora made any attempt to leave the cable car platform for a minute. Nothing else moved in that time.

"Stick close to me," Denise said, swinging her Nitro Express around. Moving with some reluctance, she stepped forward onto the rubber matting in front of them. Metrodora followed half a step behind.

There were stacks of spare motor sledge treads, pallets of salt for traction, and shelves of miscellaneous equipment. Some of it might be handy to have on hand for when they left Merovée Station. A lot of it was worthless to them. Denise had to be judicious in what she grabbed.

The thing she was still most enticed by was the emergency supplies. This was an emergency, and they needed supplies. She was still hoping to find more weapons. If everyone was armed, it would bump their chances of survival up quite a bit. Right now, Metrodora was serving as a second set of eyes and ears for her, but that wouldn't Denise much good if a monster got the drop on both of them and started clawing her guts out.

They didn't have much of anything at the moment. Even if the emergency supplies were partially depleted, it would still help them. Guns. A first-aid kit. Anything would help.

The storage area down here wasn't very well kept. A number of crates had been knocked down from where they'd been stacked. Some of them had burst open and spilled their contents out. Others hadn't broken but were now blocking the path forward. Denise tried to avoid the paths with debris in them. Her footsteps were quiet when she stayed on the rubber mats. There was something else in the cavern with them, lurking beneath the trash heap. She didn't want to alert it by crunching across broken slats and shattered test tubes.

Denise stepped past a tall stack of crates and noticed an alcove carved into the far wall. A little metal sign hung above it, anchored directly into the ice. The words *équipement d'urgence* were printed on the sign in neat letters. That was what they were looking for.

"Bingo," Denise muttered more to herself than Metrodora. Now, she just had to hope there was something left in there. She picked her way along the path toward the alcove, which was uncomfortably close to the near edge of the debris field surrounding the rubbish heap.

She sidestepped around as much of the garbage as possible, keeping the Nitro Express pointed in the direction of the main heap. She flicked her eyes in a steady pattern. Sideways to keep herself moving toward the alcove, down to avoid kicking any of the pieces of trash that had accumulated around the edge of the matting, and forward to make sure there was nothing slithering through the debris toward her like some sort of garbage shark. So far, everything remained still and undisturbed.

Despite the piles of refuse sitting around, including old food, the smell wasn't as bad as it could have been. The temperatures prevented most of it from rotting. There was some odor, probably from deep inside the pile where things were more insulated and could build up their funk in comparative warmth.

After some shimmying along the pathway, Denise reached the alcove. She ducked inside the narrow corridor and stood at the edge of the Promised Land. The end of the alcove opened up into a medium-sized room lined with shelves loaded with crates. A gate separated her from crate after crate of supplies. All the crates were more or less identical. Each one was rectangular, long enough to hold carbine rifles or medical supplies or almost anything else. They were all boxed up, with no way to see what was inside. They would just have to crack a few of them open to see what they contained and then select the ones they needed to bring back to the station.

The bigger problem right now was the gate. It had a lock and chain that prevented it from opening. There was no way to climb over the metal fencing that blocked them off from the cache of supplies. They might be able to dig under, but it would take forever to scrape away enough ice to slide one of the boxes under the metal.

Denise eyed the padlock keeping the gate closed. Obviously, there would be a key for it somewhere, but she had no idea where to find it. It could be in a drawer in a desk back in the security office. It could be in the pocket of a corpse shambling toward the South Pole. Colonel Dagenais might have it right now while he sat on the bridge of the cruiser. They needed to get in there, though. Fortunately, Denise had brought a lock-pick.

"Cover your ears," she said to Metrodora. She raised the elephant gun and held the barrels out a couple of inches away from the lock's clasp. Wincing in anticipation of the noise, Denise pulled the trigger.

The entire lock blew apart and went skittering off toward the rear of the alcove. What was left of it looked like a clump of molten metal that had accidentally fallen out of the forge and cooled in any random shape it pleased. It certainly wasn't identifiable as a padlock anymore. The gate flew open.

The noise smote Denise's ears. For a few seconds, she was almost completely deaf except for a high-pitched ringing noise. The ringing faded a little after a moment, but she still couldn't hear the brass shell as it clinked onto the floor. She popped a fresh round into the Nitro Express and turned around.

"Get behind me and grab a box," Denise said, not really sure how loud she was speaking. She could see out into the main chamber through the narrow hallway. The trash was beginning to stir.

A hand shot up through the debris. Another hand joined it, and the head and torso of a ghoul emerged from the layers of rubbish. It was like watching some campfire story fiend rise from its grave to seek fresh blood. There were more figures breaching the surface now, and not all of them were strictly human. Protruding compound insect eyes stared at her from inhuman faces.

Denise wondered for just a moment what the creatures were doing under a massive pile of trash. Then, she aimed and fired. A jet of pure fury shot out of the elephant gun's right barrel, and the first of the ghouls pitched over backward, disappearing into the trash with most of his head missing.

Another dead man waded out of the garbage. He was wearing a parka with the hood pulled over his head. All Denise could see of his face was a set of crooked teeth. His lips had been chewed off some time ago. Maybe he'd done it himself. Denise fired the second barrel of the elephant gun, and that shambling figure went down in a puff of blood and pulverized brain matter.

Denise broke the Nitro Express open and fished two more rounds out of her jacket pocket. She stuffed them home and checked on Metrodora. Any recovery her hearing had made since destroying the lock was now completely gone. All she could hear was that high-pitched ringing noise again.

Metrodora had grabbed one of the crates and was dragging it across the floor. It looked heavy. Good. Hopefully, that meant it had lots of useful equipment inside. She wished there was time to inspect what was inside and maybe mix and match with the contents of the other crates or, better yet, grab a whole bunch of the crates and cart them all back to the station. Beggars couldn't be choosers, though. Right now, they needed to make a tactical retreat with their prize.

One of the weird bug men managed to claw its way free of the trash heap, and it started toward them. It moved with the same jittery, hopping movements as the creature that killed Poole in the warehouse. It bounced around with surprising speed for anything its size.

Another squeeze of the trigger, and the abomination was thrown backward. Ichor sprayed out of the gaping wound in its torso. More of the creatures were coming, though. They looked a bit like a cross between a human being, a beetle, and the combined illustrations from a textbook on exotic skin diseases. Denise fired at another one of the creatures, and the monster's arm flew off, but it didn't seem to mind too much. It continued to disinter itself from the trash heap, even as foul fluids spilled from the gaping wound.

Denise reloaded and then bent down and grabbed the far edge of the crate that Metrodora was dragging. Together, the two of them managed to lift it up a little and move a bit faster. The wooden edges bit into Denise's fingers. She'd been right earlier; the box was heavy. She could feel things shifting around in there as they half-dragged, half-carried the box out of the alcove.

There were more of the creatures than Denise wanted to try to deal with. Her Nitro Express could only hold two shots at a time. Once she fired both barrels, she had to reload. That didn't give her a lot of time to work with when the monsters kept coming out of the woodwork. She could pick a couple off at a time, but they had the numbers. It was better to get what they could and get out than risk being overwhelmed.

She slung the Nitro Express over her shoulder and grabbed the crate, trying to get a better grip on the sides. She and Metrodora started to scuttle away in an awkward, crouched shuffle as the monsters continued to spill out of the trash. Between the walking corpses and the bug men, there must have been at least ten monsters hidden within the station's landfill. Denise had taken a couple of them out, but it was only a matter of time until the bug men started spitting acid at them.

Denise still couldn't hear much of anything. The ringing in her ears was just starting to fade ever so slightly again. It was being replaced with a dull humming noise, though. She wondered if maybe she hadn't permanently damaged her sense of hearing. Firing the Nitro Express was like pulling the cord on a small artillery piece. In close quarters like this, the noise level was well above the threshold of pain.

However, the humming noise wasn't fading at all, either. In fact, it only seemed to be getting louder. Was that the sound of the blood rushing through her ears? Was she actually going completely deaf, and this was the sound of her eardrums dying? The noise built louder still, and then Denise realized what it was.

She'd heard that noise before. In fact, she'd heard it for the first time only earlier today. Now, it seemed like a lifetime ago, but she remembered that noise from her ride on the snow tractor. It was the sound of the dragon creature flying.

This was not the time. If that thing was flying around over the crater, Denise wasn't sure that they could use the cable car. The giant creature might very well attack and knock them right off the cords. It wouldn't even have to spray their bodies with acid after that. The two of them would simply be a couple of red smears at the bottom of the crater if the cable car line snapped.

Fortunately, the creature wasn't interested in hanging out around the exterior of the crater. Unfortunately, Denise learned where the dragon was planning to go because it crawled through the entrance to the cavern, scrambling right over their parked cable car in the process. The thrumming noise ceased as it landed on the wall and climbed sideways through the narrow gap until it was in the chamber with them.

Denise and Metrodora both froze. They were behind a particularly tall stack of boxes, mostly obscuring them from the entrance to the chamber. The gigantic creature apparently hadn't noticed them yet. It must have heard the sound of the gunfire and come down to investigate.

Oh hell. Denise looked over her shoulder. A couple of the bug men were moving toward her at an alarming clip. She and Metrodora needed to get out of here. They'd leave the emergency supplies if they had to, but Denise really didn't want to do that. They'd just have to come back for them later.

The creature moved across the floor of the chamber, picking its way between the aisles of crates and supplies. Sometimes, its tail would flick out and nearly tip a crate over with a loud *thwack*, or a foot would knock something else off balance. The monstrosity moved quickly but not without a certain delicacy.

For the first time, Denise could see the creature's face. But for the head, the creature really did look like some sort of dinosaur. The similarities ended there, though. It had the same iridescent compound eyes as the smaller bug men. These eyes were huge though, larger than a basketball. They never blinked or showed any sort of expression. They were completely inhuman. If the eyes were the window into the soul, these were the sort of windows that birds accidentally flew straight into and snapped their necks.

While most of the body looked like some sort of oversized tyrannosaur, the mouth was another big difference. Like the smaller bug men, it didn't have any jaws. There weren't any cruel teeth to chomp and bite at prey, like a dinosaur. Instead, the creature had a lengthy, flaccid-looking proboscis. The proboscis flared out at the bottom a little, a bit like an oversized suction cup. Some sort of unpleasant-looking liquid dribbled from the end of the proboscis. Thick, ugly bristles sprouted around the creature's head.

The monster's compound eyes made it hard to tell where it was looking. Then Denise realized that it was looking more or less everywhere at once. Its exact visual acuity must not have been very good, though. It hadn't spotted her peeking around the edge of the crates. Denise couldn't begin to imagine how a creature with hundreds of different eyes viewed the world, but it was probably a bit like looking through a kaleidoscope. It would have trouble focusing on any one spot or object because its attention was diverted in a hundred different directions.

Two large, mostly translucent wings were attached to the creature's back. On the ground, the wings were tucked tight against its armor. The nearly transparent material glimmered in the diffused light that reflected off the icy walls. Even though the wings were mostly clear, large, snaking veins and cartilaginous filaments ran through them in places, giving them some structure and definition. They looked like the wings of a fairy with syphilis.

If they were in here with only the hulking, dinosaur-like monster, she and Metrodora might have been able to sneak the crate of emergency supplies out to the cable car unnoticed simply by creeping around behind the crates and only moving at opportune times. However, they didn't have the luxury of moving only at opportune times right now. There were still two more of the bug men approaching with their odd, juddering walk, and they were getting too close for comfort. In another few seconds, they'd be in range to start launching gobs of burning mucus at Denise and Metrodora.

Metrodora was standing very still, the crate of emergency supplies in her grasp apparently all but forgotten. Her eyes were glued to the gigantic, bristly abomination. Denise gave a quiet whistle to snap Metrodora's attention back.

She readjusted her grip on the crate to free up one hand, and then she mimed a quick plan. It was simple enough. She jerked a thumb at the approaching bug men and then made her thumb and forefinger into a gun shape. Then, she gestured to herself and Metrodora and pointed to indicate that they would have to speed around the next corner fast. Metrodora's lips thinned into a bloodless slit.

Denise set her end of the crate down and unshouldered the Nitro Express. She took one last glance at the dinosaur-bug making its way across the room. It still hadn't given any indication that it knew where she or Metrodora were. In fact, it seemed to be proceeding toward the rubbish heap.

She suddenly realized that the garbage dump was in such disarray because the creature had been using it as a nest. The old food scraps and other organic material in there would provide plenty of food for a monster that wasn't too choosy about what it ate. Bears and other omnivores could be a big problem around some landfills. This thing wasn't so very different.

Before, she'd thought that the creature probably had some sort of den around Merovée Station. It had disappeared in this direction after attacking the snow tractor earlier. Now Denise was pretty sure she knew where the abomination made its home. She was standing right in the middle of it. It was relatively protected and it had ample food resources. This cavern was a veritable haven for a primeval monstrosity.

Leveling the elephant gun, Denise took aim at the closer of the two approaching bug men. She placed her sights on the easiest part of the target, right in its center of mass. The arthropodal figure showed no expression on its malformed face. Its compound eyes were so different from anything mammalian, that Denise wouldn't have known how to read anything in them even if there was an expression.

The Nitro Express kicked Denise in the shoulder like a steel-toed boot. The first of the bug men all but blew apart, tumbling backward in a broken mass of tangled limbs. Viscera squirted across the ice in quivering heaps.

On the other side of the cavern, the dragon spun its head around. It knew they were in here with it now.

Denise swiveled the elephant gun around and blew the life out of the second bug man with another thunderous blast. She didn't even bother to reload as she whipped around and grabbed her end of the emergency supplies crate and started lugging it as fast as she could. It was heavy and awkward, making it all but impossible to move quickly.

They needed to move quickly, though. There were more insect-like figures approaching from the direction of the trash heap, as well as a couple of slower ghouls. However, the bigger problem was the tyrannosaurus-sized behemoth lumbering across the room to investigate the noise from the elephant gun.

Puffing and shuffling, Denise and Metrodora managed to move past several rows of crates and then angle themselves down another aisle just as the creature reached their side of the cavern. Denise held her breath as the creature made it to where she had been standing in only a few loping strides. It stopped and seemed to sniff the air.

Denise held her breath as she waited to see what the beast would do next. If it found them, she wasn't sure there was much she could do to prevent it from spraying hot acid on them and reducing their bones to sludge. She could hear the monster's heavy, wet breathing, like the sort of noise that might come out of a backed-up gutter. Gooey liquid dripped from its proboscis as it moved. Stubby antenna twitched questioningly as the creature searched for the source of the loud noise.

Biting her lip, Denise watched as the creature lingered for another moment. She stood as still as she could, wishing with all her might that the monster would continue on toward the trash heap as it originally intended. *Don't come this way. Don't come this way. Don't come this way*. She hadn't even reloaded the Nitro Express. She was afraid that the sound of mechanical parts in action or the jangling of brass in her pocket might alert the creature to their continued presence only a few short strides away.

Finally, after what seemed like a minor eternity, the monster turned the opposite direction. Its long tail swept over Denise and Metrodora, briefly casting a shadow over them. The creature had spotted the corpses of the two bug men and it went over to them, its tarsal claws clicking on the ice as it moved.

The monster's proboscis patted the dead bodies as if frisking them for wallets. The lobes at the end of the proboscis left smears of mucus on the bodies wherever they touched. A second later, it unloaded a torrent of yellowish slime on the bodies. The corpses began to dissolve, melting into piles of sizzling lumps. It looked like someone had tried to make scrambled eggs and sausage only to give up halfway through the process.

Denise nodded to Metrodora, and they continued their shuffle toward the cable car platform. A couple of the undead ghouls had stopped and tried to eat the half-melted remains of the bug men. Their hands melted into meat jam as they tried to pick up the acid-covered chunks. One of them managed to stick a chunk of sizzling goo into his mouth, and his entire jaw started to soften and liquefy.

Denise still didn't really understand the biology of these things. The slugs were dangerous all on their own. Once they curled up inside a human brain, they could hijack the central nervous system and pilot the corpse around, though. In such cold weather, where it would take a very long time for the bodies to rot, they could presumably drive the dead bodies around almost indefinitely. In warmer climes, the corpses would start to fester in due course. Here, they could probably wander around the ice for months or maybe years. The wind would strip the flesh from their bones before they started to decay properly. Even though they were impervious to pain, as evidenced by the man with the melting jaw, they weren't in the least bit intelligent.

A couple of the bug men ignored the smorgasbord in favor of continuing after Denise and Metrodora. Denise moved as fast as she could, given the awkward load she was sharing. She didn't want to stop to shoot. Another blast from the Nitro Express would only draw the attention of the bigger beast.

They reached the cable car platform and hustled up the short ramp. Wedging themselves through the open doors, Denise set the crate down and grabbed the cable car controls. Metrodora pulled the doors shut as the car started moving.

Apparently realizing that their prey was escaping, the two bug men sped up, lunging toward the cable car platform with their disturbing, twitchy movements. They almost looked like they were moving under a strobe light.

Denise had the car controls pushed as far as they would go, but they couldn't move much faster than a brisk walk. The bug men reached the platform a few seconds after the car clanked and wheezed away down the icy entryway to the cavern.

A gob of acid appeared on the window as the nearest of the bug creatures spat after them. The glass made a strange sound, something like a tea kettle with a case of gas. A lot of steam appeared, and the section of glass covered with slime turned black and slightly pitted. It didn't actually shatter, though. They were safe for now.

Breaking her Nitro Express open again, Denise fed two more shells into its hungry mouth. The weapon's barrels were hot to the touch, and her ears still had a high-pitched ring. The elephant gun had served her well, though. She still regretted not getting Cornelia's gun out of Delambre Station before the place was leveled, but hopefully, there was another weapon in the crate of emergency supplies. Denise wasn't sure what kind of emergency the scientists had in mind when they prepared these crates, but obviously the worst-case scenario had come to fruition. She wanted to crack the crate open right now and check what was inside, but she needed a pry bar.

The front end of the cable car had just passed out of the ice tunnel and into the open when there was a thud from overhead. Denise looked up from the single crate they'd worked so hard to smuggle out. She was just in time to watch as the second bug man skittered across the wall of ice and took a flying leap at the cable car.

Smacking onto the side of the car, the creature reached out and managed to grab onto the side of the car with its claws. The other one was already on top of the car, scratching away at the metal and trying to find a way inside.

Cursing, Denise stumbled backward in surprise. She bumped up against the far wall, and the entire car swayed on its cable. The wind buffeted the compartment anew as it emerged from the cavern, sending the little car swaying even more.

The bug man spat another gob of slime onto the window. The glass made that awful noise again, like someone was dissecting live rodents, and the area became scorched and blackened. Rather than trying to spit through the glass again, the bug man punched a claw through the window and reached for Denise. Glass tinkled to the floor as the creature tried to pull itself inside the car, paying no attention to the sharp edges of the jagged glass. A gnarled claw reached out to grab them.

Denise had other plans. She raised the freshly loaded Nitro Express so the barrels touched the creature's diseased-looking skin right between its compound eyes. "Sorry, this car is full."

She pulled the trigger, and the creature flew off the side of the cable car. Denise leaned over just far enough to see the mangled body plummet through the air toward the bottom of the crater far, far below.

That just left their friend on the top of the car. The monster was still banging away at the metal, trying to dig its way inside. Denise pointed her Nitro Express upward, but she didn't fire. Blasting the elephant gun straight upward might accidentally sever the cable they were riding on or damage the motor mechanism and leave them stranded in the air above the middle of the impact site. Neither option was exactly appealing.

Instead of firing, Denise took the Nitro Express and jabbed it upward like she was trying to tell some noisy upstairs neighbors to shut up by banging a broomstick against the ceiling. The mad scrabbling and thumping noises ceased for a second. Denise poked the barrels of the Nitro Express upward again a couple of feet to the left. There was a scraping sound as the bug man moved to follow the noise. The cable car swayed more violently.

Stepping over to the shattered window, Denise tapped on the roof of the car right next to the edge. A second later, an inhuman head poked over the side to look at them. Denise was waiting for it. She pointed the elephant gun straight at the misshapen head. Try as she might, she couldn't think of anything pithy to say. She'd had something that sounded cool when she blew the first bug man off the car, but apparently, those opportunities had to arise naturally. Damn.

She pulled the trigger. A second later, the now headless insect creature slid off the side of the cable car and into the frosty abyss below. Denise reloaded the Nitro Express yet again. The adrenaline was still flowing through her body, making her movements shaky. The inside of the cable car smelled like spent gun smoke and old bile.

"Nice shooting," Metrodora said.

"Thanks. It's not exactly hard from this range, though. Pretty much fish in a barrel. Do you know how to shoot one of these?" She held up the Nitro Express.

"I've seen you do it enough times now to get the gist."

"The basics are easy. You can open it up here to reload. The triggers are pretty obvious. The most important part is to make sure you're holding it right. Like this." Denise demonstrated. "Otherwise, it will do its level best to wrench your arm out of its socket when you fire. If I don't make it, Cornelia is pretty good with a gun, too. But you should know the basics in case things don't work out."

"That's a morbid thought."

"Pretty much everything within a thousand miles in every direction wants to kill us. It inspires morbid thinking for some strange reason."

"You raise a good point."

"I think we're safe for a few minutes, though. Here, hold the gun for a minute so I can make sure you're handling it right." Denise handed the Nitro Express over.

"Like so?"

"Here. Let me adjust you a little." Denise pushed the stock a little more into the proper position. "Alright. You've got it. Nothing will prepare you for the kick the first time you fire it, but that comes with experience. I don't want to waste ammo while there's nothing to fire at, though."

"Uh…we're about to have something to fire at," Metrodora said, her gaze drifting off to something behind Denise.

"What?" Denise turned around to Metrodora was looking at.

Behind them, the monster crawled into view, pushing its way out of the ice tunnel. It spread its wings and beat them until they became a blur of movement. The noise of its flapping wings grew into a steady thrum as they built up remarkable speed. A second later, it was airborne and heading straight for the cable car. It must have heard the shots from the Nitro Express.

"Aw, crap," Denise said.

FIFTEEN
MERDE

Denise snatched the Nitro Express back from Metrodora. Now was not the time for a lesson in marksmanship and weapons handling. She moved to the window and readied the weapon.

Maybe the monster couldn't see them inside the cable car. Maybe it had more pressing matters it had to attend to. Maybe it would pass them right by.

Flying through the air, the creature reminded Denise of a dragon more than ever. It had tucked its legs tight against its body, and it flew with its long, flexible tail sticking out almost like a rudder. That position gave it a streamlined shape, almost like an elongated, sideways raindrop.

The creature started its flight slowly, gathering speed. Denise glanced the other way. The cable car was nearing the terminal back at Merovée Station. If they could just make it into the terminal and stop in the little bay at the platform, the oversize creature would have trouble reaching them.

There were a couple of figures standing in the terminal. Cornelia and Fletch must have seen the cable car making its way back across the chasm and come out to see what they were bringing back. Denise looked down at the long crate on the floor of the cable car. Whatever was inside had better be worth it.

It soon became apparent that the dragon creature wasn't going to fly past and ignore the cable car. The beast was heading straight for them, picking up speed as it went. The creature could move fast when it wanted to.

The loud thrumming noise of the creature's wings built up, growing louder and louder. Denise gripped the Nitro Express tighter. They weren't going to make it to the cable car terminal in time.

A second later, the monster reared back and hovered directly next to the cable car. It reached out and tore the car's doors off with a claw and threw them down into the chasm below. The squeal of metal was even louder than the sound of the monster's beating wings. The entire car jerked and wobbled on its cable.

Denise grabbed onto the handrail inside as the car swung back and forth. She kept her other hand locked on the Nitro Express. The crate of supplies started to slide toward the open doorway, and Denise had to stomp her foot down on top of it to hold it in place for a second.

The monster hovered next to them and reached a gigantic claw through the gap where the doors used to be. Massive talons scraped across the metal floor, trying to reach Denise and Metrodora like someone trying to fish the last olive out of a jar.

Denise brought the elephant gun around and fired. One of the oversized claws cleaved off in an explosion of foul-smelling meat. The flesh under the armor was pale and veiny. Bits of pulped meat sprayed across the far window. Their color and consistency made the globs look like the world's largest boogers. The creature's arm jerked out of the car, leaving the digit behind.

Unlike the undead ghouls the slugs were piloting around, this creature felt pain, apparently. Denise tried to turn the elephant gun around to get a good shot at the creature's midsection, but it smacked the side of the cable car in anger at the loss of its finger.

The car went sideways like a malfunctioning carnival ride, throwing Denise and Metrodora against the far wall. The metal siding crumpled inward and tore, and the supply crate slammed into Denise's leg. She shouted in pain. It was like bonking a shin into furniture in a dark room. The pain was sharp and swift.

Gravity sent the car swinging back toward its normal orientation like a pendulum, and the sudden swing back sent Denise sprawling onto the floor. She threw her hands out to cushion her fall and landed flat on her chest. Even through layers of cold weather gear, the bullets in her pocket pressed uncomfortably into her torso.

Outside, she heard a steady pop-pop-pop. A second later, she realized that Cornelia was firing her pistol at the monster from the terminal, trying to distract it. Denise pushed herself up to her knees and then lurched to her feet. In the space of ten seconds, she'd earned half a dozen new bruises, but nothing was broken. Her body screeched at her about the places she'd just injured, but she pulled herself up and grabbed ahold of the handrail again.

The creature had been temporarily distracted by the pistol shots. It flew a short distance away from the cable car and seemed to debate with itself whether it could fit inside the terminal and reach Cornelia. The sudden abundance of prey pulled its attention in several different directions for a few precious seconds as the cable car neared the endpoint of its run. In less than a minute, it would reach the platform.

The creature zipped a little closer to the platform as Cornelia fired a couple more rounds at it. Denise saw a little blast of sparks as one bullet deflected off the monster's black carapace. There was no way the pistol rounds could penetrate the thick armor. It was like firing spitballs at an enemy fortress. Cornelia and Fletch backed off as the creature moved closer, slipping back toward the doors leading inside.

Instead of trying to pursue them, the monster backed off. It evidently realized that it couldn't reach Cornelia and Fletch. The real prize was inside the cable car, if it could just figure out how to crack that particular nut.

Denise stepped up to where the doors had been a minute ago and lifted the Nitro Express again. The creature might be able to shrug off pistol rounds, but could it deal with something big enough to give most guns bullet envy? She tried to keep her aim steady as the cable car swung in the wind.

The creature turned around and zoomed back toward the cable car. Denise realized what was about to happen and sidestepped behind the nearest intact portion of the car. A second later, a stream of acid poured onto the car, some of it splashing through the entrance in a nauseating wave. Denise backed away from the sizzling puddle on the floor. Metrodora was on the far side of the car, pressed back into the corner. The goop covered the windows and the outside of the cable car. Denise could hear it corroding the paint and warping the window seals. The glass on the affected windows started to turn brown and then black. Little pockmarks appeared in the glass, and some of the slime started to leak inside. The entire cable car groaned.

Denise tried not to breath in any of the noxious fumes rising around her. She could feel a slight burning sensation on her skin, and her eyes watered just being inside the cable car with the vile substance.

She looked out through the open doorframe, the only view not obstructed by foul ooze. They were no more than thirty feet from the terminal. They'd be safe in ten seconds.

They didn't have ten seconds. The monster grabbed onto Denise's end of the cable car. The acid it spat on the car wasn't able to eat through the metal and glass all on its own, but it was enough to structurally weaken parts of the wall. The metal had gone brittle in places. Other materials were as soft as a chocolate Eater bunny left out in the sun.

The car shook as the creature grabbed hold. There was a terrible shrieking noise as the creature's claws punched through the weakened walls, jutting into the car toward Denise. Everything started to crumple and collapse around her.

She leapt forward, launching herself over the puddle of ooze that had spilled through the open doorway. She landed next to Metrodora and pushed herself up against the far wall as the rear end of the car tore away in a shower of sparks and the agonized scream of warped metal.

The monster was staring directly at them now through the gaping hole where the far wall used to be. Denise realized she was shouting curses at it. She hadn't even been aware she was yelling. It was just a litany of barely coherent screams. Things were slipping out of control, like she was a passenger in a bus doomed to slide over a cliff.

There was now a ragged edge where the floor of the car simply ended. Below that was a straight drop down the edge of the crater. The wind howled and tugged at Denise's jacket as she stared out into the frozen abyss. Their supply crate was only a couple of feet away from the edge of the gap. Denise bent down and pulled it in front of them.

A huge claw reached for them just as the cable car lurched to a halt at the platform. Denise fired the Nitro Express again. The massive rounds tore off another claw, but the creature didn't pull back this time. It latched its claws onto the interior of the car and shook it, snapping it entirely free of the cable. A high-pitched twang filled the air like someone had just plucked a giant guitar string.

Denise grabbed Metrodora by the arm, and they heaved themselves out of the car as the creature wrenched it off its supports. They landed hard on the concrete platform below. A second later, the crate landed a hand's breadth away from Denise's head as the creature twisted the cable car and lifted it up.

Heaving herself up to her feet, Denise dragged herself up and scampered under the protection of the terminal bay. Metrodora followed a couple of feet behind. Cornelia and Fletch stood against the rear wall, next to the doors. They rushed over and helped the two of them limp over.

Still holding the ruined cable car, the creature hovered in front of the transport bay for another few seconds. Ropes of scuzz-colored drool dribbled from the lobes of its proboscis as it watched them. Denise looked up at those giant, compound eyes and broke open the Nitro Express again. Maybe she could hit one of those ghastly, expressionless eyes.

Before she could load another couple of rounds into the Nitro Express, the monster backed away from the cable car terminal and turned around. The loud thrum of its wings faded as it passed over the crater again, heading back toward the cavern on the opposite side of the impact site. Halfway back, it released its grip on what was left of the cable car, and the crumpled remains dropped into the open air.

Denise took a step forward. She eyed the empty cable car wire. There was no way back to the other side of the crater anymore. Looking out over the lip of the platform, she could see little clumps of the cable car sitting on the floor of the crater far below.

The crate of emergency supplies sat on the edge of the platform. Some of the boards on the sides were cracked from the tumble it took out of the cable car, but it was still here. Denise grabbed one end of the crate and started dragging it toward the doors. Cornelia and Fletch rushed over to help her drag it. Metrodora hung back and nursed her shoulder a little. She might have banged it up while tumbling around the inside of the cable car or during their hasty exit. With three people, carrying the crate was a lot easier, though.

"You alright?" Denise asked when they got it back to the doors.

"Yeah," Metrodora said, not very convincingly.

"What did you find over there?" Cornelia asked as she pushed the doors open. The heater suddenly hit Denise with some blessed warmth. She just wanted to lie down and bask in it for a while.

"Trouble," Denise said, dropping the crate on the floor. "Got a crowbar? Let's get this thing open."

"I saw one earlier," Fletch said. "I'll grab it."

"Looks like you two really stirred up a hornets' nest over there. You should have let me come with you to help," Cornelia said. She turned to Metrodora. "Here. I'll help you out of that jacket. Let me take a look at that shoulder."

"Metrodora did alright for herself."

"Thanks," Metrodora said, struggling out of her jacket with some obvious effort.

"Besides, we were doing okay until that damn thing turned up." Denise nodded in the direction the creature had disappeared. "Three people with one elephant gun aren't a lot better off than two people with a gun."

"Fair enough. I was able to work on some things while you were away," Cornelia said as she checked Metrodora's shoulder.

Metrodora hissed as Cornelia probed at her arm. Cornelia clucked at it and continued poking.

"What sort of things?" Denise asked.

"Just a second," Cornelia said. She turned her full attention to Metrodora. "Lay down on your back. I just want to check something."

"Is there a problem?"

"I just want to see something."

Metrodora sat down and laid herself out on the floor. Cornelia stepped over and started checking Metrodora's wrist. Denise had a pretty good idea what was coming next, and she chose to find a spot on the floor to stare at.

"My wrist is fine," Metrodora said.

"Don't worry. I'm a trained professional. I've seen wrist injuries like this before. Wrist injuries often don't hurt right away, but later…" Cornelia was standing over Metrodora, straddling her. She took Metrodora's arm by the wrist and stood straight up.

There was a *clunk* noise that made Denise wince followed by some of the blackest profanity she had ever heard.

"—with an outhouse bucket!" Metrodora finished up. Denise made a mental note to steal a couple of the choicest phrases for herself at some point.

"Your shoulder was dislocated. I reset it for you," Cornelia said. "Your wrist is fine by the way. I just didn't want you tensing up too much before I pulled it back into place."

"Thanks… I think."

"I don't have a sling for you, but you'll need one. You shouldn't use that shoulder too much for the next month or so. You should put some ice on it, which should be easy enough around here."

"Got it." Metrodora gave Cornelia a look that was equal parts thankful and suspicious.

A voice came on over the station's public announcement system. "This is Colonel Dagenais, speaking to anyone from Delambre Station."

"Fletch figured out how to hook the radio up to the speakers," Cornelia said.

"Your window to surrender is drawing to a close," Dagenais said. "You may have seen certain things in your present location. You have my personal assurances that the French government is willing to let you go after swearing to a secrecy affidavit. However, you are running out of time. You have no doubt seen signs of infection at your present location. You may yet still be fine. Surrender now, and you will be tested and released. After this time limit has elapsed, my men will approach and apply demolition charges to your structure. They will assume that anything inside is hostile, and they will shoot to kill. I repeat, they will shoot to kill after that. There is nowhere else for you to go. Surrender now." Dagenais signed off with a click.

"Have you or Fletch contacted him?" Denise asked.

"Hell no. It's been nothing but conciliatory promises and needy threats since you left. He doesn't even know for sure that we're in here right now, and it's been driving him wild."

"Yeah. You saw his office just off that cell block. He knew about what was happening here. If we talked to the right people, he'd probably end up in prison. There's no way some of this was authorized. Or, if it was, his commander is going to jail with him. He wants to get his hands on us so he can shut us up. I'll bet he's been fretting about how to cover his ass ever since this station went belly up. The fact that they inserted a smaller team at Delambre Station must have given him fits, knowing what was left behind out here. I get the feeling he's kind of relishing the fact that things got out of hand again. It gives him a chance to play the hero and also wipe out the evidence here."

"Any good news from the radio?" Denise asked.

"Well…it's complicated. Kind of a good news, bad news situation."

Fletch reappeared with a crowbar in his hand. He walked up and wedged the end of the crowbar under a slat on top of the crate. "Let's get this open. You did the hard work. Either of you care to do the honors?" He looked over at Denise and Metrodora.

"I will pass," Metrodora said, rubbing her shoulder.

Denise waved the offer off. She might not have dislocated her shoulder, but she'd accumulated a nice collection of scratches and bruises over the last half hour. She wasn't particularly eager to tug at the crowbar right now.

Fletch went to work, leveraging the prybar under the first board and pushing. Nails squealed as they came loose from the wood. A second later, the first board popped free. "What have we got here?"

Denise leaned in close to see what she'd risked her life to haul back. Everyone bent in and peered into the box. There was a layer of wax paper on top. She reached down and peeled the paper aside to see what lay beneath.

"It's meat," Cornelia said.

Denise stared down into the box. As Cornelia said, there was just a layer of raw meat under the wax paper. What in the hell?

Fletch bent lower and took a loud whiff. He pried another board loose and peeled back more of the wax paper, revealing more neatly sliced meat. It looked like an upscale butcher's display.

"It's horse meat," Fletch said.

"Horse meat," Denise repeated.

"Yeah. Horse meat. Were all the supply boxes identical to this one?"

"Yes, they were." Denise's mouth was dry. Then she asked a question that might have been dumb but was nonetheless quite pertinent. "Why is it full of horse meat?"

"Pretty common practice on Antarctic expeditions. The crew starts out using a combination of horses, dogs, and machinery to carry their gear. The horses can't graze here, though. It's not efficient to try to bring enough hay to keep them going, either. The party gets started on the horses, and when the animals start to give out, they get turned into emergency rations and food for the dogs. Then, the group continues on with the dogs and sledges. If things get truly bad, if they get stranded somewhere, they can eat the dogs to hold out longer, too."

"But why is there horse meat in the emergency supply boxes?" Denise felt like she'd just been stood up on a date. She'd been hoping for guns, medical supplies, anything that would give them an edge. This was like some sort of mean-spirited practical joke.

"I'm guessing that they did the same thing when they built this place. Dragged in as much as they could with horses and then killed them. With the temperatures preventing everything from rotting, the station would always have an emergency supply of food, even if they were cut off for an entire winter. That's what we have here. The supply of emergency backup food for the station."

Denise looked down at the box of frozen horse steaks. Merovée Station had plenty of abandoned canned food that they could live off of. A crate full of horse parts wasn't going to help them. She rubbed her eyes and resisted the urge to try out some of those choice phrases Metrodora had used earlier. Taking a deep breath, she looked up and focused on Fletch and Cornelia.

"Okay. Let's scratch that off as a bust. Cornelia said there was some good news and bad news regarding the radio situation. Give me the good news. I could do with good news. I'm downright hungry for good news. Spill it."

"Alright," Fletch said. "The radio equipment here is designed for long-range communication. It's very good. I was able to contact someone. It took a little while to convince them that this wasn't some sort of prank. They radioed out to another ship that radioed authorities on Australia who contacted someone with the Squires, and everything got relayed back to the ship I was able to contact. They're coming to rescue us."

"Thank God."

"Here's the bad news, though. They're a commercial fishing vessel out of Tasmania, maybe a day away on their current route. They're not an ice-breaker ship. The only way they can get anywhere close to the coast is to anchor out near Delambre Station."

"But Dagenais and his warship are out there."

"You see the gist of the problem. If that ship gets too close, they're going to end up like the *Sulaco*. The closest ice-breaker is even further away."

"The soldiers will be here by then."

"Right. And if we set out from here, we won't have the supplies to defend ourselves. Dagenais has that scout plane. It would spot us pretty quickly. And then there's your friend from the cable car to consider."

In the span of a couple of minutes, Denise had felt her heart sink, rise in hope, and immediately sink again. There had to be something they could do. They weren't completely helpless. They just needed a plan.

The speaker system crackled to life again. "This is Colonel Dagenais. You are running out of time. Anyone still alive and listening to this message needs to surrender soon. Your options are rapidly dwindling." Dagenais continued his spiel, again promising safety to anyone who surrendered. It was tempting on the surface. Remembering how he shelled the *Sulaco* and drove them out here in the first place punctured any false hopes, though. Dagenais wasn't a sneering radio drama villain, but he did have ice water running through his veins.

Denise thought back to those pictures in the colonel's office. She wondered if the man's wife and sons were fully aware that the husband and father in their lives was a major dick. She wondered if Dagenais thought about them and the shame they would go through if he failed when he justified what an asshole he was to himself. Or maybe, like so many dicks, he was blissfully unaware of what a sack of turds he was and saw no need to reflect on it. From her experience, a lot of jerks were taken completely by surprise when they were informed they were jerks. It was like someone going to the doctor and being told they had had a terminal disease. The diagnosis was met with shock and disbelief. The world would be a much better place if more imbeciles were aware of their condition and had an interest in treating it. A lot of them just stuffed any news that they might have personal flaws right down the mental garbage chute, though.

People would go to enormous lengths to justify to themselves that they were the sort of person they believed themselves to be. Sometimes that meant great acts of kindness and selflessness from flawed individuals. But there was a flipside to that. There were many types of frightening personality defects out there. Psychopaths. Crazed murderers. Lawyers. No type of person was scarier than a jerk who had managed to convince himself that he was in the right, though. Denise heavily suspected that was the category Colonel Dagenais fell into.

"This fishing vessel you mentioned. Did you warn them about coming here?" Denise asked.

"Yeah. I was a bit vague on the specifics because I didn't want to sound like a loon. They know things aren't safe, though."

"Good," Denise said. The cogs in her head were turning. She didn't have that plan she needed yet, but the parameters were coming together. A lot of their options were hemmed in, but the contours of the problem were starting to take shape in her head. Once she knew where the trouble spots were, she could formulate a plan to avoid them. And once she had a plan, she could improvise off it when everything inevitably went to hell.

"There's something else," Cornelia said, speaking up again.

"What?" Denise asked.

"I learned something about the meteor while you were out. I think it tells us something about the monsters, too."

"Do tell."

Cornelia grabbed a clipboard off a nearby desk and handed it to Denise. "Anything stand out to you?"

Denise took the clipboard and looked at the neatly typed paper attached to it. The words written on it were all in French, so most of it might as well have been written in Sumerian cuneiform. She could tell a few things just by looking at the format, though.

It was a report of some kind. The sentences were all arranged in neat paragraphs. There was an official-looking stamp at the bottom as well. Denise was pretty sure that the stamp translated to something along the lines of Top Secret. There was also a signature, signed with a flourish, near the stamp. The document looked like it was probably some sort of internal memorandum, the sort of thing that might be passed around to a few people in charge of this operation. Not necessarily a scientific paper. More of an internal report.

The other thing she noted was that someone had gone through and underlined a single word that kept reappearing throughout the document. *Merde*. It appeared in the memo seven times on one page.

Denise's French was quite limited. *Merci. Bonjour.* But it was usually the niceties and the curse words that spread the furthest in any given language. *Merde* was French for "shit."

She stared at the page for another few seconds, unsure of the significance, if any, of what she was looking at. It seemed a bit odd that the French researchers here would have been using such a phrase in their internal communications. Especially so frequently. It was in every paragraph at least once. The second paragraph had three instances of the word.

She glanced up at Cornelia. "Did you do the underlining, or did you find it like this?" Denise handed the clipboard to Metrodora so she could examine it. Maybe she could puzzle out something more.

"I did the underlining," Cornelia said. "Once I noticed it, it grabbed my attention. I didn't come back and underline it until I had looked at a few of the meteor samples that the research team chipped off, though. Here, follow me. I want to show you something."

Denise's bones ached as she followed Cornelia over to the edge of the room. There was a table with a series of rocks sitting under glass cubes. For some reason, the setup reminded Denise of meals hidden under serving trays at a fancy restaurant.

Cornelia lifted one of the glass cubes up and plucked out the hunk of rock beneath. It was about the length of a bottle of wine. The portion had come from the outermost layer of the meteor. One end of the chunk was blackened, but the scorching faded further along the sample, toward what would have been the interior. There was a weird groove along part of the sample that looked like someone had accidentally hit it with a glancing blow from a large drill.

She handed the sample to Denise. It was lighter than she'd been expecting. It wasn't exactly the weight of a feather, but it was easier to heft around than it looked. Denise still could have used it to smash someone's skull in if she wanted, but she could tell that there was something unusual about the weight. By the standards of solid stone, it must have had a relatively low density.

"Feel that?" Cornelia asked.

"It's light. Well, light-ish."

"Yup. And I think I've found out the reason why. Metrodora, do you still have those pictures you first showed us? The ones that observatory took when the meteor entered the atmosphere."

"Here." Metrodora pulled a tightly folded photograph out of her pocket and pulled it open. It was creased in every direction, but the image was clear enough. It was the same photo she'd presented them with back in Cape Town. It showed the meteor apparently breaking off an even larger celestial object, a large blot in the sky, just before it fell to earth.

"I can tell you're excited about whatever you think you discovered, but would you mind just telling us what this is all about?"

"I want to walk you through my reasoning here. I'm just showing you some of my evidence before I take you straight to the conclusion," Cornelia said.

Denise turned to Fletch. "Has she told you what this is all about?"

"Yeah. I think it's a big load of crap," he said, crossing his arms.

Cornelia gave him a look but then turned back to Denise. "Take a good close look at that chunk of meteor. Especially the parts that were closer to the interior. Tell me what you see."

Denise decided to play along. She held the meteor up to the light and stuck her face in close. "Let's see here. There's bits of different material. It's not all the same kind of rock. Kind of lumpy."

"Yes. It's what geologists call a conglomerate. There's lots of things suspended in a matrix of other material. It almost looks like someone fossilized a cross-section of a mixed berry pie. You can make out some distinct elements. That's very unusual. Most meteors are made up of an iron and nickel alloy. This one isn't. In fact, it's not even really a meteorite at all."

"You want to slow down and unpack that for me?"

"Those are organic materials in that matrix. They've just been processed a bit, though. The matrix itself is organic in nature too, really. They're both just highly compacted, the same way coal is just carbon from the biosphere that's been crushed and crushed and crushed until it's a little lump. This stuff was first compacted and then baked a bit when it went through the atmosphere. It probably lost a lot of its mass in the process, actually."

Denise was starting to feel dumb. "I still don't get it."

Cornelia took the meteor sample back and held it up. "As my colleague over here so eloquently put it, what you're looking at here is a big pile of crap. It's just been flash baked into rock."

"I...wait...you mean...?"

Cornelia pointed at the picture showing the larger blot in the sky. "We assumed that this meteorite broke off from a larger chunk of space debris. I don't think that's true. This big, dark shape here? I think that's a creature. A really big space-faring creature."

"And you're saying it dropped a load as it passed by Earth?"

"Exactly."

"And that's what we're looking at over there." Denise pointed to the meteorite up on its pedestal. The thing was bigger than the statues most tin-pot dictators ordered erected in their likeness. And that was after a lot of it had burned off in the atmosphere.

"That's it."

Denise looked at the sample she'd been holding. She felt the sudden urge to wash her hands.

SIXTEEN
ESCAPE PLAN

"But time is running out. If you do not surrender in time, we will have no choice but to assume the worst. For your sake and the sake of everyone you love, please contact us, and we can sort this out." Colonel Dagenais signed off on the radio again. His calls increasingly reminded Denise of some sort of surreal radio pledge drive. *Act now, and you'll receive hours of great programming, this free tote bag, and certain doom.*

There was technically still time for them to contact Dagenais, if they wanted. None of them had any intention of doing so, though. Listening to him preach their imminent destruction over the speaker system was picking at their nerves, but no one seriously thought that Dagenais was offering them a square deal.

At this point, he probably knew that they were either dead or not going to answer him. Denise was pretty sure that he was just trying to make them nervous or drive a wedge between them by counting down to their potential destruction and ratcheting up the tension.

She wasn't going to pay any more attention to him than was necessary. She was still trying to wrap her head around what Cornelia had just told her, as a matter of fact.

"Alright, so let's assume you're right," she said. "Let's assume that the meteor is just one big pile of baked dung. Where does that leave us with the various monsters down here? Maybe the slugs could hitch a ride on that thing as it plummeted down to earth. There's no way for the bug men or that giant creature to fit inside, though. The dragon-thing is about the same size as the meteor. It's the size of a dinosaur."

"I think I know what's going on there, too. I found a few other documents scattered around here. Can't read any of them, but there were some informative bits anyway. I think it reinforces my theory about the meteor's composition, too. Come over here." Cornelia waved them over to a nearby desk with a couple of binders stacked on top.

She lifted one of the binders off the desk and flipped it open, pawing through the pages until she found the section she wanted. It was a diagram of one of the slugs. Apparently, someone had autopsied one of the creatures and catalogued its innards at some point. The drawing labeled each of the organs and other points of interest as best it could. A lot of the points of interest had asterisks near the label. Apparently, the creatures were alien enough that the scientists here had to make educated guesses on some elements of the creatures' inner anatomy.

Cornelia handed the binder over to Denise. "While I was looking at the meteor samples, I noticed a lot of boreholes leading through the layers. They don't seem to be related to any process having to do with entry into the atmosphere. I'm pretty sure the slugs made them as they burrowed through the material. But that tells us something about the slugs."

"Yes, that they arrived on the meteor." Denise was still calling it a meteor. She wasn't sure it really qualified for that phrase, knowing what she did now. She couldn't quite bring herself to start calling it a space turd, though.

"That's right. The samples also don't show any larger boreholes. Certainly not large enough to house anything human-sized or larger. That means that only the slugs arrived with the meteor. What does that tell you about the other creatures?"

"That they arrived separately? Either before or after." Denise didn't really like being led around by the nose like this, but she could tell Cornelia was trying to lay out all her evidence in a way that she thought made sense. She'd indulge her friend a little bit longer, but what she really wanted was some straight answers.

"That was what I first thought, too." Cornelia took the binder back from Denise and flipped ahead past large sections of graphs and French to another series of diagrams. These illustrations showed a cross-section of a human skull with a slug nestled inside its brain. There was a cutaway diagram that showed the creature's jaws clamped onto a nerve near where the spinal cord connected to the base of the brain.

"Okay," Denise said, making a little hand gesture for Cornelia to speed it up.

"Well, the answer seems to be a little more complicated than a matter of the other monsters arriving at a different time. It has to do with the slugs themselves. We were wrong about them. They look a bit like slugs, but they're actually a lot more like a different kind of animal. Maggots."

Cornelia flipped another page in the binder and revealed another set of diagrams. The first was similar to the previous one. It showed a slug-maggot inside a human skull, but this time the creature was significantly engorged. It took up a lot more space than before. In the next illustration, the creature was barely recognizable. Some sort of extensions had formed around its form and were spreading down through the corpse's central nervous system.

There was a third diagram, too. This one showed that the entire human body had been mostly hollowed out and consumed. There was nothing left that was recognizably human in there. Instead, a second form had been weaving itself together inside the cadaver's body. It was one of the bug men that had killed Poole and emerged from the rubbish heap.

Denise thought back to some of the weird, husked bodies they'd seen. There wasn't anything left but a crust of skin. At the time, she'd assumed that something had scooped everything out of the body. Some exterior force. Now, she could see that was wrong. The bodies were like cracked eggshells after the chicken hatched. Something had emerged from the inside and clawed its way out.

"Maggots," Denise muttered, more to herself than anyone else. "Maggots turn into flies."

"Exactly," Cornelia said. "When the meteor over there was, ah, expelled, something laid eggs in it. The same thing happens on Earth a million times a day. The eggs hatched into maggots, and they started eating their way out of their nest here. Then, the French research teams discovered them, and the maggots discovered a new source of food."

"But the maggots needed even more food to pupate and turn into their next form," Denise said, letting herself extrapolate from what Cornelia was saying. "So they took over dead bodies and used those to actively hunt for more food."

"Yeah. That's why there's been dead people trying to eat us. A belly full of meat doesn't do a corpse any good. It's vital for the little critter in that dead man's skull, though. The maggots need food to reach the next stage of their lives. On this forsaken continent, human beings are basically the only thing edible for miles."

"Great," Denise said.

"In some ways, what Colonel Dagenais is doing is smart military tactics. Scorched earth. Remember from the history books when Napoleon invaded Russia and ran out of supplies, so pretty much his entire army starved to death?"

"Not exactly a moment to look back on with fondness for the French military."

"Probably not. Apparently, it's a lesson learned, though. Destroy the food stocks, and the enemy can't do anything. An army marches on its belly, and all that. If Dagenais can deny the maggots food, they can't reach the next stage in their life cycles. Eventually, they'll starve and die off in their shells. Problem solved."

"That sounds like a spiffy strategy and all, but it loses some of its charm when you realize that we're the potential food sources that need to be destroyed. I don't like being thought of as a food stock."

"It's almost flattering if you think of yourself as a strategically important resource."

"Way to look on the bright side. I'll be sure to include it on my résumé in the future. Denise DeMarco: strategically important food resource for space maggots."

"There's one last thing, though." Cornelia flipped another page. It showed a series of cross sections from a fully-fledged bug man. They showed something peculiar happening to its insides. Based on the timescale printed under each diagram, it was occurring fairly rapidly.

"I think I see what's happening."

"Before this place was overrun, it looks like the scientists here were speculating that it was possible there was a third life stage for the maggots. They thought the insect men that hatched out of people were an intermediary before the creatures reached true adulthood. Once it got enough food, it would molt again and assume its final form."

Denise thought back to the dragon creature with its proboscis and compound eyes. It bore a clear resemblance to the scabby bug men, and it certainly fit the bill for what Cornelia was talking about.

"That thing that attacked your cable car…" Cornelia said.

"It's basically a flyrannosaurus," Denise said.

"Pretty much."

Denise handed the binder back to Cornelia and pulled out the chair in front of the desk. She sat down and rubbed at her temples. Assuming any of them survived, the Squires would have the information they wanted about what was going on here. Earth had been inadvertently invaded by bug-eyed aliens who arrived on a giant turd from outer space. This was not the sort of encounter the pulp writers described when they wrote about gleaming spaceships and high-minded alien federations.

There wasn't any point in worrying about that too much right now, though. They all still needed to escape from this place. They had a few different pieces to work with. The problem was trying to chain them together into a workable plan.

The big choke point in all her ideas for how to get out of here was the rescue ship. The fishing vessel Fletch contacted could reach the coast relatively quickly, but there was only one place it could access. And that section of the coast was being guarded by a French cruiser.

That seemed to leave them at an impasse. They needed that fishing vessel. The fishermen needed to pull in close to the shore near Delambre Station. If they pulled in close to that shore, they'd be blown out of the water. Denise rolled the elements around in her head like someone swishing wine around in their mouth to work out the flavor.

There were three elements to work with, so if Denise could just find a way to short-circuit any of them, maybe she could work something out.

She didn't see any way out of their need for that fishing boat. They just didn't have another way off this continent. Maybe they could hike a thousand miles across the interior and find some help in another nation's territory, but that was like finding a needle in a haystack while blindfolded and the haystack was on fire. There were a million deadly risks, and the odds of success weren't very good. They needed that fishing vessel, or they weren't leaving this hunk of frozen rock alive.

She also didn't see a good way around the second problem, the fact that the fishing vessel needed a clear path through the ice. If the area near Delambre Station was the only safe area, the fishing vessel could reach, that was pretty much the end of that discussion. It wasn't an ice-breaker like the *Sulaco*. Its options were painfully limited this far south. Large stretches of the sea were still too choked with ice to navigate for a ship like that. They'd put a hole in their hull and sink, which didn't do anyone a single bit of good.

There was also the option of directing them to some far away section of the shore and trying to hoof it. That had a lot of the same problems as trying to reach another nation's territory, though. The journey would be dangerous, and by the time they actually reached where they'd asked the vessel to go, the ice could have shifted and blocked that route, too. And that was all assuming that they were able to evade the French scout plane and troops. Denise wasn't at all sure they'd be able to do that. There wasn't anywhere to hide on large stretches of that great, white expanse.

That left her with the third piece of the puzzle to go over in her head. Dagenais and his cruiser. They were parked squarely in the way of her plans. What she needed was some way to get them to move. Even if it was only for a little while, just a few hours, the lot of them could rendezvous with the fishing vessel and be on their merry way. It would take Dagenais a while to realize what had happened, and that would give them the time they needed to make it back to civilization.

It all sounded perfectly simple in her head. Just get Dagenais to leave for a little while. Of course. Perfect solution. Gold stars for everyone.

The problem was, how did she get him to do that? Get on the radio and ask him to give them a few hours of alone time? Use harsh language? Maybe tell him there were some cookies at the next nearest

Antarctic outpost? Those all seemed like they'd be about equally effective.

There wasn't really anything she could say to Dagenais that would get him to move the cruiser. He'd suspect a trick instantly, and then he'd park his butt right there in that harbor and never move again, if that's what it took.

If there wasn't anything she could say, maybe there was something she could do. Time was of the essence, and they didn't have many supplies. Eventually, the French troops would reach Merovée Station, and Denise knew she wouldn't be able to hold off a sustained assault for long. She didn't trust the attack to come exactly at the end of the two hours Dagenais had specified, either. It could be early, a surprise. It might come late, letting the tension build up until they were all bedraggled and easily picked off.

She needed something that they could put together quickly and working with what they had. Damaging the cruiser would force Dagenais away for a while. With more supplies, that probably would have meant a torpedo of some sort. Something that they could sneak in close and either fire or attach to the ship's hull to disable it. They didn't have any explosives, though. They had fuel for the generator, which would burn and create all sorts of chaos under the right conditions, but it wouldn't chew through a warship's hull or damage it much.

Explosives were out. They just didn't have anything that would help them in that regard. So what did that leave them? Denise mashed her brain cells together and tried to come up with something.

Radioing information out for the fishing vessel to pass on, sort of like blackmail? No, that wouldn't prevent Dagenais from killing them, and the evidence would disappear once the facility was destroyed. Some sort of Trojan horse scheme, where they could sneak something onto the ship? No, they would need something the French wanted to take aboard their warship, and they didn't have that. Tricking Dagenais with some fancy radio work and making him think that he had suddenly been recalled by the French high command? That one almost seemed promising given the amount of classified information and code books that seemed to be just sitting around, but none of them could even speak French.

Dagenais obviously wasn't stupid. He had them backed into a corner, and he knew it. By slowly and steadily advancing his men, he would have every advantage when they got here. He wasn't going to throw all that away because of some cheap ploy. This was going to take more than a little ruse. Denise needed something unexpected, something that would set Dagenais back on his heels.

What about a distraction? If Denise had one truly great, God-given skill in life, a sort of natural calling, it was for creating uncontrollable messes. She looked around at her surroundings.

There was a large amount of fairly basic office equipment, some meteorite samples, and a crate of horse meat. She could work with that.

SEVENTEEN
DEAD SILENT

Denise realized that she'd never really heard true, absolute silence before. No matter how far away from South Africa's cities and towns she travelled, there was always some noise. Just because she had escaped the rumble of cars and trucks didn't mean that the world was quiet. There were always birds singing and arguing. Insects buzzing and humming. The distant sound of flowing water or the rustle of the breeze through the grass.

There was none of that right now, though. The katabatic winds had finally abated for a short time, which made the outside seem positively balmy. However, she'd grown used to the constant sound of their buffeting gusts and the low moan they made as they swept across the white landscape.

Now that they were gone, Denise felt the true loneliness of the land down here. There was no wildlife squawking or running through the underbrush. There wasn't even any underbrush. There was just a seemingly endless expanse of ice.

No matter how Denise strained her ears, she couldn't hear anything beyond a low, dull hum. That was the baseline sound of existence, barely audible. Normally, it was drowned out altogether by the rest of the world. On the rare occasions when it was actually quiet enough to hear, such as in the darkest hours of the night when self-doubt and guilty consciences poked at restless sleepers, people usually couldn't hear it over the sound of their own thoughts.

Denise wondered what made that little humming sound. Was it just the blood flowing through her veins in a steady rush? Was it individual air molecules bouncing off her eardrums? Were the auditory nerves just not built to handle such perfect silence, and they kept misfiring in a vain attempt to pick up something…anything? Maybe it was just a sort of baseline test noise so the body could be sure it hadn't gone completely deaf. She had no idea.

She took a step across the ice, and the crunching noise her boot made on the ground seemed like it was as loud as anything her Nitro Express could do. With nothing else in the auditory landscape, each little bit of noise seemed like it was a hundred times louder than it actually was. Her next footstep seemed like Colonel Dagenais ought to be able to hear it back on his cruiser.

There was something deeply unnatural about the silence, but it seemed even worse to disturb it somehow. It was like sitting next to a closed casket at a wake and suddenly hearing something scrabbling at the wood from the inside. It was like a lone bubble rising to the surface of a murky, perfectly still pond where someone had drowned. It was like shadows moving in an otherwise empty house.

Denise did her best to ignore the unnerving quiet as she marched across the packed ice toward one of the station's outbuildings. There were a few benefits to the silence as well. She'd be able to hear any approaching buzzing noise from a considerable distance and run back to shelter before it could pass overhead. That went for French scout planes as well as monsters. She'd also be able to hear anything walking toward her across the ground. It was impossible to move silently across the ice. If the approaching soldiers or anything else wanted to come at her, she'd hear them from a good distance away. And she still had her Nitro Express, which was a handy tool for dealing with threats from any distance.

There was another advantage to the wind dying down, too. She stepped in front of the station's hangar and looked inside. There weren't any dead bodies lurking in the corners, moving or otherwise. Nor were there any freakish insect monsters.

However, there was a two-seater airplane. It was more or less identical to the one she and Fletch took out earlier. She'd seen the aircraft when they first arrived at Merovée Station, but she hadn't thought about it much after that. Since coming up with the broad outline of her plan, she'd remembered it, though.

The little aircraft didn't have the range to carry them across the continent to safety. Even if it did, it could only take two people at a time, and Fletch would have to be one of those people every time. It would take three trips to get everyone someplace safe, and they didn't have that kind of time. Even so, the little airplane was about to become very useful.

At least, Denise hoped so. Anything less than useful meant a swift and probably unpleasant death. A minute later, Cornelia and Fletch opened the station door, each holding up one end of the crate of horse meat. Denise gave them a wave to indicate that everything was all clear, and they started lugging the crate over toward the hangar. Metrodora followed behind them, holding the pistol they'd found earlier. With her wrenched shoulder popped back into place, there was only so much she could do right now, so her job was mostly to serve as an extra set of eyes while they were preparing.

When Cornelia and Fletch reached the hangar, Fletch set his end of the crate down and went straight to the plane. Denise ignored him while he started to check the equipment and make sure everything was in working order. The plane had been sitting unused in freezing temperatures for months. It needed some maintenance and tender loving care to get everything in proper working order again.

Denise and Cornelia had a simpler job. Denise grabbed some twine and started to strap slabs of horse meat to the tail of the plane. They'd cooked the meat a little first by starting a bonfire out of old papers and books in the research station and sticking the horse steaks over it.

Now, they weren't just rock-hard meat bricks anymore. Their time in icy storage had preserved them, but it had also left them the consistency of cinder blocks. A little cooking had softened them up, but more importantly, it had given them a certain meaty aroma. It wasn't a particularly good aroma, but it was there.

Some of the meat hunks were partially blackened. Others were basically raw inside. Some were black on the outside and completely uncooked outside. It would have gotten them fired from any restaurant kitchen. Denise wasn't exactly researching an article for *Housewife Recipes Quarterly*, either.

She was just hoping the smell would help with her plan a little. She took more of the meat and attached more of it around the plane's tail.

"Don't tie it around any moving parts. The twine could get stuck on something it shouldn't and lock up the controls," Fletch said.

"Way ahead of you."

"And make sure you have some up near the front, too. Balance the weight out a little."

"Will do. And...thanks. I appreciate that you're willing to do this," Denise said.

"Well, nobody else here knows how to fly a plane, and it's not like I have a better idea."

It was an odd world where the first step of any plan involved strapping a bunch of meat to the outside of an airplane. Then again, it was an odd world where someone could find herself stranded at a research station built to study aliens that hatched from space poop. Life was just full of surprises like that sometimes.

"You contacted our friends on the fishing vessel, too?" Denise asked.

"Yeah. They know not to get too close. They're approaching, but they'll stay out of range until someone signals them in."

Denise strapped some more meat to the front of the plane. Her plan was simple enough. All they had to do was raise as much hell as possible. It was just a matter of getting Dagenais and his cruiser out of the harbor for a short time. They could do that either by distracting him with something or damaging his ship enough that it would be forced to turn around. Either one would get the man out of their hair long enough to get off this ice cube.

She could think of one way that might accomplish those goals. Maybe even both of them. They just had to lure the flyrannosaurus over to Dagenais. It sounded simple enough in the abstract, which was just how Denise preferred to think about it. Focusing too much on any given detail made her think about just how completely insane the whole scheme was.

They didn't have any other good options, though. They couldn't wait for backup. The French would eventually take Merovée Station. Denise had seen the troop transports when the cruiser first arrived. She didn't have the weapons or the people to hold them off. Nor would they be much better off trying to plunge across the continent on some overland expedition through monster territory.

That left her to choose between a bunch of crazy options. Hopefully, "crazy" would also translate to "unexpected." One benefit of her plan was that it was relatively simple.

All they had to do was attract the flyrannosaurus. There was no way to outrun it on the ground, but they didn't have to. Once it was in the air, the plane ought to be able to outpace the oversized creature. The smell of the roasted meat should grab its attention and keep it following them, too.

Technically, putting a giant, acid-spewing space freak hot on her own trail was what Denise would consider a bad idea. If she were to ever write a manual for prospective monster hunters, that would probably fall into a "Don'ts" column somewhere toward the front of the first chapter.

The trick would be to keep ahead of the monster long enough to lead it somewhere. In this case, she intended to lead it straight to Dagenais. That would give them a chance to shake the creature and deliver a massive problem straight to the cruiser's doorstep. Dagenais would have to redirect all his attention and resources to deal with it, and that gave Denise and the other survivors a window of opportunity to escape. Hopefully, the creature would destroy enough equipment and sow enough chaos that Dagenais would be forced to sail back to the nearest naval base to resupply and regroup.

Dagenais knew he had them exactly where he wanted them, even if they were being stubborn. He knew better than anyone that their options for escape were quite limited. He also knew that he had them outnumbered by twenty-to-one odds. Given how lopsided things were, he wouldn't be expecting an assault straight on the seat of his strength.

Of course, the biggest flaw with her plan was that she didn't necessarily know for sure that their airplane could stay ahead of the flyrannosaurus. She'd seen the creature fly through the air, and it looked like an airplane was faster.

However, Fletch couldn't pilot the plane and defend it at the same time. The best he could do was evasive maneuvers. Denise would sit in the passenger seat with the Nitro Express and try to help out. There was no guarantee that she'd be able to. Sitting in a moving airplane and trying to hit another flying object was not an easy task. She'd only be needed, and she'd only be useful, if the flyrannosaurus came incredibly close. Even then, her elephant gun might not be enough to dissuade the creature.

The plane only held two people, which meant that Cornelia and Metrodora would have to stay behind. Denise had come up with this harebrained scheme. It was already risky enough to inflict it on Fletch. If it didn't work out, it seemed only fair that she should be the one to deal with the consequences.

Fletch had finished warming the engine up, pumping fuel, and checking instruments. After some maintenance, the plane was ready to fly again. The propeller started spinning as Fletch finished up his final tests. He gave Denise a thumbs up. "Ready?"

Basically, she was about to hop inside a flying snack bar and use it to lure a giant monster straight toward a hostile warship. What could possibly go wrong?

"Ready."

EIGHTEEN
TURBULENCE

The airplane rolled out of the hangar and onto the long, flat stretch of ice ahead of it. Denise sat in the rear seat, the Nitro Express propped straight up between her knees. She hoped she could just keep the gun there the whole time without ever having to lift it. Everything would go exactly according to plan, and the flyrannosaurus would follow them out to the coast without ever buzzing close enough to pose a real threat. They'd reach the coast, and the creature would break off to investigate the other humans. Denise would cut the hunks of meat free from the plane, if that helped direct the creature's attention. She and Fletch would be safe as lambs the entire time.

That was the goal, at least. Denise had seen enough bad situations to know that things never went as planned, though. Never. That's what the Nitro Express was for. She waved one last time to Cornelia and Metrodora as the plane moved down the ice away from the rest of the station.

Grimacing, she turned back around as the plane picked up speed. The engine's putter turned into a roar, and they bounced and slewed their way forward. The katabatic winds had temporarily died down, but the movement of the plane meant that cold air kept blasting Denise in the face anyway. Her tinted goggles kept her eyes relatively safe from the buffeting winds, but even her facemask could only do so much to keep her warm. Before, she'd almost gotten used to the cold, or at least she'd come to accept it. Now that she'd had some time to warm up in the heated station, the cold was more savage than ever. It felt like tiny wolves with freezing teeth were biting her face and trying their best to tear her skin off. Everything prickled and hurt.

After gaining a bit more speed, the plane lurched up into the air. Fletch patted the controls like he was saying hello to a faithful dog.

"Everything's working the way it should?" Denise asked. She had to yell over the wind and the sound of the plane's engine.

"We're good. It only needed a little maintenance after being left out in the cold for so long. Nothing a little elbow grease couldn't make normal again."

That was something, at least. It would be bad enough if some essential component gave out while they were still clawing their way into the freezing air. Plunging right back down to the ice in a blazing fireball would be unpleasant, but at least they'd die warm.

Unpleasant though a massive failure right now would be, there was at least a chance Fletch could divert course and limp back to the hangar. They wouldn't have that option if the plane broke down while the monster was hot on their tails. They'd either be battered out of the air and crash, or they'd get sprayed with acid and get to watch their flesh melt off their bones before they hit the ice.

"Let's get this show on the road," Denise said. The plane circled upward, banking around until it was high above the station. Looking down, Denise could see a couple of dots near the hangar. That must be Cornelia and Metrodora. There were a few more dots congregated around the far side of Merovée Station. They moved aimlessly between the buildings. From up here, Denise couldn't tell if they were merely ghouls or more advanced insectoid horrors.

Still gaining altitude, the plane finished its long, slow return angle and flew the rest of the way over the station. They reached the rim of the impact crater after a few seconds.

Denise had trouble telling exactly how fast they were moving. The scale of everything from up high was so much different than when she was on the ground. There was no way to estimate just how much faster they would be moving than the flyrannosaurus. Hopefully, it would be enough to keep a comfortable distance between them the whole way.

When she first brought up her plan, Fletch said that it would be about a ten-minute flight from Merovée Station to the coast when they flew a direct route at maximum speed. Even if the French scout plane spotted them right now and tore back to Dagenais, that wouldn't give them much time to prepare for what was coming.

Ten minutes out. Ten minutes back. Not even long enough for a lunch break. Then, Fletch would drop Denise off to wait for the ship. Once they contacted their rescue ship and gave the all clear, Fletch could bring people to the coast one at a time. Faster and safer than using their motor sledges to travel back.

Denise didn't think Dagenais knew as much as she did about the creature. The research notes at Merovée Station indicated that none of the bug men had pupated to their final, horrible form yet. Even Benoit and his team seemed unaware of the creature's existence. Its attack on the snow tractor had been the cue Dagenais needed to level Delambre Station without too many pesky questions about appropriateness afterward, but Denise didn't think he had a clue what the thing was or the expertise to deal with it quickly. Hopefully, the French soldiers would be able to mortally wound it after it served its purpose. If it was still alive and kicking afterward, it would only make Denise's plan more complicated.

Fletch steered across the chasm the fecal meteor's impact had carved in the ice and started to circle around the entrance to the storage chamber where Denise had found the horse meat. Down below, Denise could see the wreckage of the cable car at the very bottom of the crater. There wasn't much left. The car had been smashed and pulverized until it was barely recognizable. Swinging around again, Fletch kept the plane moving around in a tight circle high above the chamber entrance.

Nothing happened. Denise glanced around to the sides. She was pretty sure the creature was still inside the chamber, where it had retreated back to its trash heap nest after failing to eat herself and Metrodora, but it was possible that the monster had flown off while none of them were paying attention. She didn't think that was likely, though. Its wings made a lot of noise when it went anywhere. She already knew they could hear it from inside the station when it flew past.

However, the last thing they needed was for the damn space monster to blindside them. There wasn't any sign of it on the horizon, though.

Denise was still trying to wrap her head around the creatures. She suspected that no matter what Colonel Dagenais did, none of the research at these stations would ever make it into public hands. The French government would want to keep this to themselves. There wouldn't be any scientific awards or public laurels for this project. They were dealing with genuine aliens.

Denise kept thinking of the creatures as flies now, but that wasn't quite accurate. They were really just an example of convergent evolution. There were so many flies on Earth because they were efficient little pests. They fed on detritus and the planet's inexhaustible supplies of filth and decay.

Somewhere deep out in the wild black yonder, something had followed a similar evolutionary trajectory. Only instead of being tiny, buzzing annoyances, the full-grown specimens were the size of freight cars and capable of hunting human-sized prey. It was like peering into an alternate world where the insects had come to dominate the planet instead of dinosaurs millions of years ago. Certain environmental niches would always be filled, and certain templates were apparently quite good for certain tasks, regardless of scale.

It did make Denise wonder just what had flown past Earth and brought the fly creatures here, though. The creature must have been huge, some sort of space-faring leviathan slithering through the uncharted depths of the solar system. It was both alarming and humbling to think there might be an ecosystem out there amid the darkness.

Her musings were interrupted when a gigantic head poked out of the chamber entrance below. The head didn't need to swivel upward to see them. Its compound eyes took in everything around it.

"It's down there," Denise yelled.

"I see it," Fletch yelled back. He maneuvered the plane around and started toward the coast, moving at a nice leisurely pace for the moment.

The flyrannosaurus emerged from its lair and stood in the bright sunlight. It used its front legs to clean its head. The creature's movements were fast and jerky. Every movement it made looked like a film that was being cranked too quickly.

A second later, those huge, translucent wings unfurled from the creature's back and started to beat at the air. As it gained lift off, Denise could hear the growing buzzing sound filling the air. The flyrannosaurus tucked its legs up under its body and straightened its tail out, reducing drag to a bare minimum.

Then, it was after them.

Denise blinked in surprise. The creature moved fast. Damn fast. It came up toward them like someone had fired it out of a cannon. "Fletch, go."

Fletch glanced back at the creature and set the throttle to maximum. The plane surged forward through the air, and Denise felt an invisible hand squeeze her stomach. The force of the wind increased until it was like she was trying to shove her way through a tornado. All around her, the airplane's frame rattled and squeaked as Fletch pushed it toward its limits.

Forcing herself around, Denise looked for the flyrannosaurus. It was coming up behind them, rising like a shark about to seize a seal from below. Denise pulled the Nitro Express from up between her knees and swung it around.

This might have been a big mistake.

They were already out past Merovée Station, eating up the distance. From up here, Denise could even see the ocean and its glistening white icebergs. However, they just weren't going fast enough. The creature was gaining on them as it rose up to meet them.

"We've got a problem," Denise said.

"I'm working on it."

Denise twisted and swung the Nitro Express around to try to get a bead on the creature rushing toward them. She had to resist the nearly overpowering urge to pull the trigger right away, though. She felt like a sitting duck just watching the monster approach, but she knew she had virtually no chance of hitting it from this far out. She'd just be wasting her ammunition.

"Look up ahead," Fletch said.

Denise swiveled back around and saw something on the horizon flying toward them from the front at a lower altitude. Was there a second creature? Had she somehow not realized that there was already more than one of the monstrosities loose on the continent? If there were two of the creatures ready to box them in, they were well and truly screwed.

It took Denise a second to focus her eyes, but the dark speck moving toward them wasn't another monster. It was the French scout plane.

The pilot must have realized what he was seeing in front of him at roughly the same time, because the plane started to bank and turn around back in the direction of Delambre Station and the cruiser. He'd been cruising at a casual pace, probably watching in case Denise and her team tried to slip back toward the coast on motor sledges. The hasty effort to turn around only slowed the scout plane down even more.

However, the sound of the creature's wings was a steady gale of noise now, like a rumble of thunder that simply refused to end. The flyrannosaurus had nearly caught up to them now. Denise started to bring her Nitro Express around to aim again.

"Hold on to something," Fletch shouted over the noise of the engine and the creature's approach. Denise tucked the elephant gun back inside the cabin just before Fletch pushed the controls down.

The plane lurched into a steep dive, threatening to pluck Denise out of her seat and send her tumbling through the air toward the ground below. Her stomach rose up to the base of her throat and tied itself in a knot.

The plunge toward the earth built up the plane's speed up, letting the engine and gravity work together. Where the creature had been right behind and below them before, now it was above them and considerably further away. A second later, it realized its prey was trying to escape and it threw itself toward the earth as well.

Fletch touched the controls and brought the plane out of its dive. Denise's stomach went from the base of her throat to somewhere around her knees as gravity reasserted itself with a vengeance. She could feel the pull of the earth in her bones, like it was sucking them in. The plane levelled out and continued forward, and the feeling disappeared.

The big burst of speed had put them slightly ahead of the French scout plane, which was still gathering steam. The French plane was built for speed and maneuverability so it could survive its various outings in a war zone. Eventually, it would outrun the larger research plane.

However, the scout pilot didn't have until eventually. The flyrannosaurus came down almost directly on top of him, like an owl swooping down on a mouse. Its legs extended out from its body and latched onto the scout plane.

A claw crunched down on the left wing, first crushing it and then ripping it away entirely. Another claw sank into the fuselage, piercing the thin material. Pieces of cloth and metal rained down to the ground below. The plane's tail snapped away as the flyrannosaurus grasped at the wreckage.

Pulling the plane up to its head, it hacked a gob of vile jelly out onto the pilot. Denise couldn't hear any of what was happening over the sound of the creature's beating wings and the wind, and for that, she was grateful. She could see the man flailing for a moment, trying to crawl out of his seat in the wrecked plane. His arm fell off and sailed out into the abyss before he could leverage himself up and out, though. A second later, it looked like his entire form sort of collapsed in on itself, like a piece of paper crumpling as it burned. The flyrannosaurus stuck its proboscis down into the mess and sucked it all up while it was still moving. When everything had been slurped up a few seconds later, it dropped the crippled plane, which fell back toward the earth.

That maneuver had bought Fletch and Denise some space, but it wasn't enough. The flyrannosaurus barely even slowed down to kill and devour the French pilot. Now, it had locked onto the remaining plane again.

Denise watched as the creature tucked its legs back into their most aerodynamic position, and it started gaining on them again. She cursed and looked toward the front of the plane. They were over halfway to the coast now, but she wasn't sure they could make it before the flyrannosaurus caught up with them. The plane had lost about half its original altitude, which meant that Fletch could make another dive for one more quick speed boost. After that though, they'd be skimming the ice. Gaining altitude again would only slow them down and make them easier to snatch.

The pieces of horsemeat smacked against the plane's skin as they flew. Denise had thought that they might need a scent trail to help lure the creature along behind them, especially if they got too far ahead. It didn't look like that was going to be a big problem. She leaned as far out of the plane as she dared and cut one of the lengths of twine anchoring the meat to the side of the plane. The slab of meat plunged away from them and landed far below, creating a small explosion of horse jam. She repeated the process on all the lengths of twine she could reach, lightening the load ever so slightly.

She felt like a sailor on a doomed ship throwing furniture and cargo overboard as the water threatened to swamp them. The pieces of horse meat were dead weight, but the real problem was simply that the monster was too fast for their airplane. They'd had a head start, and Fletch's maneuvering had bought them some time, but it was like some nightmare version of a fifth-grade math problem. If a plane leaves the station going one hundred fifty miles per hour, and a monster leaves the station a minute later going on hundred sixty miles per hour, how long until the plane's occupants are eaten alive like screaming soup? Right now, it wasn't a question of *if* the creature would catch up to them; it was a matter of *when.*

Denise swung her elephant gun around and fired at the fast-approaching creature. She could actually feel the plane jilt a little in the air from the gun's recoil. The monster didn't slow down. She couldn't even tell if she'd managed to land a hit on it. The Nitro Express had blown off a couple of its claws earlier, but its armor was probably fairly weak there. She had no idea if the elephant gun could even penetrate where the creature's plating was thicker.

She fired again anyway, hoping for a lucky shot. Screw her original plan of luring the thing out to Dagenais. They weren't going to make it that far at this rate. If she actually managed to down the creature somehow, they'd fly back and try to take the motor sledges overland to safety. The French scout plane was gone now, so Dagenais had lost his eyes in the sky. Maybe they could do it.

Her second shot didn't do any noticeable damage either. She couldn't even tell if it connected. The monster didn't slow down or jerk in the air. It only continued to draw closer.

She loaded two more rounds into the Nitro Express and snapped it closed. There wouldn't be too many more opportunities to fire at the creature before it caught up to them. She wanted to save her next shot until it was close enough that she could aim for the monster's eyes. Just about every other part of its body was covered in iridescent chitin. Those bulging eyes were her best targets at this point.

"I'm going to try something," Fletch shouted.

"You better try it fast." Denise turned back around and looked at the creature again. She could practically spit at it now.

"Okay. Hold on tight." Fletch jerked the stick straight back, and the plane shot upward. Denise suddenly found her back to the ground as the plane went vertical. The gravitational forces at work made her vision swim for a second. It was like being strapped into a ride built by mad carny geniuses, and the contraption was trying to break free from its restraints to attack the authors of its misbegotten existence.

The sudden ascent dramatically slowed them down, but it had happened too quickly for the flyrannosaurus to snatch them out of the sky. Momentum sent the creature barreling ahead before it could change course. It slowed, turned around, and buzzed upward, heading straight for them again.

Fletch kept the controls angled back, and the plane went from angling upward to looping back. They spent a second completely upside down before switching into a steep dive. Fletch had just sent them into a tight vertical coil. The flyrannosaurus was now directly ahead of them instead of behind them. If their plane had machineguns attached, they could have raked them across the monster's armor and maybe done some damage, but all they had was Denise's elephant gun.

They were moving toward the coast again, but the flyrannosaurus was coming straight at them now. The plane and the monster came at each other like two trains on the same set of tracks. Denise clutched at the Nitro Express and aimed over Fletch's head at the approaching abomination.

At the last second, Fletch dipped the plane again and shot straight underneath the creature, gathering speed as he swept into another dive. The plane bounced in the air as they passed through the creature's wake. He pulled out of the dive, and Denise's vision seemed to fade for a second as gravity tried to pull all the blood in her body down to her boots.

Behind them again, the monster had to slow and turn around once more. Denise watched it swing around in a slow, arcing path that opened up some distance between the creature and the plane. The aircraft was engaged in a sort of aerial bullfight, dodging the rampaging beast before waiting for it to charge them again. The only problem was, matadors had swords and a crew ready to help them if the bull got lucky. She and Fletch couldn't do much more than run, and if the creature caught them, there was no help coming.

Denise could see the smoldering remains of Delambre Station ahead of them. Most of the structures had been reduced to rubble by the rain of shells earlier. The ice was cracked and cratered all around the area. The few outbuildings that hadn't been destroyed had been gutted by fire and were just empty shells now.

Further out, she could see the cruiser anchored out in the water. It had steamed in close to shore, muscling its way into the protective center of the bay not far from where the *Sulaco* had gone down. Its troop transport craft were all empty at the station's docks as men unloaded equipment from them.

The soldiers had seen what was coming toward them and started to scatter, though. They left behind pallets of equipment and motor sledges, all the things they would need to mount an assault on Merovée Station in the coming hours.

The plane zoomed over the first pile of burnt rubble. The flyrannosaurus followed close behind. Fletch angled the plane down again, sending them into a shallow dive over the station wreckage, gaining speed as they went. From here, it was only a short distance to the cruiser.

But the distance from the monster to the plane was shorter. The plane clawed its way forward, pulling out of its descent once it was no more than twenty feet off the ground. The ground zoomed past beneath them as the propeller roared.

Soldiers in white parkas fled in every direction, diving for cover amid the rubble. They would have been far safer if Dagenais hadn't destroyed the station. There was no place to hide now.

Denise heard a noise like someone tearing a giant sheet of wet burlap. She looked over and saw someone firing a machine gun in their direction. She ducked down in her seat a little, but she couldn't even tell if the man was firing at the plane or the monster. They were such a fast target that actually hitting them would be as much a matter of luck as skill.

No bullets punched through the plane's skin or its passengers, though. More bullets shot up through the air in their general direction, but they came from rifles. They couldn't fire quickly enough to have much hope of hitting the airplane.

All the activity caught the monster's attention, though. It broke off from following the plane and landed directly in front of a group of French soldiers on motor sledges. The sledges went flying into the air, spilling men and supplies across the ice, as the creature lashed out with its claws. Blood and alien digestive fluid splashed over the ground amid a wave of screams.

The gunfire started to draw away from the plane and shift toward the flyrannosaurus. If Denise's Nitro Express hadn't been enough to do any serious damage, the smaller rifles weren't any more effective. The creature lumbered over to a makeshift foxhole made from rubble and tore the men inside apart with its claws.

A man with a flamethrower dashed over and blew a jet of fire at the creature. The flyrannosaurus made a shrieking noise as some of the burning fuel landed on its leg. Rearing its head around, it sprayed a gout of acid at the soldier with the flamethrower and buzzed back into the air. The unfortunate man started to come apart like wet cotton candy. A second later, the caustic slime ate through one the weapon's hoses, and the tank exploded in a massive orange plume. Burning fuel fell from the sky on the positions nearby. Men ran out of cover as flames sprang up all around them.

"We need the creature to attack the ship. We're not going anywhere unless it forces the cruiser out of the harbor," Denise shouted.

"Right." Fletch wheeled the plane back around, trying to get the creature's attention again. They needed to draw it out over the water and to Dagenais. Even if the creature wiped out every single soldier who had landed at Delambre Station, Dagenais would still be able to keep everyone bottled up on the ice if he controlled the sea.

Getting the creature's attention again wasn't going to be an easy task, though. There was so much prey scattered around the remains of the station. The machine gunner who had started firing at the plane a minute ago turned into a bubbling puddle of chunky soup as the creature attacked him. The monster paused long enough to slurp some of the remains up before turning to the next cluster of soldiers.

Denise heard the whistling sound, but it took her a moment to process the noise. Then she realized what it was. "Pull up! Pull up," she shouted.

Fletch yanked the plane upward just as the first shell hit the scarred and blasted ice. Pieces of broken cement and shards of ice leapt into the air, shooting away from the explosion. Dagenais and the crew of the cruiser had seen what was happening and started firing the ship's guns at the monster.

The scene below was absolute bedlam. The flyrannosaurus moved too quickly for the cruiser to hit it with its big guns. By the time any given shell reached the monster's previous position, the creature had already buzzed across to the other side of the compound and begun devouring the liquefying remains of more of the landing party. The big guns hit more positions where their own men were hunkered down than they came close to the creature. It was a massacre.

Dagenais hadn't known about the flyrannosaurus anymore than Benoit and his team had. The creature hadn't eaten enough trash and corpses to pupate into its final form yet when Benoit's expedition retook the first station. Colonel Dagenais had brought plenty of equipment capable of dealing with the undead research teams and insectile humanoids, but they didn't have the sort of gear they needed to deal with the devastating force and power of the flyrannosaurus. Maybe if they'd had more time to finish setting up defenses, they would have had a better chance. Right now, the entire expeditionary force was being slaughtered in short order, though.

Another man with a flamethrower charged across the ice toward the rampaging creature. A shell burst near him, and the fuel tank erupted in a massive plume of flame. Denise could feel the sudden burst of heat even from well above the battlefield. Meanwhile, the flyrannosaurus had already darted over to a new location, knocking down a storage shed to grab at the men huddled inside.

Denise fired down at the monster. Her goal wasn't necessarily to save the remaining men trapped in the remains of the station. They would have marched out and murdered her and everyone else at Merovée Station eventually. They were clearly loyal to Dagenais, even if it meant killing the odd civilian here and there. Instead, she was actually concerned about the creature.

The monster might be able to shrug off small arms fire. It might even be able to take the hammer blows of larger weapons like her elephant gun. But she knew damn well that it wouldn't be able to survive a strike from the cruiser's guns. Those shells were meant to punch through solid steel ship armor, and they were packed with high explosives. A direct hit from one of those would turn the flyrannosaurus into something resembling burnt guacamole. Even a near miss would likely cripple the creature. The shells had completely levelled a reinforced, concrete research station. They would pulverize living flesh.

The plane jerked slightly in the air as Denise fired the elephant gun downward. She had no illusions about hitting the creature; she just wanted to get its attention again. No such luck. Denise fired again, but there were apparently more tempting targets. She was almost out of ammo now.

The few remaining French troops broke and made a mad dash toward the transport boats at the docks. They couldn't fight the creature without a tank or some sort of defensive positions. They didn't have those, though.

None of them made it to the docks. The flyrannosaurus swept in, plucking men off the ground and tearing them apart. Others were doused in corrosive slime, and they folded in on themselves as their bones and ligaments turned to mush.

Only then did the monster turn its attention back to the plane. It shot up into the air straight at them. Fletch banked away and poured all the power he could into the engine, angling the plane directly toward the cruiser.

Something exploded in front of them. For a moment, Denise thought one of the ship's big guns had fired a defective round that burst in midair, but the explosion was too small. Then she saw a succession of small muzzle flashes at the front and rear of the cruiser.

The ship's crew had stopped firing the heavy weapons and switched to a pair of anti-air flak guns. The guns fired rapid bursts of small shells that exploded in the air, leaving debris trails of fire and shrapnel. Another burst of smoke appeared off to their side, and another behind them.

Denise slid as low as she could down into her seat. There wasn't anything she could do about the anti-aircraft guns. After seeing what had happened to their colleagues on the shore, hopefully, the crews were aiming for the monster and not the plane. The creature was coming up behind them again, the sound of its buzzing wings filling the world around Denise.

Fletch aimed to fly right over the ship's deck. That would give the creature an eyeful of the crew moving around and hopefully entice it to land and continue its rampage anew. Denise knew she should feel bad for the poor sods about to come face-to-face with the creature, but they'd blown up the *Sulaco* and tried to kill her as well. Even if they were just following orders from Dagenais, they should have known better than killing defenseless targets.

As the plane sped closer, the men on the flak guns started to find their aim. The bursts of smoke came closer and closer, faster and faster. She could smell the acrid burning scent of the shells after they burst. Denise didn't dare turn around to see where the monster was anymore. The air was full of jagged, tearing metal scraps.

Finally, the inevitable happened. A shell exploded directly in front of them. Twisted spall slammed into the propeller with a noise like someone dropping a handful of coins into a lawnmower's blades. More metal claws shredded the skin of the wings, tearing it to flapping pieces of tattered canvas and metal.

Fletch was in the front seat. His body protected Denise from most of the tiny buzz saws whipping through the air. He jerked violently as a dozen pieces of scrap metal dug into his body all at once. One piece missed him and tugged at Denise's jacket, slicing part of her hood off and missing her head by a finger's breadth.

Denise couldn't tell if she was screaming or not. She wouldn't have been able to hear herself over the sound of the plane's engine tearing itself apart and the rapid-fire bursts from the flak guns and the angry buzz of the flyrannosaurus. The entire world was full of furious sound. One scream amid the chaos was nothing.

The plane bled speed as the propeller snapped and broke apart, sending debris spiraling off in a hundred different directions. A fire was already starting to spread from the engine, the flames clinging to the sides of the plane for dear life as the wind beat at them. In front of her,

Fletch clutched at himself before slumping down in his seat. They were going down.

The plane had dropped precipitously low for its intended pass over the cruiser. They didn't have very far to go. The plane didn't plunge straight down. The basic airframe was still intact enough that momentum allowed it to glide forward a little bit even as the engine lost power and died.

Denise held on as the plane's nose dipped a few degrees at a time, taking her along for the ride. The plane went from forty feet off the ground to thirty to twenty. She tried to look past Fletch's body to see where they were going. Maybe if they landed flat on the plane's belly, it would skim along the surface of the water for a minute before coming to a stop and sinking. That would give her time to bail out. All she needed was a relatively clear landing path.

The landing path ahead wasn't clear. There was a small sheet of ice directly in their path. The plane remained relatively flat as it sank down to ten feet above the water. A moment later, the landing gear kissed the top of the waves, sending up huge geysers of white froth.

At the same time, the flyrannosaurus swept past over Denise's head. The downdraft from the creature's wings stirred the water as it passed. The shadow zipped over Denise, and then it was gone, heading toward the cruiser. The sailors running for cover on its deck and the flash of the flak guns had caught its attention.

Denise didn't have long to watch what was about to happen, though. The plane's struts hit the floating ice sheet. Unlike the hull of an ice-breaking ship like the *Sulaco*, the plane's landing gear was never designed to cut through floating debris.

In an instant, the front of the plane smashed downward into the ice sheet exactly like someone with their shoelaces tied together falling on their face. The plane's engine block augured into the ice and came to a crunching halt.

Unfortunately for Denise, the force was like sitting in the bucket of a catapult. The rear of the plane rose up in a sudden upheaval as the front plowed into the ice. There weren't any straps to hold her in place. The force of the crash launched her forward like a car crash victim plunging through their own windshield.

Visually, the world stopped making any sense. Everything became a blur of perfect blue sky, even bluer sea, and the white-blue ice that covered the land. She was spinning and flailing through the air, completely out of control. It was impossible to know which direction was up or down at any given moment. She couldn't orient herself, couldn't think, couldn't do anything but submit to the forces of physics.

A blow like the business end of a freight train struck Denise on the thigh and she whipped around in the other direction so hard that she thought her head was going to twist off. For a single, incoherent moment, she thought the flyrannosaurus had snatched her out of the air with one of its claws and was carrying her away. Another blow hit her on the back and sent her tumbling, and she realized what had happened.

She'd hit the water and skipped like a stone. Going as fast as she was, the impact was like falling out of a tree onto concrete. Another blow sent her bouncing and crashing and sluicing across the surface of the water in a shower of stinging, freezing droplets.

Her entire world was spinning when the pain hit her. It was so intense and so sudden that she tried to scream, and then the pain was inside her, too. The sensation was like taking a sudden slap to the face, but it was all over her entire body. At first, she didn't even realize that she was underwater.

She'd slowed enough that she hadn't skipped on her last impact with the water. She'd gone under in a sudden, savage plunge. The pain covering her entire body was from the sudden, intense cold of the water.

She fought to draw breath, but she only sucked down a lungful of the freezing water. Denise gagged at the sudden stabbing pain in her throat and lungs, but all she accomplished was swallowing more water. Her lungs burned. Everything hurt. All her senses were disoriented and scrambled.

She was going to die down here.

NINETEEN
BOARDING PARTY

Denise thrashed against the cold, fighting it like she was thrashing against a nightmare in her sleep. Her legs kicked out, and her arms grasped for something, anything she could grab onto. More than anything else, she needed air.

She kicked out, trying to breach the surface. Then, she saw a flash of light down by her feet. And then another. It was the burst of an anti-aircraft shell. She was upside down in the water, her head pointed down toward the seabed.

Hands clawing out, she paddled and kicked her way toward those flashes. Her soaked clothing felt like it weighed a thousand tons, dragging her down and resisting her every movement. Her boots felt like shackles tethering her to the sandy seafloor below.

The initial, furious pain from the cold had faded somewhat, mellowing into a sort of burning sensation that covered her entire body. In another five minutes out in this water, she'd be completely numb. In fifteen, she'd probably be dead. Actually, scratch that. If she didn't get some air in the next few seconds, it wouldn't take any fifteen minutes for her to die.

Her head breached the surface of the water, and she wretched up some seawater. Taking big, gasping breaths, she flipped her hair out of her eyes and looked around. She was maybe two hundred yards from the cruiser and considerably further from the shore and Delambre Station. There was no way she could make it back to the docks. Even if she could, there was nothing for her back there.

The research station itself was burnt rubble. There was no way to get warm or dry. Cornelia and Metrodora might find her blue corpse covered in ice eventually, assuming the flyrannosaurus didn't fly back and eat her.

Instead, she started swimming toward the cruiser. There were some nets over the side leading down to the water so the assault troops could climb down into the now absent transport boats. No one had dragged the nets back aboard the ship. None of the sailors thought anyone was stupid enough to make a swim for the nets to try to board them.

She looked back to try to see the plane. Aside from a few pieces of debris floating on the surface, there was nothing left. It had slid off the ice and promptly sunk, taking Fletch with it down to the bottom. Denise wished there was something she could have down for him, but he'd taken an entire blast of shrapnel. He'd been dead even before the plane hit the water. Even if he hadn't been, Denise sure couldn't do anything for him now. If she tried to dive beneath the surface of the water a second time, she didn't think there was a good chance that she'd make it to the surface again.

Her jacket was slowing her down. It was waterlogged and heavy, only serving to drag her down after Fletch and the airplane. She stopped paddling for a moment and nearly sank beneath the water again as she ripped the jacket off and threw it away.

The water was almost starting to feel warm compared to the air. The thin sheen of water on her face and in her hair wanted to frost over in the air. Denise knew she had to keep moving. If the water was actually starting to feel vaguely comforting, it meant her body was already unable to cope with the cold, and her internal temperature was plummeting.

She swam toward the netting on the side of the cruiser, her arms and leads growing leaden as she moved. Even though she was determined to keep moving, each stroke was harder than the last. Denise had already lost the ability to feel her fingers, and a shark could have swum past and eaten her feet off, and she wouldn't even know. She knew that her soggy boots were only slowing her down as she moved, but she didn't think she'd be able to tread water and take them off at the same time.

As she reached the side of the cruiser, she could hear thumping and small arms fire from overhead. Metal scrapped and scratched as the flyrannosaurus tore after the crew, trying to dig them out of hatchways and other hidey-holes. They couldn't use the big guns or the flak cannons on something that had landed on their ship. They didn't have anything designed for this kind of situation. Screams drifted down from above. It didn't sound like the ship's crew was doing any better in defending themselves against the monster than the soldiers on the ice had. Anyone below decks would be relatively safe, but not everyone had made it down there before the creature landed.

Denise reached out and clutched the netting dangling from the side of the ship. Her hands didn't want to grasp anything. She could bend them around the ropes, but it was hard to pump the strength into them required to actually get a grip. It was like trying to climb a ladder with flippers.

She stuck her arm through one of the gaps in the netting all the way to her elbow and hauled herself up a little bit that way. Her feet scrabbled at the base of the netting and finally found some purchase on the ropes. Flailing her other arm upward, she hooked it through the next section of netting and managed to pull herself most of the way out of the water.

Her entire body shuddered. The cold breath of Antarctic air hit her all at once. The wind felt like frozen steel scalpels raking across her flesh, slicing it off a layer at a time. Water poured from her clothing and dribbled back down into the sea as she managed to lift herself up a little higher. All the liquid that had soaked into her remaining clothes felt like it weighed a ton. It felt like a hand was hanging onto the back of her shirt and gently but steadily trying to pull her back into the water.

She clung to the ropes for a moment, unable to control the quivering in her limbs. Denise didn't have a plan anymore. The plane was destroyed, and Fletch was dead. Her Nitro Express was somewhere at the bottom of the harbor, lost during the crash. She had no way to defend herself, and no way to get back to shore.

However, she knew she didn't want to go back into the water. That meant death. If she wanted to live, she could haul herself up onto the ship. There were no other options. There was no other plan. She could keep climbing and maybe survive. Maybe. Or she could die right here and now.

Denise reached up again and pulled herself a little higher. Her breath came in ragged, painful gasps, and she couldn't stop her teeth from chattering. Just being exposed to the chill air was still shockingly painful. It wasn't quite cold enough for the saltwater on her body to freeze into a sheen of ice, but it was still trying its damnedest.

She kept most of her weight on her arms as she moved upward, hooking her elbows through the netting because she didn't trust her hands to grip properly. Her feet weren't any more reliable. In order to make sure they were secured on the netting, she had to look down and inspect them. It was like trying to control her body via remote control.

Finally, she reached the railing over the side of the cruiser's deck. Denise flopped over the rail and laid on the deck for a moment. Her body wanted to curl into as tight a ball as possible and lay still, but she knew that wouldn't do any good.

A closed hatch stood in front of her. She looked to the right. The flyrannosaurus stood in front of one of the big guns, its claws wedged through an opening where it had torn the crew door off. There were shouts and screams from inside as the creature tried to fish out some of the sailors trapped inside.

Denise pulled herself to her feet with what felt like a Herculean shown of strength. She took a step forward and ended up stumbling into the bulkhead next to the door. Using the wall to support herself, she flopped sideways and grabbed onto the wheel to unseal the door. Her fingers still didn't want to cooperate, so she dug in with the heels of her palms and forced the wheel to turn a few degrees at a time until it came open.

One of the ship's smokestacks had been toppled, and a couple of small fires had started near the cruiser's bridge. Denise knew she wouldn't be able to stay in here for long, but she needed to get inside. If the cold didn't get her, the flyrannosaurus would eventually.

The door creaked upon, and she fell inside. Denise shoved herself back up onto her knees and looked around. There were red emergency lights flashing overhead, but no people anywhere. Most of the crew was probably below decks or dead.

There were, however, parkas and cold weather gear hanging on pegs near the door, waiting for the crewmembers forced to work out on the deck. Denise flapped at her own soaked clothing with her nearly useless hands and ripped off the waterlogged items. She tossed them aside and grabbed a complete set of gear from off the racks.

She threw on a jacket with the name "Langelaan" stitched onto the front. With some effort, she managed to pull a pair of insulated boots onto her feet. All the clothes were a couple sizes too big for her, but she didn't care. She was dry again, and that was all that really mattered.

Warming up wasn't an entirely pleasant experience, though. The rush of blood back into her hands and feet stung as her body tried to recover from being dunked in the cold, cold sea. The sensation of feeling coming back into her extremities was a sort of ugly ache.

After a few minutes, she was able to stop shaking quite so badly, though. Still a little wobbly, she took a few steps down the hallway and looked around. Outside, she could hear grinding metal as the flyrannosaurus stomped its way across the deck. Every once in a while, a gunshot would ring out, sometimes followed by shouting in French. Other times, there was screaming.

In some ways, her original plan was a roaring success. The losses to equipment and crew meant that Dagenais couldn't keep the cruiser anchored here. The damage was too great. Even if his men managed to kill the monster, he would have to take the cruiser back to the nearest dry docks for repairs and restocking. Mission accomplished for Denise.

The problem was, she never intended to find herself aboard the cruiser while the creature was attacking. She was supposed to be waiting for the rescue ship to arrive while Fletch flew back and got Cornelia and Metrodora. Now she was alone and unarmed on a ship with the monster, and a bunch of crew members who wouldn't be any too happy to meet the woman who had lured the creature to their vessel.

There was a loud squealing noise, and then something outside exploded. Denise was pretty sure that someone had just failed in an attempt to kill the monster, and they'd probably paid for it with their lives.

She moved down the hallway, walking in an awkward limp from her earlier impact with the water after the crash. There hadn't been enough time to form a bruise yet, but Denise knew that her thigh and most of her back was going to be an ugly shade of purple in a few hours.

That was assuming she lived that long, though. She needed to find a way off the cruiser. Eventually, the crew would find her here. The only reason they hadn't already was because they had other, bigger concerns to deal with right now. Outside, she could hear the pop of rifles followed by more shouting. Once the crew did find her, she wouldn't last too long. Battered as she was, she couldn't do much against a press of sailors. As it was, she probably couldn't win a brawl with a seventh grader.

Half-leaning against the wall she came to a staircase. She could go up, which would take her up to the bridge, or she could go down below decks. She wasn't sure there was much point in going up. The bridge seemed to be on fire.

There was a sign on the side of the wall with arrows pointing up and down. She couldn't read most of the labels because they were all in French. There was one she could actually puzzle out just fine, though. *Radio.*

She started down the stairs. If she could reach the radio equipment, she could at least contact Cornelia and Metrodora back at the station and tell them what had happened. She limped down the stairs as something huge struck the deck overhead. The impact was followed by the screech of metal and the boom of a couple of grenades. The flyrannosaurus screeched like a scalded cat, and then there was more shouting and screaming.

Denise didn't think the creature could destroy the entire cruiser. The ship was made of tons and tons of armored steel. One forty-foot insect couldn't wreck the whole ship just by itself. It couldn't seem to burrow through the reinforced decks or the hull, even if it could rip off doors and equipment.

However, just because the creature by itself couldn't destroy the ship didn't mean the cruiser wasn't in serious danger. If no one stopped the fire in the bridge relatively soon, it could spread to the rest of the ship and maybe even the ammo stocks or the fuel storage. If the flames reached either of those areas, the damage would be catastrophic.

She pushed down the stairs one level and followed the signs pointing her toward the radio room. She turned a corner and saw figures moving down the narrow hallway toward her. Denise ducked back into the opposite hallway and tucked herself into a narrow space between some lockers.

The sailors had seen her, but she didn't hear any shouted orders or feet pounding toward her. She realized that they didn't know who she was. All they saw was the outline of another human being in a military jacket before she disappeared. They didn't see enough for them to register that she didn't belong here.

A minute later, they walked down the other hallway, and Denise could see them hustling away. They were each holding what appeared to be a propane tank, probably scavenged from the kitchen. No doubt they were taking the canisters up to the surface in some kind of scheme to blow the creature up, probably by luring it over the propane tanks and then igniting them. Not a bad idea. It might even work.

A modern military vessel like this didn't really have defenses against something landing directly on its deck. Cruisers like this were supposed to lob shells at other ships from miles away and help protect the massive battleships. The days when pirates might swing aboard and attack the crew with drawn cutlasses were long gone. Even if they hadn't been, nothing could have prepared the sailors here for dinosaur-sized pirates that could spray acidic digestive juices and shrug off weapons fire from anything smaller than a howitzer. The crew was doing its best to improvise, just like her.

For now, Denise knew that she needed to get in touch with the others at Merovée Station. They were still expecting Fletch to fly back and pick them up. They needed to know that the plan had changed. Then, she needed to find a way to get off this ship before the crew found her or the situation deteriorated even further.

She could smell smoke in the air now. It was an unpleasant chemical odor, the smell of burning paint peeling off the walls, melting equipment, and spilled fuel. The air increasingly smelled like the inside of a truck engine. That wasn't a good sign. Some of the crew must be trying to extinguish the flames, but it couldn't be easy with the flyrannosaurus picking off anyone who popped their heads above deck at the wrong moment. There was a decent chance that the ship's command structure was pretty scrambled as they took casualties, too. That would only slow down efforts to issue commands and deal with the situation.

Denise crept down the hallway and spotted the door to the radio room. There was a figure in front of the equipment, his back to the entrance. He was speaking rapidly in French into one of the handsets. There were multiple banks of equipment, and voices came through several receivers, all speaking over each other.

She recognized the voice of the man speaking into the handset, though. She'd been hearing it all afternoon. It was Colonel Ozias Dagenais.

If she hadn't heard his voice, Denise probably wouldn't have recognized him. She'd seen pictures of him in his office, but he didn't look like the man in those photographs anymore. His face was puckered with burns that hadn't healed very well, and a series of gashes that Denise recognized as claw marks ran down the side of his cheeks.

Denise had known that he'd made it out of Merovée Station when the security protocols broke down, but evidently he hadn't made it out whole. There wasn't much resemblance between the scarred and burned man in front of her and the man from the pictures in that office.

He must have sensed her presence standing behind him. Dagenais stopped speaking into the radio and turned around, his eyes popping open when he saw her. He reached for the pistol holstered at his hip.

Denise had already picked up a stone paperweight off a pile of messages, though. By the time that flicker of recognition appeared in the colonel's eyes, the paperweight was already clutched in an angry fist above Denise's head.

"Surprise, jackass," she said, bringing the heavy paperweight down on the side of the man's head. There was an unpleasant sound, and Dagenais went down with a thud. Denise bent down, ready to bash his brains out in case he was still conscious and trying to reach for his pistol. He was out cold, though.

Denise tossed the paperweight to the side and grabbed the man's pistol out of its holster. She pointed the gun downward at Dagenais, feeling the smooth, hard metal in her grip. Her finger moved toward the trigger before stopping.

A gunshot from here in the interior of the ship might bring unwanted attention. Denise still had to avoid the rest of the ship's crew as best she could. Pulling the trigger now might send that group with the propane tanks running. Better to just do what she needed to do and get out of here.

At least, that was what she told herself. Dagenais had already caused her untold problems, but he was passed out and defenseless at her feet. He wasn't going anywhere. Murdering sonofabitch or not, Denise didn't feel right shooting an unconscious man from point-blank range. Leaving him behind while his ship fell to pieces around him? She could deal with that. Someone might very well yet come by and drag Dagenais to safety. It was more of a chance than he'd given to the crew of the *Sulaco*.

She stepped over his prostrate body and stepped over to the radio equipment. After a bit of fiddling, she found the frequency for Merovée Station. "Cornelia? Metrodora? Are you there? This is Denise."

There was a pause, and then a tinny version of Cornelia's voice came over the airwaves. "Denise? Where are you broadcasting from? What's going on?"

"Listen. There's been a change of plans. I'm on the French cruiser right now."

"You're *what*?"

"Things didn't work out the way we planned. Fletch is dead, and the plane is wrecked."

"Are you alright?"

"For now, yeah. I don't have a lot of time to explain. The area around Delambre Station has been cleared. There's not much left except for rubble, but you can get to the coast safely now. The big problem is going to be the fly creature. It's attacking the ship. Call our rescue party. Tell them to pick you up in a few hours. The French cruiser is either going to have to retreat or it'll be sunk by then. The monster will probably have gone back to its cave, and you should have a straight shot to whatever's left of the docks by then. Take the motor sledges and get back to the coast after that. It'll be your best chance to get picked up safely."

"The creature might actually sink the ship? Denise, what about you? You're on that ship. What the hell are you going to do if it goes down?"

"I'll think of something," Denise said.

A loud warning siren had started to wail throughout the cruiser, threatening to drown out her response to Cornelia. Cornelia said something else, but it was difficult to hear her over the klaxon's angry caws. Brisk French started to pour out of the speaker system, issuing orders to whoever was still alive to follow them.

Denise set the handset down. Now all she needed to do was think of some way to avoid getting killed in the next few minutes.

TWENTY
SWAT

Denise backtracked until she found the stairs again. She needed to get the hell off this ship and fast. The burning smell was only growing stronger. If she could just get to one of the lifeboats, she could row her way back to shore and wait for the rescue ship to pick her up. Every minute she stayed on the cruiser was another chance for her to be discovered. The fact that she hadn't been yet was partly because the crew's attention was spread pretty thin already and partly because they weren't expecting her here. As far as anyone but Dagenais knew, she'd probably died with Fletch when their plane went down, and no one had given it a second thought since.

She could hear more loud banging noises from overhead. It sounded like she was in a bunker that was being bombed. Some of the clangs and thuds and screeches echoed across the entire ship, sending rumbles through the floor plating.

The air was growing warmer as Denise angled her way back toward the staircase she'd come down. Under other circumstances, the heat would have been greatly appreciated. However, as she turned the corner, she saw that the entire stairwell was awash in flame. Obviously, no one had been able to control the fire in the bridge, and it had only spread downward. The ship's entire command center was completely screwed.

Denise turned around and went back around the hallway. There were other places she could get back up to the deck. She took off toward the front of the ship, in the direction where she'd seen the sailors with the propane tanks headed. They must have been trying to get up to the main deck near where the flyrannosaurus was. That meant there had to be an exit somewhere up ahead. Now all she had to do was find a stairwell that wasn't blocked off or guarded by sailors.

She stayed close to the wall as she moved. That was partly so she could lean against it a little to help support herself and partly so she'd be able to duck into some other corridor if she had too.

Ahead of her, two sailors dashed down an intersecting hallway without giving her a second glance. The red emergency lights were working to her favor. If people saw her out of the corner of their eye or from a distance, she was just another figure in a familiar style of jacket. Even so, she held the pistol she'd taken from Dagenais tight in her hand.

Ahead of her, part of the ceiling had been blasted open. A severed arm with a tattoo on the bicep lay untended on the floor. Something had exploded up on the deck directly above her. Maybe it had been a cluster of propane tanks. Denise could see a sliver of perfect blue sky overhead. Then something loomed past and blocked her view of the sky for a second. Denise caught a glimpse of iridescent black armor and a pair of bulging eyes.

Then, a claw slammed against the tear in the ship's armor and tried to peel it back. A long, pointed talon slipped through the gap and reached for her. Denise scurried out of the way and continued down the hallway. Behind her, the claw withdrew, but she could hear the monster stomping across the surface directly above her.

Continuing forward, she found a closed door. Maybe it could lead up to the surface and away from the creature. If she could just get to the lifeboats, then maybe she'd be able to escape. She unlatched the door and pushed it open.

The door didn't lead outside. It led to the ship's forward storage area. Normally, there would have been a small freight platform to quickly raise and lower supplies from the surface down into the belly of the ship. Food, shells, medical equipment, it would all be brought down the shaft and offloaded here so it could be dispersed to the proper part of the ship.

However, the freight platform had collapsed down into the hold. There was a tangle of thick cables and clasps from the collapsed elevator. In addition, the stacks of supplies had been tossed about and flattened. What was worse, the fire had started to spread down here as well. Even as Denise watched, some flaming debris fell down from the upper decks and landed on a crate full of rations, which began to smolder and blacken. Soon, little tendrils of flame were beginning to lap at the wood.

The fires weren't too intense down here yet. Only a small section of the hold currently had open flames actively chewing through the stacked items. Denise would have turned around tried to find another route to the upper decks but for one thing amidst the debris.

There was a small pontoon boat lying on the floor. Calling it a "boat" was probably giving it too much credit. The little platform barely qualified as a raft. It was just a simple, collapsible platform attached to a couple of runners and a small engine. Most likely, it was some sort of maintenance craft, something they'd send out to inspect the ship's outer hull once a month and make sure there wasn't any corrosion or buckling. It had one small seat and a rudder.

Perfect. If she could just drag it out of here and get it on the water, she'd have a ride back to shore. Then, all she had to do was lay low and avoid being eaten until the flyrannosaurus retreated to its den. That wasn't necessarily an easy task, but she'd worry about it when she got to it. The mere fact that she was aboard the French cruiser right now was a pretty clear indication that a key part of her original plan had gone straight down the crapper. She was just going to have to riff together the last part of her plan on the fly and hope it worked.

Ideally, she would have also come up with some way to kill the damn monster rather than allowing it to escape back to its lair. She was a professional monster hunter, after all. That's what she was supposed to do.

This time, there was nothing she could do about the situation, though. She had a pistol, but that wasn't going to do anything against the creature's armor. Even if she had her elephant gun, the creature had the fortitude of a tank. The best she could do was hope that it would leave her alone long enough for the rescue ship to arrive.

Once they reached the adult stage of their lives, flies typically didn't survive for very long. She could only hope that the same was true of these things. Even if it could theoretically live for the next hundred years, she wasn't sure it would be a problem for too much longer. Antarctica couldn't support these things for too long if they were just left alone. Eventually, they would run out of food if they were just left alone. The maggots. The bug men. The flyrannosaurus itself. They'd starve so long as no one blundered into their territory for a while. Then there would just be husks and corpses.

Right now, that was the best Denise could hope for. If she'd known what she was going up against down here, she would have asked the Squires to give her a warship of her own. Not that the cruiser the French had given Dagenais seemed to be doing him much good. The monster could probably pry the turret off a tank and get to anyone inside. The creature was too fast and mobile to hit with anything big enough to actually kill it.

If she had time to execute the perfect plan, she would need to find a way to immobilize the monster first. Essentially, she'd need a giant sheet of fly paper. Once it was pinned to a single location, it would be comparatively easy to kill. Dousing it with gasoline and tossing a match at it would probably do the trick just as well as hitting it with one of the cruiser's six-inch guns. The damn thing couldn't be invincible.

Denise crept down the stairs that led deeper into the cruiser's storage depository. Sunlight trickled down from the hole where the freight elevator had crashed down. The cold light battled with the flashing emergency lights and billowing smoke inside the storage area. She looked up as a shadow passed by overhead. The flyrannosaurus moved past the edge of the cargo shaft, temporarily blocking out the light from above. It had the crushed remains of a sailor in one of its claws. There wasn't much left of the man.

She moved down the stairs as quietly as possible. The flyrannosaurus was well above her. She didn't think it could reach down and grab her from the upper deck, but that didn't mean it wouldn't spray a gob of digestive fluids at her, if given the chance. So far, it either hadn't noticed her or was more interested in easier prey.

Cringing as she moved down the stairs, Denise did her best to ignore the pain shooting down her leg each time she put all of her weight on it. The leg wasn't broken. She never would have been able to clamber up the netting and board the cruiser if she'd broken it. Slamming into the water after the plane crash had done a number on it, though. Now that she wasn't numb all over anymore, she was really starting to feel it.

If the plane had crashed into the sea at full speed, she probably wouldn't have survived. That shrapnel burst that killed Fletch had also taken out their engine and torn up their wings, though. They'd bled a lot of speed before that ice flow launched her into the air.

She was lucky to have lived through the crash, which only made her feel worse about Fletch. She and the Squires hadn't told anyone the real reason why they'd been brought down here. That made her at least partially responsible for the events that followed, didn't it? Denise wasn't sure it would have made a difference in the end, but Fletch and Poole and the others hadn't known the risks going in, and that seemed catastrophically unfair. This place had killed everyone from the *Sulaco*.

No. She corrected herself. Dagenais had killed everyone. The job was relatively safe until he showed up. She hadn't known the full list of dangers either, and she would have left once they became clear. Then Dagenais showed up and killed most of the people she brought with her and forced the remainder right into the arms of the monsters. If it were up to her, maybe she couldn't have saved the men the flyrannosaurus carried off when it first attacked the snow tractor, but everyone else would have still been alive.

Denise almost regretted not shooting Dagenais back in the radio room. Murdering him in cold blood wouldn't have done any of the others a lick of good, though. When he sailed back to France, there would be authorities who had heard her side of the story. They'd either hear it in private, or if they didn't want to listen, they'd hear it in the papers. When Dagenais arrived, he'd have to explain not only why he'd committed a small-scale atrocity but why he'd completely failed in his mission and nearly lost an armored cruiser. Given the sort of people Dagenais probably reported to, the latter would probably be more damning. He'd have hell to pay in due course. Maybe it wouldn't be justice exactly, but neither was shooting him in the head while he was passed out on the floor.

She still kind of wished she'd shot him, though.

Denise reached the bottom of the staircase and hobbled over toward the little pontoon boat. Scuttling over, she tugged at it, trying to free it from some of the debris that had collapsed on top of one corner. Keeping an eye toward the ceiling, she glanced up every time she heard the creature shifting around above her. The hole above her was large enough for the monster to fit inside, if it really wanted to. Attracting the beast's attention was the last thing she needed right now.

The pontoon boat sat near the remains of the collapsed elevator. There was a Gordian knot of metal cables, clasps, spilled hydraulic fluid, and twisted metal. Denise pushed some of the debris aside to get better access to the pontoon boat. The fire was starting to spread down here too, and she didn't have much time.

There was a waterproof tarp caught on the side of the boat. She wrapped her hands around the tarp and pulled it free. Tossing the bunched material aside, she started dragging the little craft aside. It was heavier than it looked, and it made an awful scraping noise as she tried to pull it behind her.

Cringing, she looked up. The flyrannosaurus must have stomped away from the edge of the freight shaft, some other unfortunate soul having caught its attention. She knew she only had so much time, though. The ship was much quieter than it had been when she first dragged herself aboard. There was very little gunfire still popping from above decks. The creature hadn't eaten everyone. A ship like this might have hundreds of people aboard. It had killed almost everyone who was caught out in the open or who tried to fight it on its own terms, though. The survivors were probably lurking in doorways, firing, and retreating as the monster drew close.

In place of gunfire, the sound of open flames was fairly loud now. Denise didn't know just how far the fire had spread, but she already knew that the ship's bridge was a loss. When the flyrannosaurus knocked down part of the cruiser's smokestack, it must have spread burning material far and wide, though. Most of the crew was probably trying to fight the blazes at this point, and the sailors still firing at the monster were just trying to distract it from the crews with hoses.

Given that no one had even come to deal with the fire spreading in the freight shaft here, Denise was guessing they were spread pretty thin.

That was fine by her. It would make it easier for her to drag the little pontoon boat away and scuttle back to shore.

"You," a voice bellowed from behind her.

Denise spun around. Colonel Dagenais had moved down the stairs and into the freight shaft behind her. He had a reddening handkerchief pressed to the side of his head where she'd brained him. His scarred face was contorted into an ugly grimace.

Denise dropped her grip on the side of the pontoon boat and reached for the pistol she'd taken. It was too late, though. Dagenais came at her with a long knife he'd grabbed from somewhere. He slashed at her, forcing her back.

Now, she was really regretting not shooting him earlier. Denise managed to yank out the military pistol, but Dagenais was practically on top of her. He'd waited until he was right behind her before announcing his presence, sneaking up while she was watching out for the monster above.

She lurched backward to avoid another slash from the knife, but her footing was uneven. Her foot came down on a can of beans that had spilled out of a nearby crate. The can squirted out from under her, and her feet went with it. Denise let out a squawk as she tumbled onto her butt.

Her finger involuntarily tightened on the pistol's trigger, and a bullet shot off into the corner and sparked off the bulkhead. The impact on her already aching limbs was enough to make her hiss in pain. She tried to lift the pistol up toward Dagenais, but he was too quick.

The blow to his head should have slowed him down quite a bit. It probably had. He almost certainly had a hell of a headache and a lingering dizziness. The problem was, he'd gotten the drop on Denise, and she was in no condition for a protracted fight, anyway.

Dagenais slapped the pistol away. It flew out of her weakened grip and clattered across the floor before landing in the fire on the far side of the crashed elevator. She threw out her other hand and grabbed onto the side of a crate in an attempt to pull herself up to her feet. She wouldn't stand a chance flat on her back.

The knife arced down and stabbed straight through the back of her hand, through her palm, and into the crate's wooden slats. It took a split second for the pain to reach Denise's brain, but when it did, it exploded inside her skull. Any coherent thoughts blew away like they'd been hit with a bomb. One second, she was trying to figure out if she could get that pistol back or if she should run or if she could reach Dagenais with a good kick to the ankles and bring him down. The next second, that was all gone. There was just a single foghorn blast of pain.

The knife had landed just behind her knuckles, between her middle and ring fingers. The flesh on the palm of her hand made a tent shape where the knife exited her skin. Blood welled up from the back of her hand and welled downward. Her first instinct was to try to pull her hand back, which her body did without thinking. That only tugged at the sliced flesh and muscle, making the pain even worse. She went very still instead.

"You've ruined everything," Dagenais said. His words were a little rubbery because he hadn't completely recovered from the blow to the head he'd received. "Everything. You never should have come here. You weren't here when the creatures first broke containment. If you had seen the things I saw that day, you never would have come. They never should have sent a second research team. They never should have allowed you here. They should have burned everything to the ground when we had the chance. Bringing people here only risked spreading the creatures to the rest of the world."

Dagenais loomed over her, leaning against the crate he'd pinned Denise to. He was breathing hard, and he had flecks of vomit on his lapels. Denise had clocked him good, and he was suffering the consequences for trying to do too much after a head wound.

Denise was barely paying attention to him, though. She was making a high-pitched keening noise in her throat, and she couldn't make herself stop. The knife in her hand quivered a little as something elsewhere on the ship exploded and sent shockwaves through the hull, and she had to bite down hard to stop herself from screaming.

Still panting, Dagenais seemed to be working up the strength to find something to finish her off with. Denise tried to reach over to the knife, but Dagenais simply reached over and applied some pressure to the blade. The sensation of the cold steel grinding another fraction of an inch through her nerves, carving through skin and muscle, sent her into a paroxysm of pain. She shrieked, and her boot heels tapped against the floor of the cargo hold.

Dagenais coughed and was nearly sick all over himself. It wasn't a sign that he was squeamish about the sight of the blood pouring out of her hand. That was just a common result of recent head trauma. He managed to tamp down his gorge and backed away a few feet.

"Stay right there," he said.

"You son of a bitch," Denise managed to spit out.

Dagenais didn't bother to respond. He clearly wasn't interested in explaining himself any further. What he'd done so far seemed justified in his eyes, and that was obviously good enough for him. He clearly wasn't interested in explaining himself any more to the likes of her.

He jumped as a gunshot rang out in the cargo hold. Another followed a split second later. The pistol that had fallen into the growing flames on the far side of the room. The ammunition was starting to cook off in the intense heat. Dagenais lurched behind a piece of crushed elevator equipment, shielding himself from the gunfire.

Denise flinched as each round shot off. The flinch sent another shiver of pain up from her hand, all the way up her arm, and through the entire rest of her body. There was no way to tell where any given bullet was going. She couldn't even see the pistol from where she was sitting. Any stray round could end up buried somewhere inside her body.

The pistol popped and rattled for another few seconds, making noises like giant pieces of popcorn on a hot skillet. The individual bullets shot off in random directions, slamming into burning supply crates and the metal bulkheads. One of them zipped past a few feet over Denise's head before hitting the wall with a ringing noise.

After a few seconds, the brass hail storm came to an end. There hadn't been that many rounds in the magazine in the first place. It didn't take them that long to blast apart once they reached the critical temperature.

When the pistol went silent, Dagenais stood up and grabbed a crowbar off the ground. The length of metal was probably down here to help pry open the crates of supplies. The colonel seemed to have a different use in mind.

Denise reached around and tried to tug at the knife pinning her to the crate. She was stuck on her back with the one arm extended and nailed down, leaving her like a turtle that had been flipped over. She was in a terrible position to defend herself, and it was also difficult to flop her free arm around to try to unpin herself.

Dagenais tapped the crowbar against the side of a crate like a man testing out a new car by kicking the tires a couple of times. He nodded to himself, apparently satisfied. Sweat was running down his brow now. It was springing up on Denise's skin, too.

The fire was spreading and driving the temperature up inside the freight shaft. Now, it was hot as a desert inside the metal room. As the fires spread, the walls would begin to heat up and turn the place into a convection oven. That was assuming that the fires didn't reach the stores of ammunition first and blow the entire cruiser out of the water. But some of the sweat steeping on Denise's face was cold fear.

She knew that Dagenais hadn't grabbed the crowbar to open any of the nearby crates. If he had a firearm, he would have finished her off by now. Maybe he could have pulled the knife out and done the deed with that, but he had to assume that she'd fight like a wildcat the second he freed her from the crate. With his head in its condition, he knew there was no guarantee he'd end up on top in that situation.

He was going to take the crowbar and beat her to death with it while her hand was still pinned. Simple as that.

TWENTY-ONE
SHIP OF THE DAMNED

Denise reached over and tried to get a grip on the knife handle again. If she could just pull it out, she'd be free and she could also defend herself a little. The knife didn't have the crowbar's reach, but it was better than laying there like a dog showing its belly. Her fingers touched the handle of the knife, and that alone sent searing pain through her hand.

Dagenais stepped closer, tapping the end of the crowbar against his hand as he walked. He didn't look happy about what he was going to do, but he didn't look like he was too torn up inside about it, either. It was just a necessary chore, like mowing the lawn.

The air was already dark with smoke. The emergency lighting shimmered through the swirling darkness. Suddenly, the room became much darker, though. Denise looked up.

Above them, the sunlight had been blotted out by a massive shape. The flyrannosaurus stared down at them with its bulging compound eyes. Its claws snaked over the edge of the gap and clacked on the metal.

Dagenais turned around and looked up. "*Merde.*" Still gripping the crowbar, he backpedaled toward the stairs as the beast shifted its bulk and started to climb down into the freight shaft with them, crawling down the side of the wall with surprising agility. The noise from the exploding pistol bullets must have attracted it back to the freight shaft.

Denise had stopped breathing. She stared up at the alien horror as it shimmied down inside the ship. When the creature reached the ground, it stood back up to its full height. From there, it only needed a few quick steps to cut Dagenais off from the staircase back up.

This was her chance. Denise peeled her eyes away from the scene playing out in front of her and turned her gaze back to the knife sticking out of her hand. Keeping her pinned hand as still as possible, she reached out again for the knife. Every little movement jangled the sliced nerve endings against the blade, and she had to keep her breath coming in sharp little gulps to keep from screaming.

She grabbed hold of the knife's handle and took a deep breath. This was going to hurt. There was no way around it. She knew she couldn't stay here, though. The flyrannosaurus wasn't coming toward her. It either hadn't spotted her yet, or it thought the colonel looked a little tastier. Even if the creature didn't spot her at all, she knew that the fires would eventually roast her. There was no help coming.

If Cornelia was here, she'd probably have some advice on how to deal with a situation like this. The best way to pull the knife out. How she should protect her hand after it was free. Denise didn't know a better way than to count to three, though.

One...two...*three!* She tore the knife free in one quick movement. It was like being unexpectedly hit with a brick. There was no transition period. All of a sudden, her entire world was just a bright flash of pain. Her senses couldn't even figure out what signals to send her brain for a second because everything was being jammed out by the overpowering sensation coming from her hand.

Somehow, she managed to avoid screaming. Instead, she made a low, guttural noise that seeped out from between her clenched teeth. She yanked her hand back and held it flat against her body. Blood seeped out and stained the military parka as she pulled herself up into a low crouch and peeked over the nearest crate.

Dagenais was moving backward through the debris around the crashed elevator, trying to always keep boxes and equipment between himself and the flyrannosaurus. The monster kicked aside debris as it moved toward him, backing him toward the rear wall. Between the monster and the crackling flames, there weren't many places he could go, and he was rapidly running out of options.

Denise slid to her feet and started toward the staircase upward. Never mind the pontoon boat. She couldn't drag it out of here unnoticed. With the creature preoccupied, she did have a chance to escape, though.

Then, she saw something. She looked back and forth between the monster and the stairwell. The monster. The stairwell. The monster. The stairwell.

She started moving toward the flyrannosaurus. She took slow, careful steps, trying to disturb as little of the debris as possible. She knew that she was only going to have a single chance at this.

More than anything else, she wanted to get the hell off this ship of the damned. Just take off up the stairs and find her way to a lifeboat. Leave Dagenais to his fate and run. It could be as simple as that.

But there was something she needed to do. She knew she wouldn't be safe just because she was off the ship. Once it was done with Dagenais, the creature would just crawl right back up to the surface, and eventually, it would fly back to shore. If she was caught out in the open, floating helplessly in a lifeboat, it would just swoop down on her, and that would be that.

There was another concern, though. Dagenais wasn't in the right about what he'd done, but Denise knew what he'd been trying to accomplish. If the maggots or the flyrannosaurus made it to civilization, the results would be cataclysmic. She didn't know just how far the thing could travel. She didn't think it could make it to another continent, but that was only a guess. Once it ran out of food here, what was stopping the creature from setting off in a new direction to search for more? She didn't know the monster's capabilities. Maybe it could reach the tip of South America or the Cape of Good Hope or Australia. Hopefully, the thing would just starve to death in due course, but there wouldn't be a place in the southern hemisphere that was completely safe until the creature was dead.

Slinking up behind the creature, she passed under its long, armored tail. Inching forward now, she ducked down and grabbed something from the remains of the ruined elevator.

Dagenais had realized he was in danger of being trapped, and he kept pushing his way blindly past the crates, trying to circle back around toward the stairs. The creature simply knocked supplies to the side as it moved, though. It was coming closer with every step.

Denise scurried up directly underneath the armored titan. She felt like the mouse about to bell the cat. The monster loomed over her, unable to see her because she was directly underneath it. Coming up directly next to one of the creature's enormous feet, she stopped.

She took the cable she'd grabbed from the downed elevator and threw it around the monster's ankle. She moved carefully, so the metal wire didn't actually come into contact with the creature's leg just yet. Then, she looped the end of the cable back around. The cable had a hook at the end with a clasp. She took the clasp and snapped it down on the cable, creating a sort of noose.

Just then, the creature pushed aside a final row of boxes and stood directly over Dagenais. The creature's proboscis twitched, and a massive glob of revolting fluid showered onto him. Screaming, Dagenais tried to thrash at the foul liquid, but everywhere it touched simply burned away more of his flesh.

It looked like someone had left a waxwork mannequin out in the heat. Flesh dribbled away in syrupy rivulets. Fatty tallow splashed onto the floor and sizzled like butter on a griddle. The scream filling the freight shaft was loud but short lived. Skin and meat slid off the colonel's skull as his clothing started to dissolve on his body. The man's skin bubbled and ran down his bones, and muscles and organs liquefied into a bloody slurry. His connective tissue started to fail, and pieces fell off the body as he flailed. An arm. His jaw. They plopped to the ground as the acid started to pit the bones. Dagenais split in half, sending his guts tumbling out onto the floor in an undifferentiated mass.

Denise knew her chance when she saw it. She darted out from underneath the monster and made for the stairs as silently as she could. Hopefully, the creature would slurp up what remained of Dagenais before it turned her attention to her.

No such luck. The flyrannosaurus noticed her before she made it twenty paces. She was standing next to the pontoon boat when it spun around to face her. The creature reared its head back, and Denise knew what was coming next.

She did the only thing she could. She snatched up the waterproof tarp she'd torn off the pontoon boat earlier and threw it over herself. A second later, the spray of acid hit her in a hot shower. It was like getting caught in a springtime storm in hell.

The odor nearly doubled her over. It made her eyes water and her throat burn. Breathing too much of it would probably burn a hole in her lungs. Coughing and gagging, she threw the tarp to the side. Its waterproof surface had repelled the spray of gunk for a few precious seconds, but now it was melting like a slice of cheese on a hot sandwich.

Reaching the stairs, she started climbing as fast as she could. Her leg ached where she'd hit the water earlier, but her hand screamed each time she jostled it. Her face scrunched itself up into a pained snarl as she moved up the steps as quickly as she could.

The flyrannosaurus took several steps, moving closer to blast another sheet of digestive fluid at her. It took one last step, and then the cable she'd tied around its leg snapped taught. Stumbling, the creature turned its head to better angle its compound eyes down at its feet. Perplexed, it jerked at the cable, but it didn't come loose.

That cable was meant to support a metal platform and tons of equipment at a time. If the creature had any significant intelligence, it would simply reach down and pluck the clasp away. Instead, it started to flail at the cable, tugging and kicking with its leg as it tried to free itself. The cable jerked and danced, but it didn't snap.

Denise lunged up the remaining steps and threw herself into the empty corridor as another spray of acid hit the stairwell. Picking herself up, she took one last glance back down into the freight shaft. The flyrannosaurus was still trying to kick its way free of the cable. Eventually, the impromptu manacle might snap, but it would probably take a while. Until then, the creature didn't have enough slack to climb back up onto the upper decks. It was trapped down in the shaft. And with that fire spreading…

Limping down the corridor, Denise took the first set of stairs she could find that led upward. She pushed open a door and found herself out in the smoky sunlight. The temperature outside, hovering around freezing an hour ago, had risen substantially in the vicinity around the cruiser. The fires were everywhere now. There were still a few crew members trying to douse them, but the flames were only climbing higher and higher, spreading further and further. Originally, it would have been easy to contain the blaze, but everyone had been too busy just trying to survive the monster's initial attack that the situation had grown completely out of control.

Shuffling toward the railings, Denise saw that there were already a number of lifeboats missing from their moorings. A couple more had been damaged in the creature's assault. There were still some that were useable, though. Moving like one of the undead creatures haunting the mainland, Denise shambled her way over to the nearest lifeboat. Pulling herself inside, she pulled the winch and lowered the boat down into the water.

The lifeboat had a small motor and a cache of rations. She was mostly glad for the motor. If she had to row with a pair of oars, her arms might have fallen off at this point. As she cranked the motor, she heard another lifeboat buzz closer.

A voice shouted at her in French. She looked up and found herself looking down the barrel of a rifle. There were six French sailors in the boat, all of them covered with soot and grime. One of them had his arm in an improvised sling. The man with the gun shouted at her again and jabbed the rifle in her general direction.

Goddammit.

The man with the sling apparently spoke English. "You are one of the quarantined individuals we have been looking for." There was a brief but furious discussion inside the other lifeboat. The man with the rifle jabbed at her again and said something to the man with the sling. None of the others had a gun. They were trying to decide whether or not to shoot her on the spot.

Finally, the man with the sling spoke again. "You are now our prisoner. Two of our men will board your boat and steer it to shore with us. Do not attempt to escape, or you will be shot."

As promised, to sailors transferred themselves over to Denise's boat. They cranked the motor to life and steered the boat after their companions as they sent the little vessels toward shore.

Denise sat still and grimaced as they bounced along the waves. Her hand still hurt, and her leg grumbled each time she rocked in her seat over a new wave. She didn't know what the sailors were going to do with her. Dagenais wasn't around to order them to kill her. The fact that they hadn't executed her on the spot was another good sign. They weren't sure what they were supposed to do with her, so they were going to wait until they found a more senior officer to tell them what to do. Depending on just how onboard the rest of the team was with Dagenais's leadership, that could either go badly or very badly. At the very least, she suspected there was a good chance she'd disappear into a French military prison in some backwater part of their territories.

There were more lifeboats already sitting on the shore. They'd pulled in next to the abandoned landing craft. The boat ahead of her pulled up to the shore and beached itself on a narrow strip of sand. Her boat slowed and puttered in next to its companion a few seconds later.

One of the sailors pushed her out of the boat, and she stumbled onto the shore. The sailor with the rifle was already waiting, as was the man with the sling.

Even from here, Denise could feel a trace of heat from the flaming ship. She turned around looked at the floating pyre. More lifeboats were streaming away from the cruiser. Fire danced from bow to stern. Even from here, it was obvious that the vessel was a complete loss. There was no sign of the flyrannosaurus. It must still be shackled down in the freight shaft. Whether it was alive or dead was up for question, though.

Then, the question answered itself. The fire must have finally breached one of the ammunition storage chambers. There was a flash like a bolt from heaven, and the entire ship annihilated itself in a single instant. The colossal fireball shot into the sky and spread outward. It looked like the end of the world peering over the horizon.

A second later, the shockwave hit the beach. Denise covered her ears against the gigantic roar as sand and water pelted her. A wave crested on the water and rocked the lifeboats that hadn't yet reached the shore as bits of flaming metal and debris rained down into the harbor. After a few moments, the sky stopped belching debris, and the hot glow in the distance faded. There was no sign left of the cruiser.

Denise watched the entire scene with weary eyes. She'd done it. She'd killed the creature. There wasn't any guarantee it would do her any good now, though. That would all depend on what the sailors decided to do with her.

Her hand still hurt. Really, everything hurt. All she wanted to do now was sit down on the sand and wait for her fate to be decided. She couldn't fight the sailors. They had the only gun, and there would be more of them arriving in the next few minutes. Even if she could run away from the little group that had captured her, which was unlikely given that her leg was stiffening up, more sailors had already landed. She just didn't see the rest of them yet because she was down by the shore. The rest of them must have been up near the remains of Delambre Station.

Her captors weren't interested in letting her sit around, though. The one with the rifle poked at her, prodding her up the shore in the direction of the shelled rubble. She imagined that eventually, the group was going to head out on a mass exodus toward Merovée Station. It was the only shelter for miles, and when the katabatic winds started howling again, they would need it. She figured there was a decent chance they wouldn't bother to bring her along for that trip, though. It was even money that she'd be left right here with a bullet in her skull so they could overtake the other station unencumbered.

They crested the slight slope up to the remains of the station. A conversation buzzed around Denise in French. She couldn't understand any of the words, but it clearly wasn't happy. The rifle was jabbed in her direction a couple of more times to emphasize a particularly vehement point.

"Good afternoon, gentlemen," a female voice said. Denise's head whipped up.

Cornelia stood near some of the battered ruins, a scratched-up elephant gun pointed casually in the sailors' direction. Metrodora stood next to her, a pistol in her hand as she watched the sailors who had already landed ashore. A couple of motor sledges sat nearby.

"Look what I found in the rubble," Cornelia said, raising the elephant gun a little. "Had to dig it out, but it still works fine. Metrodora and I decided to come over and visit after you called us on the radio. Figured that maybe we could lend a hand. Our ride should get here in a couple of hours, and then we can go back home."

Cornelia poked her elephant gun in the direction of the French soldiers. Metrodora had her pistol trained squarely on the man aiming at Denise. The sailor holding Denise at gunpoint cursed.

Denise smiled as the sailors raised their hands in surrender. The one with the rifle threw his weapon down on the ground, and the group stomped off to join the rest of their comrades in the makeshift POW camp. Cornelia stepped over, picked the rifle up, and tossed it on a pile of discarded weapons.

Apparently, they'd been capturing each boatload of soldiers as they arrived. Metrodora kept her pistol pointed in the general direction of the captives. If all the sailors bum rushed their captors at once, they could probably wrestle the guns away, but a good number of them would get shot first. They already looked pretty demoralized. No one wanted to be one of the guys who got shot.

"Boy, am I ever glad to see you two," Denise said.

"We're glad to see you, too," Metrodora said. "Was the creature still aboard the ship?"

"Yeah. So was Dagenais. Or what was left of him."

"Good. I think, all things considered, I can arrange for the Squires to pay you a bonus for all this," Metrodora said.

"Just another day at the office."

TWENTY-TWO
THEY DIDN'T MAKE CARDS FOR THAT SORT OF THING

"Got any threes?" Denise asked.

"Go fish."

"Crap." Denise sat at her desk and drew another card. Enough time had passed that her hand was mostly healed up. There was a rather unpleasant-looking scar, but she could make a fist without flinching now.

She leaned back in her chair and rubbed her eyes. The same old Cape Town office remained as quiet and empty as before. The main difference was that she didn't have to worry about making the rent payment on time for a few months.

The proper reports had been given to the Squires. Merovée Station had been firebombed from the air, and the surviving French crew members had been sworn to secrecy. A couple of French generals had been fired in disgrace, and the wider world would never know exactly what happened down in Antarctica.

A French diplomat had informed Denise and Cornelia that they weren't allowed to speak of the situation either, or they might just meet with an unfortunate accident. Denise had kicked the man out of their office. Technically, she'd thrown him through the front window. She didn't react well to threats. She intended to take the man's advice, though. So far, she hadn't told anyone about the incident, and she intended to keep it that way.

Cornelia had a brand new employee of the month trophy on her desk. Given that Denise didn't have anyone else working with her, it hadn't exactly been a difficult choice over who to nominate. She'd bought Cornelia a couple of fancy dinners, too. The Squires had paid them well enough to splurge a little, and it seemed like a nice enough thanks-for-not-letting-me-get-killed-by-a-mob-of-sailors gift. They didn't really make cards for that sort of thing that she could just buy in the store.

Despite everything, Denise was pretty happy with life right now. When she discovered that she couldn't force herself to go sport hunting anymore, it turned her life upside down. She'd worked for a research company for a little while and at a game preserve, but neither option really worked out. Now though, now she was pretty sure she'd found her niche. So long as she could keep helping people with her skills, it could work out to be a pretty good life. She just needed to make sure that she didn't get roped into too many situations where things could spiral so far out of control. Surely it couldn't be that hard to stay out of trouble, could it?

There was a knock at the door. Denise and Cornelia both looked up. A second later, the door opened and a familiar figure walked in.

"Metrodora?" Denise asked.

"It's good to see you two again. How are you doing?" Metrodora's tone was a little odd. Her voice was flat and heavy, and she moved like she was carrying a heavy weight.

"We're fine. Are you alright? You don't look so good. Did the Squires send you?"

"No, the Squires kicked me out." Her voice quavered a little.

"What? Why? You told us they raised you basically from childhood. You're one of their experts down here."

She reached into the satchel bag she was carrying and pulled out a book. It was fairly hefty. Maybe three hundred and fifty pages. Big enough to smack someone upside the head with, and they would feel it. She laid the book down on the desk.

Denise looked at the cover. *Monsters of Sub-Saharan Africa: A Survival Guide*. The author was listed as Hendrik Meltebeke.

"Your book," Denise said.

"The Squires were able to trace it back to me. They bought up the entire print run, burned them, and cast me out. I was able to save a couple of copies, but the rest are ashes now. I thought you should have a copy. I ended up taking your advice. General locations only. No specifics."

"Oh, Metrodora. I'm sorry. That's awful, but…"

"But?"

"Now that you're free, I don't suppose you're looking for work? I think I know a place that could use a person like you," Denise said. She leaned back in her chair and smiled.

Bio: Jonah Buck wanted to learn eldritch knowledge and commune with pale, inhuman creatures that flit across the sunless landscape to terrorize the living, so he became an attorney in Oregon. His interests include history, professional stage magic, paleontology, and exotic poultry. He's written dozens of short stories, and his published novels include *Substratum*, *Carrion Safari*, *Carrion Shadows*, and the forthcoming *Cesspool*.

CHECK OUT OTHER GREAT DINOSAUR THRILLERS

WRITTEN IN STONE
by David Rhodes

Charles Dawson is trapped 100 million years in the past. Trying to survive from day to day in a world of dinosaurs he devises a plan to change his fate. As he begins to write messages in the soft mud of a nearby stream, he can only hope they will be found by someone who can stop his time travel. Professor Ron Fontana and Professor Ray Taggit, scientists with opposing views, each discover the fossilized messages. While attempting to save Charles, Professor Fontana, his daughter Lauren and their friend Danny are forced to join Taggit and his group of mercenaries. Taggit does not intend to rescue Charles Dawson, but to force Dawson to travel back in time to gather samples for Taggit's fame and fortune. As the two groups jump through time they find they must work together to make it back alive as this fast-paced thriller climaxes at the very moment the age of dinosaurs is ending.

HARD TIME
by Alex Laybourne

Rookie officer Peter Malone and his heavily armed team are sent on a deadly mission to extract a dangerous criminal from a classified prison world. A Kruger Correctional facility where only the hardest, most vicious criminals are sent to fend for themselves, never to return.

But when the team come face to face with ancient beasts from a lost world, their mission is changed. The new objective: Survive.

CHECK OUT OTHER GREAT
DINOSAUR THRILLERS

THE VALLEY
by **Rick Jones**

In a dystopian future, a self-contained valley in Argentina serves as the 'far arena' for those convicted of a crime. Inside the Valley: carnivorous dinosaurs generated from preserved DNA. The goal: cross the Valley to get to the Gates of Freedom. The chance of survival: no one has ever completed the journey. Convicted of crimes with little or no merit, Ben Peyton and others must battle their way across fields filled with the world's deadliest apex predators in order to reach salvation. All the while the journey is caught on cameras and broadcast to the world as a reality show, the deaths and killings real, the macabre appetite of the audience needing to be satiated as Ben Peyton leads his team to escape not only from a legal system that's more interested in entertainment than in justice, but also from the predators of the Valley.

JURASSIC DEAD
by **Rick Chesler** & **David Sakmyster**

An Antarctic research team hoping to study microbial organisms in an underground lake discovers something far more amazing: perfectly preserved dinosaur corpses. After one thaws and wakes ravenously hungry, it becomes apparent that death, like life, will find a way.
Environmental activist Alex Ramirez, son of the expedition's paleontologist, came to Antarctica to defend the organisms from extinction, but soon learns that it is the human race that needs protecting.

CHECK OUT OTHER GREAT DINOSAUR THRILLERS

SPINOSAURUS
by **Hugo Navikov**

Brett Russell is a hunter of the rarest game. His targets are cryptids, animals denied by science. But they are well known by those living on the edges of civilization, where monsters attack and devour their animals and children and lay ruin to their shantytowns.

When a shadowy organization sends Brett to the Congo in search of the legendary dinosaur cryptid Kasai Rex, he will face much more than a terrifying monster from the past.

Spinosaurus is a dinosaur thriller packed with intrigue, action and giant prehistoric predators.

LAND OF DEATH
by **Eric S Brown** & **Alex Laybourne**

A group of American soldiers, fleeing an organized attack on their base camp in the Middle East, encounter a storm unlike anything they've seen before. When the storm subsides, they wake up to find themselves no longer in the desert and perhaps not even on Earth. The jungle they've been deposited in is a place ruled by prehistoric creatures long extinct. Each day is a struggle to survive as their ammo begins to run low and virtually everything they encounter, in this land they've been hurled into, is a deadly threat.

www.ingramcontent.com/pod-product-compliance
Lightning Source LLC
Chambersburg PA
CBHW031953170626
46807CB00006B/2470